BLUE PARADISE

BLUE PARADISE

by

Matt Bloom

RED BRICK PRESS / NEW WRITERS' SERIES
New York

Red Brick Press
An Independent Imprint of Hatherleigh Press
1114 First Avenue, Suite 500
New York, NY 10021
1-800-906-1234
www.hatherleigh.com

Printed in Canada

∞ This edition is printed on acid-free paper that meets
the American National Standards Institute z39.48 Standard.

Library of Congress Cataloging-in-Publication Data
Bloom, Matthew, 1964 –
Blue Paradise / by Matthew Bloom.
    p.   cm. -- (New writers' series)
    ISBN 1-57826-002-7 (alk. paper)
        I. Title.   II. Series.

PS3552.L6393B57 1998   97-42784
    813'. 54--dc21   CIP

All Red Brick Press titles are available for bulk purchase,
special promotions, and premiums. For more information,
please contact the manager of our Special Sales department
at 1-800-906-1234.

10 9 8 7 6 5 4 3 2 1

A C K N O W L E D G M E N T S

There are many people who have made this book possible, and I would like to take this opportunity to thank them for their generous support and ongoing contributions:

John McElroy, whose energy and encouragement helped guide me during the early days of its writing.

Dede Cummings of dcdesigns whose creative talent and artistic drive made this book a thing of real beauty.

Tim Thrasher of Thrasher Graphics for his skillful assistance with the final implementation of a very classy cover design.

Andrew Flach, my publisher, for believing in this project.

TO MY PARENTS JOAN AND ROBERT,
AND MY BROTHER, JONATHAN.

BLUE PARADISE

C H A P T E R   O N E

PADDY sat by the side door and watched transparent waves of heat rise from Forty-Fifth Street. He drew a labored breath, looked up at the ceiling fans turning slow and wobbly, then down at his mug of Schaeffer and tried to figure how a beer mug can sweat like a person.

He sipped some Schaeffer, now warm and almost flat, and looked around his bar—at the chipped linoleum tile floor, at the wood paneling bulging away from the walls where moisture had seeped behind it. An American flag hung on a pole over the bar next to a yellowed painting of an unknown woman—a long-forgotten bartender's girlfriend who resembled Jackie Kennedy Onassis in hairstyle only. Her face, though pleasant, had the broad, flat working-class features of a north Jersey mall girl. Nothing else adorned Blue Paradise except the beer signs and the POW-MIA sticker in the window.

During the Eighties Paddy had bought a plastic palm tree and some thatched lamps that he suspended from the ceiling over the pool table. In an attempt to cash-in on the new Yuppie culture, he'd changed the bar's name from Paddy's Corner to Blue Paradise. Midtown's young professionals love tropical bars, he reasoned. These days most of the thatch had fallen off the lamps. The palm tree was gone, stolen one night. Paddy still wondered how someone could have stolen a palm tree without being seen.

He yanked on the cord that made the fans turn faster and dismissed the idea of installing air conditioning. They don't deserve it, he thought, looking at the regulars: Frank, Jimmy, Stanley, Dog, and Walter, hunched over their drinks at the bar, and at Gracie, the epitome of faded beauty, behind it.

Paddy considered trying to win some money from Frank tonight, but he couldn't imagine dragging himself around the pool table in this heat. And truth be told, he rarely ever beat Frank. He wiped his brow with a cocktail napkin and shut his eyes. Before dozing off he thought longingly of winter. Only a few months ago he had been looking forward to summer.

The phone behind the bar rang.

"I'm not here," Frank said, drawing his fingers across his throat.

Gracie was chewing her gum like she was trying to kill it.

"What am I, your secretary?" She answered the phone on the fifth ring. "Blue Paradise . . . . No he ain't here." She rolled her eyes toward Frank. "Yeah . . . . yeah . . . . I know. . . . I seen him a little while ago but he ain't here now. . . . yeah, right, right. . . . bye."

Gracie hung up the phone, turned to the mirror and saw Nick walking in the door behind her reflection. Nick threw a few crisp upper-cuts into the air before ducking under the worn mahogany bar. As soon as he was standing upright again, Gracie said to him, "Ya put a little color in your hair and it drives these creeps crazy." She jerked her chin toward the regulars and fluffed her thinning locks with fingers swollen by the heat.

"They comin' onto you again, huh?" Nick said.

"I can tell you stories, honey." And Gracie proceeded to tell the one she often told about her dead husband, Harry, and how it wasn't two days after he died of a heart attack that his lousy, "good-for-shit" friends started coming around asking if they could do anything for her. "Oh, I'm sure they had one thing in mind they could do for me, those worms." Gracie stopped talking and gazed again at her newly blonde hair and at her body that seemed to inflate a little more each week. "He never complained, my Harry. I remember the time it was so cold he and his friend Scrag had to drink wine all day to keep from freezing out on the dock. When he came home that night he didn't look so good. He tried to eat the steak I cooked him and threw up all over the kitchen. It was like someone'd been murdered with a butcher knife with all the red wine everywhere." She paused to dislodge a piece of food from her teeth with her tongue and went on. "But he didn't complain. He just went to bed. I cleaned the kitchen. In the morning I made him his coffee and he was back to work again."

"You sure it wasn't your cooking that made him

sick?" Frank said, his alcohol-widened face concealing a smirk that his eyes could not.

"You sure it was the cold that made him drink?" Jimmy piped in.

Gracie glared scornfully across the bar at both of them, then frowned at the watch her current boyfriend bought her. Rick Buehler was his name, not that anyone in Blue Paradise had ever met this latest installment in the soap opera of Gracie's life. "Jesus H, you're five minutes late!" She barked at Nick. "You think I work here for my beauty? Mr. Handsome bought me this watch so I wouldn't be late meetin' him no more!"

Gracie slung her heavy, brown pocketbook over her shoulder. Paddy wasn't looking, so she slipped a bottle of Reingold beer from the ice bin into it. Her eyes met with Nick's for a split second before she grabbed a crumpled dollar bill off the bar and hurried out the door and into the middle of 11th Avenue where a cab slammed on its brakes to avoid hitting her. The cab's body jerked forward and back. Gracie flipped her middle finger in the air and screamed a soundless curse at the driver before hurrying to the other side.

"Crazy bitch," Jimmy said, his dark, deep-set eyes watching her through the window as she scurried across the avenue and up 45th Street.

"Too bad that cab's brakes worked," Frank said.

"Her name certainly doesn't match her personality," Walter added without looking up from the New York Times crossword puzzle he was nearly finished with.

The bar quieted now that Gracie was gone. Paddy slept with his mouth open just a little, his head tilted back against the wall.

"So, did you fuck her?" Frank asked Jimmy, continuing the conversation his wife's call had interrupted.

"Of course I fucked her. When a woman invites you to her apartment, you fuck her."

"What's the problem, then? You had a nice dinner, you fucked her, you left. A perfect evening. What the hell are you so scared about?"

Jimmy swallowed hard to keep chills from running up his spine.

"I don't know. Maybe it's not for me anymore."

"What's not for you?"

"Well, after we finished drinking some kind of after-dinner drink she asks me if I want to go into her bedroom. I say yeah, of course. No problem." Jimmy wiped his nose on his sleeve and snuffled loudly. "So, I go in her bedroom and sit on the bed and I hear her doing something in the living room. Then she starts turning out all the lights in the apartment. The next thing I know she walks into the bedroom stark naked with a lit candle in her hand."

"Nice body?"

"Tits sagged a little but you gotta expect that with a girl in her forties," Jimmy answered charitably. "So, I just sit there checking her out. Then she turns the lights off in the bedroom and, with this candle held under her chin, she looked just like death. I nearly had a fuckin' heart attack. Her eyes were like black holes. And her mouth looked all twisted and evil. She stood there for, I don't know, maybe three minutes not saying a goddamned word. I nearly lost my hard-on I was so spooked."

"But you fucked her anyway."

"At that point I didn't have a choice." Jimmy raised his hands in consternation. "And I could swear, after we done it and we were lying there in bed, I could feel hair on her ass. The next time I put my hand there it was gone. I put my hand on her ass a little later and the goddamned hair was back again."

"Did she have a cat and a broomstick?" Frank smiled.

Jimmy cradled his head in his palm a few inches above the bar. He'd missed Frank's joke. "I don't know . . Yeah, I think she did. What the hell would the cat be doing on her ass? I mean, I don't know if I'm going crazy or not, but I know once you fuck death like I did, you're a goner." He gulped some beer, brooded for a few moments, then said, "Sometimes I wish I hadn't split with my wife. Lately I'm thinking all women want me for is my money. Yeah, I dress nice and I got a few expensive watches, but I don't got real money." Jimmy pulled at the leg of his matching nylon sweatsuit, one of the closetful he owned and took pride in. "And now all the women, they got this G-spot thing. Every one of them wants you to hit her fuckin' G-spot. Like I got a corkscrew-shaped cock or something." He lowered his voice and shot an accusatory glance at Walter. "I'm not saying I've gone homo or nothing, but lately when I'm with a woman I feel like she's sucking the life outta me. I never used to feel that way."

Three stools down, Stanley and Dog sat next to each other, stunned into silence by the hot, stale air and too much drink.

"You're better off without them," Stanley slurred.

Frank pointed his thumb over his shoulder at Stanley. "Listen to Stanley," he said sarcastically. "A man speaking from experience. What do you think, Walter? You must have an opinion on the subject of women, or then again, maybe you don't." He let the implication hang in the air.

But the taunt got no rise from Walter who kept working on his crossword puzzle. His eyes shifted back and forth behind his thick glasses. Stanley smiled. It felt good to hear Frank refer to him as a man who knew something.

X

The darkness that fell over Blue Paradise at about eight only made the heat feel closer, more immediate. Jimmy insisted on turning in early to stay out of trouble. He also had to take care of his other business, the one he did when he wasn't fixing the sewing machines he claimed to fix for a living. It was the business he never discussed with anyone beside Frank and Paddy.

"Who you fighting next Friday, Nick?" he asked before going.

"Leroy Johnson. At the Paramount. The undercard of the Hearns fight."

"The big time. They paying you anything?"

"Ten grand."

"Chicken feed." Jimmy waved dismissively. "I'll bet a lot of people are gonna make more than that off the fight."

"It's more than you make fixing sewing machines," Frank said.

"Yeah, but if you can fix a sewing machine, you can fix anything." Jimmy winked at Nick. "You ever need anything fixed, Nick, you let me know."

Nick stopped wiping up a spill and wondered what Jimmy meant by that. Jimmy looked over at Paddy, still sleeping, his beer-keg belly expanding with each breath.

"Kiss fatso goodnight for me," he said.

"Why dontcha do it yourself?" Nick smiled.

"All right, I will."

Jimmy walked over to the oblivious owner and laid a wet one in the middle of his damp forehead. He wiped his lips with the back of his hand with cartoonish exaggeration, rubbed his hand on his leg and left. Paddy began to snore.

Walter finished the crossword and started jotting notes on a cocktail napkin. He was well into his sixth or seventh glass of cheap port. His lips moved as he silently mouthed the sentences he wrote to himself.

Margo had come in at eight and sat at the end of the bar furthest from the window. She was unusually quiet tonight. Nick brought her Gimlet. She smiled and said, "Thanks, Nick," but she seemed far away.

Dog remained on his stool in the corner under the TV. The rum and coke Gracie had poured him before she left hours ago was still two inches away from being finished. But miraculously he was quite drunk now.

"You want another one, Dog?" Nick asked, studying Dog's blank face and small, round eyes. Dog's habit was to doctor his drink in the bathroom from the flask of rum he carried in his back pocket. His one rum and Coke usually took him through an entire evening, lightening in direct proportion to his reddening complexion.

"No. I'm alright," Dog answered.

"You been drinking that one pretty slow. I haven't seen it go down in almost an hour. Whaddaya piss in it when you go the bathroom?"

Not wanting to incriminate himself, Dog just grinned instead of answering. Nick turned his attention to Stanley who was leaning dangerously to one side, ready to fall off his stool.

"I think you've had enough for tonight, Stanley," he said.

"Don't gimme that shit, Nick! I'm dead sober!" Stanley's eyes were glassy. Nick rubbed away the tiny drops of spit that flew from Stanley's mouth and restrained the urge to jump the bar, grab him by the collar and march him out the door. Stanley finally left but returned a few minutes later with a Budweiser tall boy from the 24-hour deli next door.

"You can't bring that in here, Stanley."

"I can do whatever I want!" Stanley was staggering now, his arms flailing out. "You're not the president! You're not God! You're not even the owner of this bar! At least the camel jockeys next door own their place."

"Maybe I don't own this place, Stanley, but I am the guy who can kick your ass out of it any time I want!"

Stanley barely kept his balance. He hadn't been on his feet since coming in at 5:00 PM. Nick knew that punching him would feel great. Too great. He was glad when Stanley saved himself by stumbling out again, this time for good. The next day he wouldn't remember any of it. He never did.

Nick resumed polishing bottles, hoping to finish them without interruption. Paddy required him to polish them once a week. Nick did it every night. When he finished, he stood back to admire the shine he'd rubbed into them.

"They look wonderful," Walter mocked in a friendly way. "You missed a spot on the Galliano." Walter looked over at Paddy who was now slumped forward on the table, his arms folded beneath his head. "Nick, don't worry about what Paddy says," he said quietly, his voice tender with concern. "I know it bothers you."

Nick hadn't thought much about Paddy's latest

drunken tirade. "You'll never be shit!" Paddy words had sprung from some alcohol-fueled resentment. "You'll be here until I fire you!" Nick had walked away so he wouldn't have to listen anymore. He'd heard it before.

"Naw, he don't bother me." Nick buffed the Galliano bottle and put it back on the shelf between the Remy Martin and the Hennessy that no one ever drank unless they were mixed with cola.

"Even if he doesn't, you should know that he gives you a hard time because he likes you. He doesn't want to see you leave."

Nick started cleaning ashtrays with a damp rag.

"How do ya figure that? If he liked me I'd think he wouldn't break my balls."

"You have a lot to learn about the ways of the mind, Nick," Walter said with gentle condescension. "I know all about it from my short career in advertising, believe me. What he's doing is telling himself that he doesn't like you so when you make it big as a boxer and leave, it will be easier on him. You're the son he never had. No father wants to see his son leave him behind."

Nick looked out the window at the midtown skyscrapers looming in the dark, their lights cutting a hazy path, making the heat visible. The buildings seemed to be unreal, one-dimensional, part of a city far removed from the one he lived in.

"I never understood that psychology stuff," he said. "I don't believe in it. All I know is Paddy's a big pain in my ass. Gracie robs him blind. Every other dollar goes in her tip cup, but he thinks she's the second coming of Christ. Me, I only take what's mine, and I'm a no good prick." Nick shook his head. "Ah, it don't bother me."

✕

Margo sat at the bar with her legs crossed and a long, thin cigarette held in the crook of her first two fingers. She had a "talker," as Walter liked to call them. The talker was an insurance salesman for Metropolitan Life. If Margo was with another client, he would wait and patiently drink vodka on the rocks until his turn came. Margo told Nick she was staying sober tonight, so he poured her Gimlet from a gin bottle he kept filled with water.

"I know it sounds cliché," the talker said in a solemn voice that suited his Brooks Brothers outfit. "But she doesn't understand me. My wife is the classic old-fashioned housewife. She doesn't understand a guy needs to let loose once in a while."

"How do you like to let loose?" Margo whispered seductively.

The talker's grin turned to a leer that spread slowly and unevenly across his face, bunching his pudgy, lightly bearded cheeks.

"I think you know how I like to let loose. We talked about it last time, remember?"

Margo laughed and shimmied her bared shoulders in feigned delight.

"Oh, that way. I remember now."

"Would you like another drink, Margo?"

"I would love one."

Nick made Margo another virgin Gimlet. He poured the talker a Stoli, taking three-fifty for the Stoli and ten for the Gimlet and then marking the Gimlet and its price on Margo's list. This way he'd know how much he owed her at the end of the night.

"Thanks for the drink, sweetheart," Margo said to the talker.

"It's my pleasure." The talker raised his glass level with his forehead for a formal toast. Before he drank, he said, "Look at you, Margo. Look at you. You're so powerful, so in control of every situation. You're exactly what I want a woman to be." He thought for a moment, then said with quiet urgency. "You're in the position to be seen socially."

"Is she making much tonight?" Walter whispered to Nick.

"Not bad."

Nick put his hand beneath the button of his jeans to ease the sharp ache that had suddenly shot through the pit of his stomach.

"What's the matter?" Walter's eyes, magnified by his glasses, narrowed.

"It's nothing. My stomach hasn't been feeling too good lately."

"What's wrong with it?"

"I don't know. I get these pains sometimes. It's like I can feel my heart beating down in there. When I shit, it's like acid coming out."

"It's probably just nerves."

"Probably." Nick finished his Coke, slid an ice cube into his mouth and crunched it to slush between his molars. "You know, I only been here four fucking years, Walter. It seems like forever." Across the room he watched Paddy begin to stir. "Imagine what it'll seem like if I never get out from behind this bar."

Walter put his arm around Nick's shoulder and let it rest there for a moment. He took it away when he felt Nick's muscles begin to tense.

"Don't worry, Nick. You won't be behind this bar forever."

"I don't know. If I lose this fight, I might never get

another chance. In boxing if you don't win, you lose. And if you lose, you really lose."

"The world certainly isn't kind to losers," Walter said. "But, in my mind, it's the effort and not the winning that's important. If you fight hard, to the best of your ability, then that's enough. You can't do any more than that. The trouble is, our society only respects success—winning and nothing else."

"What about you?" Nick changed the subject. "You're gonna finish that book and get it published. You're not gonna be a waiter the rest of your life."

Once the answer had been easy. Walter thought about that drunken night three years ago. It seemed so obvious then, so doable and virtuous. Back then it was clear to him that looking in the mirror each day would be so much easier if he was writing words to enlighten people instead of ones to trick them into buying things they don't need. He quit his advertising job the next morning and spent the rest of that brilliant fall day walking off a surprisingly comfortable hangover, kicking the crisp, dead leaves in Central Park, breathing their woody scent deep into his lungs.

At first, ideas came to him easily, as if they were floating in the air, invisible to everyone but him. All he had to do was reach out and grab them and make them his. His world was a novel waiting to be written. But after three years he still hadn't found a way to begin. When he sat down to write, his mind would freeze and his fingers remained motionless on the keys until they cramped in that position. The walls of his apartment would close in, and the silence would become unbearable.

Blue Paradise was only a short walk away. An empty stool was always waiting, and so was Nick with his chiseled features and blue eyes that remained blue even in the permanent dimness of the bar. The Sandeman Port would be untouched by anyone since the night before, and Nick knew how to pour it without letting sediment into the glass. And more importantly, at Blue Paradise his novel was coming right along. Sure, they were all in it. Frank, Jimmy, Paddy, Stanley, Dog, Margo, Gracie, Nick. Of course he would invite them to the book-signing party and even the movie premiere, if he sold the film rights.

Walter swallowed the last of his port and eyed the bottle.

"The writing's going fine," he said. "Make sure Paddy orders another bottle soon, Nick, if you will. That one's getting below the halfway mark."

Nick picked up the bottle and shook it to feel how much remained.

"When I finish that bottle I'll autograph it for you," Walter said. He stood and counted out four singles.

Nick rapped his knuckles on the bar. "That last one was on me, Walter."

"Well, I thank you, sir." Walter left the four dollars and picked a piece of lint from the sleeve of his black and grey Herringbone jacket that matched the color of his hair.

"Gonna do some writing tonight?" Nick said, knowing Walter wasn't going to.

"I suppose I will." The urge to sit back down, order another glass and tell Nick that he had not written a single word in three years was very strong. "Maybe I'll take the night off, recharge the old batteries."

"I know what you mean. It's like boxing. Sometimes you gotta take a day off and rest your muscles so you don't burn out."

"But I assure you, Nick, you will be the first to see it when it's published. And now, my friend, I must be getting along."

"I'll see you tomorrow."

They shook hands. Walter left. Nick put the four dollars in his tip cup.

C H A P T E R   T W O

THE D-LESS diner sign across Eleventh avenue flick-
ered on and off, "_iner, _iner, _iner." Nick stood in the
doorway of Blue Paradise and watched the traffic
lights marking the blocks up the avenue. A few long-
legged whores sauntered by in no hurry, in no direction. Nick searched for Jerry, his stick-figure form, the
nervous, jerky walk he could spot a mile away. He's
probably wandering Times Square, Nick figured. He
usually does when he isn't working.

A fire engine's siren woke Paddy from his dreams.
He blinked away the film blurring his vision and
squinted at his watch.

"You were late today, Nick," he said, his voice
thickened by sleep.

"Five minutes, Paddy. Five lousy minutes."

"Like I said, you were late." Paddy stood and
walked back to the staircase that led up to his apart-

ment and his wife. "Don't miss any spots when you clean the bar," he said.

"I never do."

In a minute Nick heard Paddy creaking across the floor above him, then a short, muffled conversation with his wife. After thirty years of marriage they rarely spoke to each other in more than short, informational statements.

"What's for supper?"

"Chicken."

"Good."

Mrs. Paddy (What was her name?) never came down to the bar.

"You want another drink?" Nick said to Dog. Dog shook his head and continued staring out the window at the airplane warning lights blinking on top of the mid-town skyscrapers, at the random pattern of offices lit by late-night workers and cleaning ladies vacuuming.

"It's so hot no one wants to leave their apartment," Nick said, referring to the nearly empty bar.

"I don't have an air conditioner so I don't have to worry about that," Dog said.

When Dog left, Nick sat on the other side of the bar and watched the news on the TV that was suspended from the ceiling by chains. The first death from the heat: An old man in the Bronx. His neighbors had complained to the super about the foul odors coming from his apartment. The super found the man dead and blown up like a balloon, agony frozen on his face. He didn't have the strength to open the windows and was too proud to call anyone for help. That's what his grieving son speculated as a reporter held a mike in his face, practically against his teeth. He died in the heat, his pride intact. At least he died with that, Nick thought.

"The Canadian cold front is coming soon—any day now," the weatherman promised, pointing at a smiley-face graphic of cooler air hovering near Plattsburgh, telling New York City to go fuck itself.

The next story was about the suspects who'd attacked and raped a Fifth Avenue socialite. She was found unconscious and nearly dead in her apartment. Nick watched footage of the four handcuffed suspects, black kids from the projects on the other side of the Ninety-Sixth Street DMZ, their heads turned away from the camera. For political reasons, the Manhattan DA had pushed for a fast trial and it was going to begin tomorrow, just weeks after the crime had occurred. Nick was sure it would be just like all the other media circuses. Summer's just beginning, he thought. It's going to be a long one.

The insurance salesman was drunk now. His hand was on Margo's knee. His top button was open and the knot of his tie was pulled down into a tight ball. Margo glanced over at Nick from time to time to make sure he was paying attention.

"Being a man is tough," the talker slurred. "A tough, tough thing." His voice trailed off.

"I can imagine," Margo said. She rolled her eyes at Nick. "I wouldn't want to be a man."

"No, you wouldn't." The talker moved his hand up Margo's leg and strengthened his grip. "I like you as a woman, Margo. Promise me you'll stay a woman."

"I promise."

The news ended. Nick turned off the TV. No one but Margo and her client remained in the bar, so he shot a game of pool, then practiced pivoting his back foot when he threw his right hand. More power that way. He wondered what Leroy Johnson was doing now. Was he also training in this heat, sucking the foul city air into his lungs, sweating inside his body and out? Was his chest broken out in a nervous rash? Was he shitting acid? Maybe he wasn't. Maybe he wasn't scared at all.

The talker nursed his drink while devouring Margo with his desperate eyes. It was only one o'clock but Nick decided to close early. To hell with Paddy. To hell with him. Let him fire me, the fat bastard. Let him find someone else to put up with his shit.

Nick pulled the plugs on the grit-crusted neon window signs. He wiped the bar and cleaned the last few glasses. Margo walked the talker to the door, his arm around her, his square, short-fingered hand caressing the soft, smooth skin of her shoulder. She told him to get home safe and come back and see her.

"When?"

"Soon."

"How soon?"

"Real soon," she whispered and blew a kiss off her hand. She kept her lips puckered until he finally turned and walked away.

"You gonna do your thing tonight?" she asked Nick when the man was gone.

"I have to."

"You mind if I stay and watch?"

"You can watch if you want."

Nick put the stools up on the bar and made sure the door was shut and locked. He turned off the lights so only the one glowing through the bottles behind the bar and the one coming from the jukebox broke the darkness.

"Wanna hear anything special?" Margo asked.

"Whatever you want," Nick said, unraveling his jumprope.

He took off his shirt and noticed Margo taking a quick look at his chest. She pumped four quarters into the jukebox and cocked her hip to the side as she selected songs. Nick swung the rope slowly at first, holding the handles together in one hand, then opening the rope and jumping through it, his wrist propelling it in a sweeping, continuous arc until it became invisible.

Gladys Knight was singing, *"He sure found out the hard way that dreams don't always come true . . ."* Margo searched for more songs, her hip cocked to the other side now. Her skirt curved with her ass and conformed to her legs, covering only the upper part of her thighs. Nick was studying her body and Margo knew it.

The jumprope snapped at even intervals against the floor. Nick crossed it over, kicked out his right then left foot, sprang up and spun the rope twice beneath him before coming down on his toes quietly, like a panther.

Margo took a beer from the bin behind the bar. She sat at a table and drank straight from the bottle. Patsy Cline was singing, *"I'm back in baby's arms, how I missed those loving arms."* Margo sang along with her for a while.

"Why don't you ever wear sneakers and shorts?" she asked, looking at Nick's sweat-soaked jeans and the black leather work boots he always wore.

"Why bother?"

"You run in those boots, too?" She squinched up her nose.

"Running shoes cost a lot."

Nick put the rope down after jumping for twenty minutes. Without resting, he began to move around the bar, fighting with a phantom, chasing then retreating from an opponent only he could see. In the dim, uneven light, Margo thought the shadows made his muscles look bigger.

Nick tried not to look at her, to lose his concentration, to see her face instead of Johnson's. You lose concentration, you look away—that's when you get hit. But he couldn't help it. The way she pursed her full lips when she wasn't talking, the way she crossed her legs, creating a cleft between her thighs that led into the dark shelter of her skirt. She was thirty, maybe. Nick never asked. He could see it in her face, though: the hint of lines at the corners of her eyes and on either side of her mouth.

"Are you going to see Alice tonight, Nick?"

Nick stopped shadowboxing and grabbed the clean rag he had left on the bar.

"Yeah. I think so," he said, wiping his face and torso. The rag chaffed his damp skin.

"You gonna go home?" he asked her.

"I guess so. I don't know." She came over and touched his hair which was wet, like after a shower. "Maybe we could—"

"Take a cab, Margo."

Discipline. Discipline, Nick thought to himself. He pulled away from her and reached into his left pocket where he kept her money from the night. The bills were slightly damp. He gave them to her, then pulled his tips from his right pocket. From this he peeled a five-dollar bill and he held it out to her.

"You don't have to, Nick. I made some money tonight. Besides, I can walk"

"You should go right home. Take a cab."

Margo frowned.

She took the money.

CHAPTER THREE

Nɪᴄᴋ ᴋɴᴇᴡ it would be tough. He could usually tell before taking his first step. Tonight he started slowly and the pavement jarred his legs and knees as he headed west on Forty-Fifth Street toward the highway, then south past the Intrepid aircraft carrier, now a museum and lit by spotlights. He turned east on 44th and jogged back to Eleventh Avenue. 27th Street seemed far away and it was tempting to run straight down the highway instead of zig-zagging back and forth through the warehouses and tenements between 11th Avenue and the Westside Highway.

Nick forced himself to run this same route every night. He settled into a pace, throwing combinations into the air. The lights from the Jersey side shone thin, white paths on the river's surface. A barge pushed silent and low against the incoming tide on its way from Albany to the harbor. Nick tried to keep up with the barge but it left him behind, sliding finally into the darkness.

On the corner of 40th Street, he shadowboxed under the street lamp until his combinations worked fluidly: two lefts, a right, a hook, an uppercut. Across the highway, the Circle Line, World Yacht, and United States Lines terminals lined up next to each other, blocking his view of the Hudson river. Nick dropped down and did sixty push-ups, coming up with bits of cinder and glass embedded in his hands. Someone shouted out the window of a passing car and a beer bottle burst like a grenade against the sidewalk only a few feet away.

Nick got to his feet and continued running. When he reached 27th Street where it meets the Westside Highway, he stopped and shadowboxed again under the humming street lamp. The soles of his work boots skimmed the pavement as he moved from side to side and stabbed his fists into the hot air. Rivulets of sweat poured over his brow and into his eyes. He let the sweat flow. There was no use wiping it away in this heat.

Fuzzy halos of smog surrounded the tail lights of the cars dodging potholes on the highway. Nick crouched and threw an upper-cut, two jabs, a right and a hook. He dropped onto his hands. One, Two, Three, Four, Five. The sidewalk rushed toward him and receded. He did this nightly routine with an almost religious attention to detail. Sixty more pushups: twenty-five with his hands turned inward, twenty-five with his hands straight, five with a clap, five with a double clap. Breathe! Breathe! he told himself. Your head'll explode if you don't.

Back on his feet, Nick threw his punches harder. Drops of sweat created dark, wet spots on the sidewalk. He changed direction, and his fists blurred toward the river. He moved forward behind his jab, bobbing and weaving, planting his left foot most of the time, sometimes balancing only on his toes.

He imagined Leroy Johnson stalking him, slipping, and returning his punches. Johnson's mean face had a taunting smile stretched across it. He threw his overhand right, the one he always threw, the one he was supposed to throw so well that you didn't see it until it dropped on you from above like a bomb. Johnson's fists, no longer gloved, came at Nick viciously and Nick could almost feel them landing, cutting into his skin. He fired faster to counter but started to miss. A car honked. Johnson disappeared and Nick peeled off his T-shirt, wiped his face with it, and started walking east on 27th Street toward 11th Avenue.

Nobody out except a few bums collecting cans and garbagemen emptying trash baskets. Nick's heart pounded and his chest heaved as his lungs struggled to filter oxygen from the air. The pavement seemed to move, like water beneath his feet. A garbage truck's brakes squealed. On the river, another barge blew its lonely-sounding horn. The barge horn faded and was replaced by the unseen trumpet Nick heard almost every night.

The music came from a rooftop, its clear notes floating over the warehouses, across the highway to the river. The songs were always sad ones but they made Nick feel less alone. He'd imagine the trumpeter on top of one of the warehouses, blowing his lungs and heart out to the sleeping steel towers of midtown and the Jersey shoreline across the river.

Tonight the notes were especially long and rich. They seemed to enter Nick, to expand from his stomach into his throat and take him far away. He wondered if anyone else was listening. But no one was there, just him and the trumpet player.

He walked along Twenty-Seventh Street. The music faded behind him until he reached Ninth Avenue where a few of the bars were still open. Nick fought the urge to go into Connolly's and have one or two to help him sleep. Alice would smell the alcohol on his breath. She wouldn't say anything, of course, which was worse than if she did.

He crossed Ninth Avenue. On the other side, two doors down from the corner, he stopped and stood in the shadow where the building meets the sidewalk. In the third floor window of the tenement directly across the street, the familiar silhouette was there behind the curtain, now grey from years of city air filtering through it. Sometimes the man, Nick's uncle John, sat as still as a stone, sleeping in his chair with the lights on. Most of the time he was awake, his damaged nerves keeping him from sleep, watching with failing eyes the neighborhood that no longer knew he existed.

Nick didn't bother to take quick looks around him as he usually did at this time of morning. His eyes were fixed on his uncle who sat alone in his apartment with his own fights from a forgotten boxing career replaying over and over in his head. Nick nearly went upstairs to see him. Instead, he started running again, back toward the river.

A lone whore stood in the middle of deserted 27th Street. As Nick passed, her perfume smelled harsh and fermented.

"Why not do some sweatin' with me?" she said, gesturing at him with her long, snakelike tongue.

A car turned off the highway. Its headlights lit the

whore's lime green mini-skirt and the heavy makeup caking her face. The car stopped. The whore got in and Nick watched the car disappear into the night. He licked the salt from his lips, spat it to the street and kept walking.

As soon as he turned onto 26th Street a familiar pair of arms wrapped around his neck, pressing his adams apple against the back of his throat. "I'll cut your fuckin' jugular for the lint in your pocket!" The voice attached to the bony arms echoed loudly off the Lock And Leave Warehouse. Nick leaned forward into a judo throw, and Jerry's body went up and over and fell limply to the sidewalk. Nick planted his foot on Jerry's back and felt sad for a moment looking down at the fragile body that could easily belong to an awkward, pubescent boy.

"Sonufabitch," Jerry said, attempting to rise. "You oughta be a wrestler, not a boxer. C'mon, Nick, lemme up." Jerry's right eye was twitching faster than it normally did.

"Bark like a dog first."

"Oh, Jesus fuckin' Christ. Not again."

"Like a German Shepherd, not a Poodle." Nick pressed his heel down harder. This too was part of the nightly ritual.

"Oh, awright, goddamnit! Ruff! Ruff!"

"Louder!"

"BARK! BARK! RUFF! RUFF!"

Nick lifted his foot.

"Motherfucker," Jerry said, rising slowly and wiping a smudge of dirt from his T-shirt. Together they walked to the small, aluminum office shack that stood in the middle of the Chelsea Van Rental lot where Jerry worked the deadman's shift checking-in returned vans. He went inside and came out with a half-empty bottle of Seagrams Seven rye which he held up to the naked lightbulb over the door of the shack.

"No crabs yet," he said, searching the bottom of the bottle for the small, crab-like insects that grow in old bottles.

"You never give them enough time to grow crabs."

"I wonder how they manage to live in there without any air," Jerry said. "Shit, I wonder how we live in this fuckin' city with this heat." He went back inside and returned with two folding beach chairs, souvenirs from some family's Florida vacation. "Which one do you want, Miami Beach or Disney World?"

"Miami Beach."

Nick settled into the chair and a few of the aging nylon fibers ripped beneath him. Jerry twisted the cap off the bottle and took a generous pull before handing it to Nick who did the same and felt the liquor coat the inside of his empty stomach and rise quickly to his head. He handed the bottle back.

"You don't want no more?" Jerry said.

"I'm in training, for godsake."

"So why the hell are you drinking at all?"

"One shot at the end of the night's okay," Nick said. "I can't sleep without a shot of something."

"Why don't you drink at Blue Paradise before closing?" Jerry held the bottle up to his lips. "That's what I'd do."

"I know that's what you'd do. And you wouldn't wait for closing either." Nick paused to think. "I would, but I don't want anything in me before I run. Besides, I think Paddy marks the bottles and checks them against the register tape. Like I ever stole anything from him."

Jerry wiped some rye from his mouth with the back of his arm.

"That's your problem, ya hump," he said. "Why dontcha quit if Paddy's riding you so much?"

"Quit? Who's gonna pay my rent if I quit?"

Jerry sat up in his chair and changed the subject.

"What about the fight? You're favored to win it. The guy's supposed to have a glass chin, right? You'll get some good fights after you beat him."

"It's a scummy business," Nick replied. Now he needed another hit and took one from Jerry's bottle. "Promoters jerk fighters around and cut deals with each other all the time. Unless you're a big name, they make the money, not you." Nick leaned his chair back into a reclining position and shut his eyes. "I'm only getting ten thousand for this one. And Johnson's got a dangerous right hand. It's no sure shot."

Ten grand's chicken feed, Nick figured with his eyes still shut. Quit his bartending job at Blue Paradise and he could live off ten grand for six months maybe. Then what? The smell of oil dripping from the vans brought him back to the sound of Jerry sucking the last drops from his bottle. Nick could feel it. He knew Jerry was thinking hard about ways to make money off him if he won the fight and got a shot at the title. Well, it's not going to happen, buddy. It's supposed to, but I just don't see it.

"So, how's business?" Nick asked abruptly. He needed to forget about the fight for a while.

"Slower'n shit. It's summer. Everybody's out on the island getting laid. It don't matter to me. I get paid just the same."

Nick opened his eyes and focused on the US Postal plant across Eleventh Avenue. A postal truck downshifted as it drove up the ramp and vanished into the dark confines of the huge, windowless building.

"Yeah, you get paid just the same, don't you?" he

said. "Especially when you're getting side action from scumbags like Chico."

"Listen, there's nothing wrong with that." Jerry paused before adding, "Doin' a little business on the side's the American way."

"Yeah, renting Big Bob's vans to a drug dealer, that's the American way all right. It ain't honest, Jerry."

"What the hell's honest anymore? What was ever honest?"

"Plenty of things."

"Ah, shit, we'd have goddamn Indians as landlords if everyone in this country was honest."

They didn't talk for a minute. Then Nick said, "Big Bob'll catch you, Jerry. You'll be in deep shit when he does."

"He won't catch me. If he does, I'll cut him in. A little extra cash'll smooth it over."

"He won't go for the idea of renting his vans to Chico, that drug-dealing bastard." Nick picked at the nylon fibers of his chair. "What's Chico paying you, anyway?"

"Fifty a van. He uses two a night, three if he's busy. That's not bad. He gets 'em back by five and nobody knows nothing." Jerry lit a cigarette and sucked hard enough to burn the end nearly a quarter of an inch. "He's not really a scumbag," he said, punctuating each word with small puffs of smoke.

"Doesn't Bob check the odometers for mileage?"

Jerry pulled a small screwdriver from his back pocket and waved it in front of Nick's face.

"What he don't know won't hurt him."

Nick shut his eyes again and imagined that when he opened them he would be somewhere else, some other time. He found himself doing this more often lately. When the butterflies came he shut his eyes and travelled in his head until they were gone and he was some vague place he had never been before.

Jerry peered into the opening of the empty bottle before setting it down on the tarmac. "Another dead soldier," he said. He leaned forward out of his chair and walked into the office where he looked up at the Snap-On Tools calender on the wall and liked that Miss April's tender blue eyes beamed down on him adoringly wherever he stood.

He came out and sat next to Nick again and watched a whore saunter down Twenty-Sixth Street on her way toward the highway. Jerry lit another cigarette and offered one to Nick who waved it off.

"Me, I wouldn't touch a whore," Jerry said. "Not a street whore anyway. Scary-looking bitches. Just tonight I saw one with a puss like Bela Lugosi get out of this car and she sticks her head in the window and spits in the driver's face. Then she starts screaming and kicks the goddamned door. Imagine what the poor asshole's gonna tell his wife when she asks about the dent."

"'Well, you see, Betty,'" Nick said, imitating the john. "'I was getting this blow job on the Westside Highway and it wasn't worth twenty dollars. So I gave her fifteen and she kicked the car. Don't worry, I think the insurance will cover it.'"

"Yeah, the insurance'll cover it," Jerry said, blowing a cloud of smoke. "I wonder if he's got insurance for when his dick falls off. Ya hear about that guy who got his dick bitten off by one not too long ago?"

"Nah, I didn't hear that."

"It happened right around here. No kiddin'. How the fuck do you think he explained that?"

"'Honey?'" Nick mimicked in a suburban wife voice. "'What happened to your dick?'"

"What's a guy supposed to do after that?" Jerry laughed. He took another long drag and became serious. "You gotta take a gun to your head. Nothing left for you to do if that happens. No point in living if you can't fuck. You can't even pee unless you squat like a girl. Fuckin' nightmare."

"It wouldn't change your lifestyle much," Nick said.

Jerry stiffened. "What the fuckdaya mean by that?" He clamped down on the aluminum armrests. "It wouldn't change my lifestyle much? That's a fuckin' thing to say."

"Calm down. I didn't mean nothing by it." Nick nearly laughed at the hard sulk on Jerry's already pinched face and his rapidly twitching eye. "Really, I just said it. You left yourself wide open."

Jerry loosened his grip on the rusted arms of his chair and grinned crookedly. He was relieved now, but his grin disappeared when he looked at his watch. Chico should have brought the vans back by now.

Nick stood up and stretched. He started shadow boxing lightly, but the pre-morning air was too hot, too polluted. His breath became labored, like someone who had never trained before. This close to a fight, he thought. I should feel stronger.

"You hear the radio today?" Jerry said. "They're telling joggers to stay inside. Said they're waiting for this big wind from Canada to come and sweep all the goddamn pollution out to sea. But the fucker's stuck up there and won't come down."

"I can taste the fumes going in my lungs when I run," Nick said. "That's some bad shit."

"You shouldn't be running." Jerry was into another cigarette by now.

"I have to run. I have to train."

A weak breeze tipped the ash off Jerry's cigarette. Rather than refreshing the air, it only added to the dankness.

"Feels like the end of the world is coming," Jerry said. "That's how this crazy weather makes me feel. I wake up barely able to breathe. I go to bed barely able to breathe. And me: I'm in my prime. We finally fucked the planet to it's breaking point and I haven't even got the chance to do all the things I want to do yet."

Nick had stopped shadowboxing by now and was shaking the tension out of his arms. Jerry was getting on his nerves. A pang of anxiety dropped into his stomach like a lead sinker. I'll do what I have to do, he thought. No bullshit about the end of the world.

"What time you got, Jerry?"

"Five o'clock."

"I better get goin'."

"Hey, why not hang here? You can sleep on my cot."

"Where you gonna sleep?"

Jerry shrugged his shoulders to dismiss the idea of sleep. Clock time didn't mean much to him.

"I don't think I'll be sleeping today. I slept yesterday."

"No, I gotta get going. I promised Alice I'd come see her." Nick leaned down and slapped Jerry gently across his fleshless cheek. "I'll see ya later."

"You coming by tomorrow?"

"I don't know."

"Maybe I'll stop by the bar. See the gang at Blue Paradise," Jerry snickered. "Fuckin' losers."

Nick was already on his way. Jerry watched him go, punching at the air as he walked through the gate and turned toward Tenth Avenue.

Jerry went back inside the office shack to get another bottle. His heart sank when he remembered that
his supply was exhausted. He looked at the grimy wall
from which Miss April was still smiling at him.

"Don't worry, Barbara, baby," he said to her. "The
rest of the year's never gonna come as long as I'm
around." He kissed his index finger and touched it to
her glossy lips.

5:10 AM. Jerry went outside and sat in the Disney
World chair and fingered the zip stick he kept in his
pocket but had never summoned the courage to use on
anybody. The red sky had given way to pre-dawn grey.
"You better bring those goddamn vans back, Chico,"
he said loudly, fiercely to the silent van lot. As the new
day approached, he hoped the sound of his voice
would settle his nerves. It didn't. "Gonna be a hot
fucker," he said more quietly.

CHAPTER FOUR

In his dream, Nick looked down at himself as he lay on his back in the middle of the ring, framed by a pool of his own blood. He tried to move, to get to his feet, to escape the howling faces surrounding him and the relentless punches pounding him further into the canvas. But he couldn't move and the blood draining from his wounds threatened to drown him until the bell finally rang and Nick jerked awake into a sitting position.

The sheets were stuck to his body and the sun was already high and hot. Nick waited until his heartbeat slowed, then got out of bed and walked into the kitchen. He tried to stretch his ribs that felt stiff and compressed by reaching toward the ceiling that was only a few inches higher than his finger tips. The note on the counter read: "Nick, Have a good workout. Be quiet when you leave! XXOO! Love, Alice. P.S. I'm glad you came over last night! XXXOOO!"

Nick leaned down and drank straight from the tap. The water cooled the burning sensation in his stomach. He splashed some on his face, got back into bed and thought about coming in from his run last night.

Alice had been asleep but she woke when she heard the door open and put her arms out to Nick in the dark.

"I'm sweaty," Nick whispered.

"I don't mind."

He hugged her, arching his wet body away from hers. He let go. She held on.

"I'm gonna take a shower," he said.

"Just be quiet, honey. Mr. McElroy doesn't sleep well when it's this hot."

"He should use his air conditioner."

"He says he's saving it for an emergency."

Nick stayed in the shower for a long time, letting the lukewarm water massage the top of his head. He plugged his ears and heard the drops echoing inside his skull and gradually reduced the hot water until it ran cold, washing away the heat collected in his armpits.

He dried himself and wrapped the towel around his waist and sat on the edge of Alice's bed. She kissed his palm as he slid it over her face and cupped it on her forehead. How small and round it felt. Sometimes he'd sit like that for hours, unable to sleep, looking down at her, enjoying the feel of her head in his hand.

In the beginning their relationship had been fiercely sexual. Alice would be waiting for him, ready, and Nick often didn't bother to shower until the next morning. Mr. McElroy, the owner of the funeral home Alice lived over and worked in, used to complain about the noise. But over the course of two years,

Nick's interest had died down. And now he often found himself looking at other women with a longing that, for a time, had been quenched. Mr. McElroy rarely complained about noise anymore.

With Alice on the bottom, Nick did what he knew she wanted him to do, going through the motions with his mind elsewhere, on the fight, her eyes shut, his on the city lights outside her window. It isn't her, he told himself. She hasn't changed. It's me. He knew that.

After making love to her he struggled against drowsiness while she told him about the body she'd worked on that day: a woman killed by a car crossing 9th Avenue.

"How's she looking?" Nick asked.

"Like she died in her sleep. The poor woman."

"I don't know how you do this kind of work."

"I like being a mortician. It's an important job."

"I know, but you're around dead people all day."

"Someone has to take care of them."

"Why you? Just being in this apartment gives me the creeps with all them bodies downstairs."

"So, why do you come here?" Alice didn't wait for his answer. "Anyway, they're just bodies. I don't know why everyone's so afraid of the dead."

"Because they remind people of what's in store for them."

"An afterlife, that's what's in store for them. The body's just a temporary vehicle for the soul."

Nick rolled his eyes and wished he hadn't started this same conversation.

"God gave us the will to stay alive because he knows better than anyone that death ain't nothin' but being eaten by worms in the ground," he said.

"Nick, how can you talk about God and then believe that all we do when we die is rot in the ground?"

Nick turned on his side and pretended to sleep. Alice nudged his ribs with her elbow.

"What?" Nick turned back to her. "Whaddaya want me to say, that I believe in some kind of crazy afterlife? I wish it was true, but it's not." His voice softened. "Alice, I don't know about you, but I'm not going anywhere else after this. Everyone, including me, has got one life whether there's a God or not. That's it. When I'm dead, if people say, 'I remember Nick Gallagher. He was a real stand-up guy,' I'll be happy. That's all I want."

Alice was quiet for a few moments. Then she said, "You want more than that, Nick. I know you do."

Nick leaned over and nipped the top of her ear.

"You're right. I also want you to shut up." He kissed her cheek and Alice put her head into the hollow of his shoulder.

"I'm glad you're here," she said. "I feel better when you're here.

In a few minutes she was asleep and Nick lay on his back, wide awake now, listening to the even rhythm of her breathing, trying to clear all thoughts from his mind so he too could settle into a comfortable sleep. But his eyes wouldn't shut and he spent the next hour looking out the window at the lightening sky. Later, Alice woke and asked if there was anything wrong.

"There's nothing wrong."

"There's something wrong," she said groggily. "I know there's something wrong."

"Go back to sleep, baby. You need to rest."

When she did, Nick remained far from sleep. This time of the morning was when the coming day seemed like a huge wave rearing up, poised to crash down on him. He contemplated getting up now and leaving and never coming back. Forget about the fight. Forget about everything. And he couldn't get it out of his mind that one day, as sure as the sun outside was rising, he would be dead for good and forever.

Nick forced himself out of bed. He pulled on his jeans that smelled of dried sweat and keg beer and left the apartment, closing the door quietly behind him. On the landing that led into the mortuary he stopped and listened to Mr. McElroy tell Alice about the funeral they were having in the afternoon. "They want her in the green dress," McElroy said in the gentle voice he reserved for few people other than Alice and his clients. "And not too much makeup, Alice." Nick decided not to say hello. He slipped out unnoticed.

On the sidewalk, the air horn of a passing truck cut through Nick like shrapnel. Crossing 25th Street, he looked down to 11th Avenue and beyond it to the spot of river almost completely obscured by polluted fog.

He walked without counting the blocks and cut east on 34th Street to 8th Avenue where the porn shops multiplied with each uptown block. On the avenue, cars blasted their horns at jaywalking pedestrians. The crowds on the sidewalk thickened and panhandlers begging drug and booze money stood rock-like among them, unmoved by the human stream swirling around them.

A stoop-shouldered man carrying a Bible and a microphone attached to a portable speaker stepped into the middle of the sidewalk, blocking Nick's path and looking straight into his eyes. "Matthew, Eighteen-eleven," he shouted and read, "'For the Son of Man has come to save that which was lost.'" The preacher lowered the Bible, revealing a face that seemed to fold in upon itself and shake in fleshy waves with each frantic movement. He said, "If you are lost, my son, you need to be saved from the wrath of God!"

Nick tried to sidestep him. The preacher blocked his way again and expertly flipped the pages of the Bible to Romans 10:3: "For they being ignorant of God's righteousness, and seeking to establish their own righteousness, have not submitted to the righteousness of God!'" The preacher fixed his wild eyes squarely on Nick. "Hear him!" he shouted in a loud baritone. "You need God's righteousness! Without it, you go to hell! Save yourself before the time has come when it's too late! You can't do it on your own! Nobody can do it alone!"

The preacher grasped Nick's arm. Before Nick could pull away he said in a quieter, more intimate voice, as if telling a secret, "Join with me, son. I can show you the way to salvation. Join with me." His fingers dug into Nick's muscles. Nick twisted his arm free and dodged around the man. "Heaven and Earth shall pass away!" The preacher shouted after him. "But my words shall not pass! They shall not pass!"

Oh, man, Nick thought, moving away. First Alice, now this nut.

The down-and-outs buzzed like flies outside the liquor store below "Leon's Boxing and Fitness Gym," begging change for bottles of Thunderbird or Night Train, or Richard's Wild Irish Rose on a good day. A small, hand-scrawled sign in the window of the store read: "Wine is good for you." Nick stood on the corner of 40th and 8th and looked up at the boxers throwing silent punches into mirrors, stalking each other in the confines of the ring, pounding heavy bags that looked to them like their next opponent. The street preacher's words, no longer discernable, still pierced the layers of city noise.

"Yo, gotta quarta?" A filthy man held out his leathery palm, creased by white lines of cracked skin.

Nick pulled two dimes from his pocket. The man took them and mumbled, "Dime's gettin' thinna' every day," before weaving back to his post in front of the liquor store.

To Nick, it seemed like a long time that he stood on the sidewalk watching the fighters through the window above him, trying to summon the will to go upstairs and join them. Across the street, hustlers carried tourists' luggage out of the Port Authority while cars and cabs, ignoring the lanes, battled each other up the avenue. The crowd on the sidewalk hurried past. Nick ignored them and thought of his ongoing discussion with Alice about death and of what the street preacher had said about going with God and letting him do the work. It sounded like a good idea. Too bad it's all bullshit. Nick opened the door and took the stairs one at a time.

"You pay your dues yet?" Leon barked when Nick walked into the gym.

"I paid yesterday. Remember?"

Leon looked at Nick as if for the first time.

"I don't remember you paying no dues. Nobody uses my gym for free. No sir." Leon shuffled into his office and came out with a tattered spiral notebook. He licked his puckered index finger and turned some pages. "I gotta lotta fighters comin' in and out. I ain't got no time to remember who paid and who didn't." He licked his index finger again and turned more pages. "Oh, yeah." He squinted into the book. "Hold the phone! Now, shows here you paid twice in the four month and you paid in the six month. What happened to the five month?"

"I paid for May on April thirtieth," Nick said.

Leon shook his head.

"Says here you paid in the four month and you paid in the six month. It don't say anywhere where you paid in the five month."

"That's because I paid for May at the end of April. I paid for April at the beginning of April and for May at the end of April."

Leon studied his book some more.

"It don't make sense to me, payin' twice in one month. I still don't see no five month." He shut the book, shook his head and shuffled back into his office growling something about not having time or patience for all the thieves in the world.

In the locker room, Nick had to spin the combination on his lock three times before it opened. He pulled the squeaking metal door open and the acrid-ammonia smell of old sweat spilling out of it pricked deep into his nostrils. He undressed slowly while listening to two fighters in the next row of lockers.

One was saying: "Shit, I don't mess with teenagers these days. Teenagers' crazy-ass mutha-fuckas."

"Man, you look at 'em wrong they pull out their nine-millimeter and POP! POP! in ya head!" the other fighter said.

"Crazy shit goin' down now. The other day I seen a bunch of 'em running outta a bodega. So, I go in to get me a beer and I find the muthafuckin' store owner on the floor behind the counter wit' blood spurtin' outta his head. Freaked me out, man. Shot the poor fucka' right in the head. They took 'im to the hospital, but I think he dead. I took my beer, though, 'fore the cops came."

Nick pulled on his cut-off sweats, then sat on the wooden bench and criss-crossed blood-stained hand wraps over his knuckles and around his wrists. In the corner, a fighter showered under a rusted spigot coming from the wall.

"You fightin' soon?" the one fighter asked his friend.

"Gotta six-rounder in the Bronx in August. Some kid named Julio Garcia. S'pose to be good, but he ain't gonna do shit against me. I'll pop him with my jab, set 'em up, then BAM! with my right!"

"I saw you movin' around today. You got some good shit."

"Jes a matter of time, bro', and I'll be there. Gold and diamonds on every finger. I'm gettin' my shit together, man. Been doing my roadwork, laying off the drinkin'. I even been tellin' my bitch to take cold showers if she got to. She say, 'Baby why don't you make me happy no more?' and I say, 'That's what I'm tryin' to do.' She don't understand. You can't make a bitch understand you can't go in the ring all happy and satisfied and shit. Gotta keep your strength inside instead of givin' it to her."

"I hear ya, bro'. Let a bitch take your strength and you finished."

When Nick came out of the locker room Leon said, "Who you fightin' next?"

"Leroy Johnson."

"Leroy Johnson?"

"You're the one who arranged the fight, remember?"

Leon looked confused again. He said, "Yeah, well. When is it?"

"Next Friday. At the Paramount. On the Hearns

undercard."

"At the Paramount?" Leon's eyes lost focus as he struggled to fit the information into his punch-drunk brain. "Aw'right. Do your workout. Then I want you movin' with Rashid a few rounds."

Rashid, a tall, lanky black kid, was shooting straight, crisp jabs at the double-end bag tethered to the ceiling and the floor with elastic shock cords. Nick had seen Rashid fight before. The same kind of fighter as Johnson.

Nick shadowboxed a couple of rounds in front of the mirror before moving on to the heavy bag. He pushed some jabs that made a dull thud against the hard leather, not the sharp pop he wanted. Today the bag felt more solid than it usually did. Nick circled it and threw more jabs and followed with a right that felt unnatural, rehearsed, like he was throwing it under water. *Pivot the back foot when throwing the right*, he told himself. The basics felt new and unfamiliar. The bag swung back, smashing into Nick who stood flat-footed between punches. *Up on the toes! Up on the toes!*

It didn't take long for the sweat to flow. Nick kept pumping his jab until it started to loosen and make the correct sound. Leroy Johnson was supposed to be taller, so Nick adjusted the height of his punches, aiming for the yellow Everlast patch a few inches above eye-level. He doubled his jab and followed with a right.

"Keep your elbow tucked into your body." Leon slapped Nick's elbow and dug his fist into Nick's ribs. "Shouldn't be no room for me to put my fist in there." Leon's fist still felt hard and able to do some of the damage it was formerly capable of. "Keep your body turned sideways." He walked away.

Soon Nick's combinations started to flow more easily. He moved on his toes, firing punches at the bag, sometimes resting against it, then pushing it away and volleying lefts and rights and hooks. The bell rang. The fighters around him stopped working and walked in small circles, shaking the fatigue from their arms. Nick wiped his face with a towel. He glanced at his reflection in the cracked mirror. It looked lean, his unshaven cheeks, hollow.

By the fourth round Nick was swinging with controlled fury. Paddy's latest tirade came into his head. "You're nothing but shit!" Those four words played again and again in time with Nick's increasingly hard punches. "You're nothing but shit! You're (BAM!) nothing (BAM!) but (BAM!) shit!" Paddy's voice could have been Nick's father's and Nick began to relive the daily beatings he and his older brother, Tommy, once received, the beatings his mother never tried to stop. Good old dad liked to use the thick leather belt with the cowboy buckle. He used his fists when he couldn't find the belt. Mom did nothing, afraid she was going to be next. Nick could still feel the stinging slap of the belt across his back and shoulders, still feel the physical pain that stopped long before the beatings did.

Nick hit the bag harder, alternating lefts and rights until it stayed angled in the air, poised to swing back when he stopped.

"Keep your mouth shut," Leon said as he walked by. "You wanna bite your tongue off?" Nick shut his mouth and forced his breath through his nose. With ten seconds left he flurried until the bell rang and his arms burned all the way to his shoulders. Leon came back. "Get your head gear," he said.

Rashid was already in the ring, leaning against the

ropes in his corner with his headgear on and his mouthpiece in. Leon wiped Nick's face and smeared a large dab of vaseline over it. He cleaned the headgear by sticking his bent knee into it, then put it on Nick's head and buckled the strap tight so it bit into the skin beneath his chin.

"Now, Rashid's taller'n you," Leon said, close enough for Nick to smell the cheap cigars on his breath. "I want you gettin' inside his jab, bangin' 'im to the body, then coming up to the head with hooks and uppercuts. That's your fight, bangin' the body, then coming up. I don't want you tryin' no fancy Muhammad Ali shit, ya hear?"

Nick nodded and looked to the opposite corner where Rashid stood, relaxed and confident. He flashed Nick a mouthpiece grin that seemed to say, "I'm gonna get you but good." It's only a few rounds of sparring, Nick told himself, but when you're in the ring, it's a fight.

The bell rang and Nick moved to the center of the ring. Rashid met him there. Ignoring the traditional tap of gloves, he fired a jab that caught Nick high on the forehead and followed quickly with another jab, then a straight right flush to Nick's face. Nick threw his own jab, tight and slow. Rashid slipped it easily and countered with a left and a right in quick succession.

Rashid's jabs came fast after that, one behind the other, doubled and tripled. "Get inside! Get ya ass inside on 'im!" Leon yelled to Nick from the corner. "Slip them jabs!" Nick waited for the next one to come. As soon as he felt Rashid's glove thud into his palm, he crouched and moved forward and drove an uppercut to his stomach, then a hook to his chin. "That's right!" Leon yelled. "Now, move outta there, Rashid!"

The rounds seemed longer than three minutes. Nick

wondered how many Leon wanted him to fight. A few, he'd said. A few means three or four. Can't be more than that.

By the fourth round Rashid was beginning to tire and his jabs were no long landing with the heat they'd carried in the first. Nick slipped inside a high one and scored another combination to Rashid's ribs. With ten seconds left in the round and Rashid breathing deeply through his mouth, Nick drifted back against the ropes and waited for him. If you want me, come get me, he thought. I've gotten my shots in for the day.

Letting the thick, elastic ropes support him, Nick noticed the rattling, fist-driven rhythm of the speed bags behind him and the tapping of jump ropes against the floor and trainers shouting harsh orders at fighters. "What you standin' there for? Fight!" Leon yelled. Rashid advanced and doubled a jab. Nick blocked both of them and thought for a moment that maybe all he had to do was pick punches. You can't get hurt if you pick and slip punches. The bell rang.

"One more round," Leon said, wiping away the blood trickling from Nick's nose.

"One more?"

"You don't wanna go anymore?"

"I'll go one more if you want me to."

"Blow." Nick blew the blood from his nose into the paper towel Leon held. "I don't wanna see you lettin' up like that," Leon warned. "Do that in a fight and the judges gonna take the round away from you. Gotta fight the whole three minutes! You been doin' your roadwork?"

"Yeah, at night."

Before allowing Nick to leave the corner, Leon said, "I want you to plant your left foot when you jab, none of that ballerina shit up on your toes." Nick nodded and headed to the center of the ring. The two fighters circled each other warily. Nick picked a jab and countered with his own. In the background he could hear Leon urging him to get inside. He glanced out the window at the bums hovering outside the liquor store below. He looked back at Rashid in time to catch a glove in his face.

"What the hell you doin'? Daydreamin'?" Leon yelled.

Nick crouched to avoid being hit again, then circled to the right, out of Rashid's range. "You never gonna hit nobody all the way out there!" Leon's voice sounded small now, and distant. Nick backed up. The right hand came. Nick saw it, but too late and it snapped his head back and blurred his vision, like a broken TV. "You're nothing but shit!" Paddy's voice said, clearing Nick's head. He charged Rashid, hoping to land a solid right, the punch you feel travelling from your fist through the rest of your body. It was only sparring, but now, suddenly, Nick wanted to knock him out, cold on the canvas.

Rashid retreated into a corner. Nick followed him there, loading up his right. Before he could unleash it, the bell rang. The two fighters tapped gloves and let the weight of the gloves pull their arms down to their sides.

In the corner, Leon peered into Nick's face as if trying to find an answer to an impossible question there. "What's wrong with you, boy? You wait 'til the last five seconds to fight?"

Rashid tapped Nick's shoulder before climbing through the ropes.

"Good fightin', man," he said. "Don't think I'll be takin' many deep breaths this week."

Leon slapped the side of Nick's headgear to get his attention back.

"You start thinkin' he's your mama out there? Huh? Is that it? If that's it, I'll understand 'cause nobody wanna hit his mama!"

Nick took off his gloves and head gear and rubbed away some of the vaseline that slicked his face.

"I was pacing myself."

"Pacin' yourself? You don't pace yourself in the last round! That's when you try to take the guy's fuckin' head off!" Leon looked at Nick with pure disgust. "You can't wait 'til the last five seconds neither."

Nick walked away from Leon to the other side of the ring where he leaned against the ropes and looked out the window to the tiny figure of the preacher still flailing his arms at the godless throng of oblivious New Yorkers. Less than two weeks before the fight. The butterflies started swirling in his belly. To get rid of them he thought about the money he would make just for showing up. Ten thousand wasn't much but it would be something. Then what? More fights? He thought of his Uncle John. Until I end up like him?

"I'll get someone else to take the fight." Leon's voice sounded uncharacteristically calm and devoid of annoyance. "I'll give it to someone else. Don't matter to me."

"I want the fight," Nick said.

"I been 'round fighters my whole life and I know when one don't wanna fight."

Nick's back was still turned to Leon.

"I want the fight, " he said.

He turned around and was glad to find that Leon had already gone over to the heavy bags and was teaching a fighter how to bury his chin into his shoulder. If Leon was still there, Nick might have changed his mind about the fight. He didn't want the opportunity to do that.

C H A P T E R   F I V E

THE JUKEBOX blared merengue 45's while garment
workers rolled racks jammed with evening dresses
through the loading dock/bar to the trucks waiting
outside. Some of the workers sang with the music.
Some shouted in Spanish at the two barmaids. Probably something about tits, Jerry thought as he alter-
nated sips of Seagrams Seven with gulps of beer. Spics
should learn English.

Jerry liked La Cueva bar for the cheap drinks and
the barmaids who he thought of as being even
cheaper. The dim light smoothed their tan skin. They
both wore the same low-cut dress, yellow with pink
flamingos on it. Nobody but Nick would find him
here. Jerry liked that too. There weren't many people
he wanted to be found by anymore.

Nick could tell by the glaze over Jerry's eyes that he

had been there most of the afternoon. He sat next to him and ordered a Budweiser which the barmaid delivered without a smile or a glass.

"Gracias," Nick said to her.

The barmaid returned to the other end of the bar, as far away as possible.

"Don't even bother," Jerry said. "They're cunts. I come here for their tits, not their personalities."

"I knew you had a good reason."

"The best two sets in the city for my money."

"They are nice," Nick agreed.

"They're not nice. They're nice to look at."

Jerry and Nick drank and watched the barmaids while more racks of dresses wheeled through the loading dock behind them. Nick savored each swallow of beer.

"So, it could lead to something, this Johnson fight," Jerry said.

Nick shrugged his shoulders and studied the label on his beer bottle.

"It could."

"Whaddya mean, it could? Like I been telling you, when you're on the undercard of a Hearns fight, people are watching, for chrissake! Maybe you'll get a shot at the title. You win and you're set."

Nick shrugged his shoulders again. They were beginning to tighten from the workout he had just finished.

"You're never set in the fight game, Jerry."

Nick's read the Budweiser slogan on his bottle and knew that the purest water and the finest hops claim on the label was a load of crap. It was always after his workout that he wondered why he had sparred half-assed, let up when he should have fought like it was the real thing, the way you're supposed to before a fight, without thinking about your life or anything else, without needing Leon to tell you. He could have hurt Rashid if he wanted to. He knew that. Before a fight you can hurt a sparring partner and not feel bad about it. No one looks at you strange or says anything like, "Ease up, man. It's only sparring."

Jerry threw back his Seagrams Seven and ordered another.

"You want one, Nick?"

"No. Better quit while I'm still ahead."

The shorter barmaid took Jerry's money before delivering his drink. The taller one held her hand to her stomach and moved her feet and full hips in time to the song that sounded to Nick like all the other Spanish songs, brassy horns and the singer singing incomprehensibly fast.

The door opened and a man darkened the stream of daylight that poured into the windowless bar. Nick watched the man out of the corner of his eye until he was sure he didn't recognize him. Except for Jerry, Nick didn't want anyone he knew seeing him in a bar before his fight.

"Listen, Jerry. I was passing the post office, the main branch on Thirty-Third Street. I hear they're hiring." Nick stood and took a U.S. postal application from his back pocket. "Why dontcha fill it out?"

Jerry squinted at the application for a few seconds.

"Have another beer with me, Nick."

"I can't get drunk before the fight."

"You got 'til next Friday to sober up, for chrissake! C'mon, I hate drinking alone. I do it too fuckin' often."

Jerry grabbed onto the sleeve of Nick's T-shirt and pulled him back down onto the bar stool. "Say, Nick, you remember Lucille Sarducci, that girl we went to school with?"

Nick thought for a moment.

"Yeah. I remember. Pretty girl."

"I wonder what happened to her. You haven't seen her around, have you?"

"No."

"I always liked her," Jerry said, subdued and serious now. "I mean, if you were with her you wouldn't spend your time looking at other girls. She was smart too. It's like, you wouldn't have to answer a million dopey questions all the time. Most girls, you gotta lead them around by the nose."

"That was a while ago. She might not be so smart or pretty anymore." Two men came in and took seats at the bar. Nick stood, uneasy now. "I gotta get going, Jerry."

"She had them nice legs," Jerry said. "Not slutty, just nice. When the weather got warm in the spring she used to show them off. Remember that? But it wasn't like she was showing off. She was just showing them."

"She did have nice legs."

Jerry shook his head, punched his thigh and said, "For two fuckin' years I couldn't get up the balls to talk to her. I should have talked to her. Maybe if I stayed in school I would have."

Nick considered having another beer but knew there'd be no reason to stop after two. He put his hand on Jerry's back and could feel each rib individually.

"Don't worry about it, Jerry. Fill out the application, willya?"

"Do you think she's married?"

"Who? Lucille? How the hell should I know? Just fill out the application."

When he stopped thinking about Lucille Sarducci, Jerry noticed that Nick was gone. He drank for two more hours. By then the barmaids had merged into one. Four tits, four legs, two asses. That's all he saw. "Como se llama?" Jerry held out his hand to the shorter one who backed away and said something Spanish to the tall one about Jerry's twitching right eye and how she hoped he wasn't winking at her. "Cunt," Jerry muttered. Won't even shake my hand. Well, when I come in and lay down a C-note for a drink and let you keep the change, then you'll shake my hand. Then you'll fuck me and suck my dick and tell me to come back for more. Jerry crumpled his change into his pocket and stumbled out of La Cueva, leaving the bar bare of a tip.

Outside, the five o'clock sun was still strong enough to force Jerry to squint his drunken eyes. He walked without direction and soon found himself in midtown, surrounded by skyscrapers that reminded him of the giant casinos in Atlantic City. It occurred to him that both the casinos and the office buildings were built for the same purpose, to make money.

He sat on the edge of a fountain outside a building at Park and 51st and remembered his first trip to Atlantic City with his father who went there at least once a month after drinking cans of Schlitz beer at the kitchen table. "When I come back I'm takin' you to the best res'trant in the city," he always told his wife before leaving. The next morning he would stumble in and, without looking at her, head directly to the bedroom where he snored loudly until evening. He never did take her to the best restaurant in the city, or any restaurant as far as Jerry could remember.

On Jerry's tenth birthday, his father handed him the last beer in his six-pack and said, "Drink up." Jerry forced the beer down. His father looked at his watch and said, "It's about time I teach you a few things."

The other passengers on the bus to Atlantic City were loud and cheerful. Everyone seemed to know everyone else. One big, happy party. Some snuck hits from hidden flasks and bottles despite the "No Smoking or Alcoholic Beverages" sign. Jerry squirmed in his seat, light-headed from the beer while his father explained the rules of Black Jack. "Everything else in these fuckin' casinos is chance," he said. "But in Black Jack you can use your brain. It depends on the dealer too. You find a front loader and you can peek when he's dealing his hole card." Jerry's father winked. "Who knows, maybe we'll find one who likes kids."

A rush of adrenelin tingled Jerry's spine when the towering casinos finally came into view. After the long, dark ride through the New Jersey swamps, they looked like huge robots emerging from the ocean. Jerry got off the bus. The cold, salty wind from the Atlantic blew across the Caesars Palace parking lot and into his face. He heard waves breaking through the dark and the fog shrouding the deserted boardwalk. "Can we go on the beach?" he asked. His father looked at him, puzzled, and said, "The beach?"

Most of the time Jerry stayed at his father's side, intimidated by the lights and bells and screaming gamblers in the casino. He watched the stacks of chips being pushed back and forth. A chip fell to the floor. The dealer glared suspiciously when Jerry picked it up and put it back on the table.

His father gambled through the night and into the morning. After being up six hundred, the twenty-five dollars hands he started betting dwindled his small, unearned fortune considerably. And each time he tilted the last of his Seagrams Seven into his mouth, he sent

Jerry, with a dollar tip in hand, to find the cocktail waitress for another. When he was playing with the small remainder of his money, the waitress returned with another drink. This time Jerry kept the tip he held for her in his pocket.

On the way home, Jerry's father slept, his face pressed against the bus window, a timid dawn breaking over the New Jersey flatlands on the other side of it. The rest of the passengers either slept too or silently contemplated their losses against the back of the seat in front of them. Too excited to sleep, Jerry unfolded the dollar he'd kept and read the words written on it. He had held money before, but this was different because it was entirely his. He turned the bill over and over, studying the feel, the color and the smell of the worn paper for the rest of the trip back to the city.

Jerry filed the memory and picked a Village Voice out of a garbage can. He sat back down on the edge of the fountain and flipped the pages but mainly watched the workers, particularly the secretaries, leaving the building, on their way home. Maybe Lucille Sarducci was one of them. Maybe if they met again, things would be different.

Jerry lit a cigarette and tried to think of someplace to go, someplace he'd never been. He decided he had until his cigarette burned to the filter to figure out where and continued flipping the pages of the Voice until he came to the ones crammed with ads for phone sex lines and escort services and Korean massage parlours. He searched for the massage parlour he'd seen advertised before and had considered going to when he felt like he would explode if he didn't. Now, after watching the barmaids all afternoon, the reasons he used for not going seemed thin.

Jerry found the ad at the bottom of the page. He

tore it out and took small, measured drags on his cigarette until he tasted the burning filter. He dropped it
to the ground, crushed it beneath his heel and started
walking again toward a surer thing than Lucille.

Jerry's footsteps echoed up the stairwell of the East
36th Street tenement. At the third landing, he stopped
to catch his breath and swore without conviction to
quit smoking. The stale air he struggled to breath carried smells of food cooking mixed with the scent of
perfume. A cough from the landing above startled
him. He hesitated for a few moments, then grabbed
the banister and pulled himself up the next flight.

On the fourth floor landing, a solidly built Asian
man with an impassive face guarded a green door in-
scribed with gold, oriental lettering. His hands were
clasped military-style behind his back. Scary-looking
gook, Jerry thought.

"Hands in air," the man ordered. Jerry obeyed and
the man walked around him, searching him first with
hard eyes, then with his hands, patting every part of
Jerry's body capable of concealing a weapon. Jerry
was glad he had left his zip stick in the office shack.
Satisfied that Jerry was unarmed, the man whispered
into a intercom mounted on the wall, then opened the
three locks on the door and motioned him inside.

The Korean madam sitting behind the steel desk
studied Jerry coldly. Her prominent cheekbones were
smeared with makeup the color of pink bubble gum.
Behind her, six Korean women wearing cheap lingerie
and similar makeup sat on a sofa looking down into
their laps or straight ahead but not at Jerry who felt
the cartilage in his knees suddenly melting away.

Deep breaths failed to stop his knees from trembling

and his hands went numb. He couldn't feel his penis either, as if it didn't exist anymore. The door shut behind him. Keys jingled. Deadbolts slid into their slots.

"You pay me forty dollar now," the madam said in a flat, affectless voice, holding out her thickly-veined, impeccably manicured hand for the money. Jerry gave it to her and she quickly deposited it in the top drawer of the desk. "Which girl you want for massage?"

Jerry pointed to a petite girl with straight, black hair and breasts that looked too large for her slim body. He didn't give a shit that the others' feelings might be hurt because they weren't picked. Whores don't have feelings. The girl forced a smile and led him to a small room lit only by a long candle. A curtain printed with tropical flowers covered the window, blocking any daylight except for a thin band along the bottom. The girl handed Jerry a transparent, zippered purse and instructed him to put his wallet in it.

Jerry waited until she turned away before undressing and wrapping the towel she gave him around his waist. The girl took his hand and led him from the room down a narrow corridor lined with bamboo wallpaper. Still drunk, Jerry clumsily turned sideways to avoid touching a dripping wet man in a towel being led in the opposite direction. The man stared straight ahead and said nothing. Loser, Jerry thought.

The shower room reminded Jerry of the one in his high school gym. "Wash first,"the girl said. She adjusted the temperature of the water to warm before running the hand-held shower along the length of Jerry's body. Her tiny hands lathered his skin and his heart beat faster when she paused at his crotch to soap his balls and give them a squeeze. He looked down and saw that he was still limp. The spirit is willing, he thought.

When he was washed the girl led him back to the room and shut the door. She dried him with a rough towel that left his skin flushed. "On bed," she ordered. Jerry obeyed and lay on his stomach on a cot covered by a thin mattress with a light blue sheet stretched tightly over it. Muted traffic sounds seeped through the window. The girl removed her bra and climbed on top of Jerry in just her panties. He could barely feel her weight on his back.

"Now, what you want?" she cooed in his ear. Her breath smelled like she had just woken and had not yet brushed her teeth.

"Why don't we start with a massage?"

"Massage?" she said. "Just massage?" She reached under him and took his penis in her hand. "Oh, so big," she giggled. "Turn over and we have fun."

Jerry turned over. The girl straddled him again and did a slow, mechanical grind against his groin. Jerry looked up at her sagless breasts jutting straight and firm from her chest. He noticed small scars at the base of each one. Fuckin' silicone jobs, he thought with a surge of disgust that quickly rendered his semi-erect cock flaccid again.

"For hundred dollars you fuck me," the girl said. The word "Fuck" sounded strange coming from her child-like mouth. She leaned down close to Jerry's face. "You want fuck me, lover? You want fuck me now?"

Without considering any alternatives, Jerry took some bills from the purse and handed them to her. Still sitting on his sunken chest, the girl quickly counted the five twenties, then dismounted and put on a robe. "I come back, baby."

The warmth where she had been evaporated, allowing goosebumps to rise on Jerry's skin. He watched other girls lead their customers past the partially open door but felt powerless to close it. By the time the girl returned from delivering his money to the madam, the candle had burned to less than an inch and the room had darkened.

She climbed back onto him and performed the same grind. Now that she had the money, her face was set in a hard, business-like mask. Her sour breath floated down to Jerry again. *What the fuck has she been eating?* She reached back and took him in her hand.

"You no like me?" she said, pouting fakely.

"I'm not paying you to talk," Jerry answered, unable to look her in the eye. "Just do your job."

She squirted clear mineral oil from a bottle into her palm and started to rub the underside of Jerry's penis, gently first, then harder. No response. "What wrong? You no like girl?"

The only thing the comment raised was a prickly sweat on Jerry's brow. He looked up at her face and was sure she was restraining a laugh. A boozy rage expanded in his gut.

"Why don't you use your mouth, Sooky or whatever the hell your name is?" he said.

"Fifty dollar more."

"Fifty dollars?"

Reluctantly, he paid it. The girl left the room again and while waiting for her to return, Jerry noticed the light along the bottom of the curtain had dimmed. He looked up at the bare, white ceiling and had to close his eyes to concentrate, to hold back the mounting pressure pushing behind his cheekbones and at the base of his throat. When he opened his eyes, the girl was back, kneeling at the side of the bed as if praying to him. She bit open a plastic packet and held a rolled up condom between her thumb and index finger. She squirted more baby oil into her palm, grabbed ahold and pulled Jerry harder now, as if angry, as if she wanted to rip his member off and put him out of his misery.

While she worked on him, Jerry tried fantasizing to achieve an erection. He imagined the girl was someone else, Lucille Sarducci, not some skinny, fake-titted gook. But the harder he concentrated, the softer he became. The girl was starting to hurt him and the smell of her breath was making it difficult to hold Lucille's image for more than a few seconds at a time. She tried unsuccessfully to roll on the condom, then resumed the painful tugging.

Jerry slapped her face hard. He hadn't planned to. It was as if someone else had done it and he was merely a spectator. Fear registered in the girl's eyes and her mouth dropped open. Jerry worried that she would scream and bring the man outside the door. He quickly got up from the cot and put on his jeans. With her back turned to him, the girl put on her bra and robe. Her shoulders hitched a couple of times. She could have been crying but Jerry was sure she was laughing.

"I want my money back," he said, trying to keep his voice steady and calm.

The girl turned to him, revealing the redness where he had hit her cheek.

"No money back," she said before leaving the room.

Jerry figured it would be easy enough to get his cash back from the madam, but didn't relish the idea of fighting his way past the man outside the door. He sat on the cot, closed his eyes and suppressed a wave of nausea that brought up a mouthful of rye-flavored bile. He swallowed it down. His mind raced with incomplete thoughts and explosions of colors projected onto the insides of his eyelids. He knew he could borrow money from Nick if he had to. It wasn't the money he wanted back so badly.

Jerry finished dressing and took his last twenty from the transparent purse. He studied the wrinkled bill in the failing candle light and remembered again that first dollar he had made in Atlantic City and how he quickly learned that it said "In God We Trust" on the back and "This Note Is Legal Tender For All Debts, Public and Private" on the front.

"You go now!" the madame said sternly. She was standing in the doorway, her small fists clenched at her sides. "This is not hotel!"

Jerry focused on the small woman and imagined his fist busting open her tight little shark mouth, adding blood to the color of her painted face. He imagined doing the same to those bitches on the couch, saving the one he was with for last. She shouldn't have laughed.

He got up from the bed and felt nervous and weak-kneed as he walked past the madam to the reception area where the girls on the couch stopped talking and watched him. He could tell they knew. That little whore must have told them with a giggle that it was the easiest one fifty she ever made. Jerry tried the door. It was locked. He pounded it with his fist until the man outside opened it and stared at him with a glint of laughter in his eyes. He knew too, no doubt.

The residue of Seagrams ached Jerry's head as he let gravity pull him down the stairs. Reaching the street felt like breaking the surface after being underwater. He walked to the corner and stopped there for a few minutes, not sure which way to go in his anger and humiliation. He lit his last cigarette and started walking. It didn't matter where, as long as it was away. Atlantic City kept coming back to him for some reason. He couldn't get it out of his mind. He could almost smell the ocean as if he was standing right on it's edge. Atlantic City. It's a sucker's bet. That's what his father told him before falling asleep against the bus window on the way back to New York. He was right, Jerry thought. It is a sucker's bet.

C H A P T E R   S I X

Nɪᴄᴋ ᴡᴀᴛᴄʜᴇᴅ ᴛʜᴇ ᴛᴠ and rolled his neck every few minutes to keep it from stiffening. The doctor being interviewed on the 11 o'clock news said the Fifth Avenue Rape victim was recovering but the lab had not yet confirmed who belonged to the sperm specimen taken from her. At least they had other evidence, fibers from one of the suspect's T-shirts found in her apartment.

"If she died they could've gotten them for murder too," Jimmy said.

Walter put down his book and rested his eyes, tired from reading in the bad light. He looked up at the TV and said, "They're treating them like they've already been convicted."

Jimmy glared down the bar at Walter.

"You don't think they did it?" he said.

"I don't know all the facts. Do you?"

"I know enough of them."

Walter took a small sip of port.

"All I can say is thank God we have a legal system based upon proof of guilt, not conjecture and bias."

Jimmy turned to Frank.

"What the fuck is the professor talking about now?"

"His head's up his ass as usual," Frank answered even though he hadn't been listening.

"With all this news coverage, it'll be impossible to get an unbiased jury," Walter continued. "Everyone in New York's already formed an opinion."

"At least we know what the fuck's going on," Jimmy countered.

"What if they're innocent? Has that ever occurred to you?"

"If they're innocent now, they'll be guilty next time. Get those little spooks off the street before they become big spooks." Jimmy knocked back a shot of Jack Daniels.

Walter tried to read again, but the sentences no longer made sense.

"Why argue or even attempt discussion anymore?" he said ruefully. "What's the use? Thoughtful discussion is a dying art if not dead already."

"God, you're an asshole, Walter," Jimmy said.

Walter no longer cared what Jimmy thought of him. There was so much he could explain to him, to all of them if he only had the time and the energy. Tonight he was too tired to even try. Who'd listen, anyway. God, he felt tired.

"Nick, another port if you would."

Stanley pulled the book from Walter's hand.

"*Scented Gardens For The Blind*. What's it about? Gardening?"

Walter assumed an air of patience. He took the book back from Stanley and said, "It's a novel about a mother who wills herself blind in envy of her daughter who no longer speaks."

"No kidding," Stanley nodded, faintly interested. He returned his attention to the TV, to a show featuring a panel of morbidly fat people. The host of the show asked one of the obese woman to describe her eating habits.

"Man, she's fat," Stanley said, apparently transported by it all.

Jimmy and Frank each drank a shot of Jack Daniel's and let out a joint "Ahh!" Nick poured them another although neither had their money on the bar. Paddy had instructed Nick not to take any from them tonight even if they did. He preferred to get it later at the pool table, tax free. Frank cringed when he sipped his beer chaser.

"How can you serve this Schaeffer shit, Paddy?" he said.

"That's Budweiser." Paddy pointed to the three beer taps, two of them Budweiser and the third Schaeffer. "Can't you read?"

"Budweiser, my ass."

It was strongly suspected that Schaeffer kegs were hooked to all three taps. Nick, who knew, never confirmed nor denied. When pressed on it, Paddy always said, "You don't like it, go to one of them fag joints where they serve foreign beers with limes and salt and all that crap." If pressed harder he'd say, "If you knew any history you'd know that Schaeffer was what everyone in New York drank before that goddamned

Confederate beer took over!" Most of the time, though, Paddy stood by his story because a keg of Schaeffer costs half as much as a keg of Budweiser.

"Nick, get Frank and Jimmy another round," Paddy ordered. "And polish the bottles. They look like they been in some old lady's attic."

Nick refilled their glasses, pulled the rag from his back pocket and started wiping away the fine dust that had settled since yesterday.

The talker buying Margo drinks wanted to kill someone. No one in particular, just someone to rid himself of the anger building inside of him. Margo stirred her ice water gimlet with her pinky and timed her nods to the rhythm of the man's words. When he paused to adjust the briefcase between his feet, she said, "I don't know if I should be hearing this. Wouldn't that make me an accessory or something?"

The man took off his suit jacket and started to roll up his sleeves.

"If you want, you could help me do it." He spoke quickly, precisely. "We could be partners in crime. Afterward we could skip town. Go to Mexico. No, not Mexico. That's the first place they'd look." The man ran his hand over his bald spot. "How about Belize? It's supposed to be beautiful down there."

"It sounds very romantic," Margo said, pretending to shiver with excitement. "We'd be like Bonnie and Clyde. You do look kind of like Warren Beatty. Anyone ever tell you that?"

The man smiled sheepishly. "You know, Margo, I really feel like once would be all that's necessary. One final purge of all the bad things in my life. Then the slate would be clean and I could begin again. His eyes fixed on hers. "Maybe we could begin again together. Bartender? Another round, please," he said without taking his eyes from Margo.

Nick brought the new drinks, his Johnnie Walker Red Label, her water with ice and Rose's lime juice. The man paid Nick $13.50, then raised his glass. Margo looked into his dull, brown eyes and saw that he would never kill anybody. He didn't have the guts.

"_iner, _iner, _iner" The neon sign from the D-less diner across the avenue shined through the window and reflected off the bar. One night, while drinking a beer after jumping rope, Nick saw the "D" on the sign go out. He tried to attach some sort of significance to witnessing this event, like a shooting star or a meteorite landing, the kind of thing that usually happens when no one is there to see it.

On the TV, a Met slid into second base. A puff of dirt obscured the point where the second baseman's glove touched his ankle. The umpire called the runner out.

"He was safe!" Stanley yelled. "Can you believe that ump, Nick?"

"He was out, Stanley," Nick said.

"I saw it, plain as day! He was safe!"

"I think the umpire can see it better than you can. He's right there. You're watching it on TV."

Disgusted, Stanley gathered his lunch box and put his new Mets cap on his head so the visor obscured most of his face. "He was safe, Nick, and you know it!" He stormed out.

Walter came back from the bathroom.

"Listen to this, Nick." Walter marked a passage in his book with his finger and read: "'And no one knows how much the world is worn out, defaced by the continual rubbing of human sight upon its edges, corners and open pages.' The mother is explaining why she decided to go blind. It's an interesting concept, isn't it?"

"It is," Nick said, although he didn't get it.

"That's the stupidest thing I ever heard, someone making herself go blind." Stanley was back after being gone for less than half a minute. He sat on the same stool. "What she do, poke herself in the eye with a stick or something?"

"Maybe she'd rather be blind than see all the idiocy in the world," Walter said, turning to Stanley disdainfully.

"Being blind would suck." Stanley's eyes once again became glued to the game on the TV, impervious to Walter's quip.

Walter snapped the book shut and straightened the collar on his jacket, shaking his head in a hopeless, dejected manner. "Reading someone as good as Janet Frame makes me feel like I shouldn't even bother." He turned from Stanley to Nick. "I'll never be as good a writer as she is."

"That's not the way to think," Nick said.

"I know it isn't." Walter fanned the pages of the book with his thumb and repeated more quietly, "I know it isn't. I guess I'm upset because they put me on the lunch shift tomorrow. I hate the lunch shift. Obnoxious businessmen drinking martinis. Do you know how hard it is to carry a tray of martinis without spilling them?"

"I've never even made one," Nick said. "Can you believe it?"

"Well, that's understandable, working in a place like this. It's a beautiful drink if done correctly, especially when the light hits it right. I'll teach you how to make one tomorrow night." Walter tucked the book under his arm but seemed reluctant to leave. He stood and let his hand rest on the bar before putting it in his pocket. "I'll see you, Nick."

"Goodnight, Walter."

Night became early morning. Margo waited for an hour after the last talker left, but no one else came to see her.

"You did alright tonight, Margo," Nick said, trying to make her feel better. He gave her the money from the drinks her customers bought her. "A couple of real drinkers."

"Not bad." Margo put the money in her purse without counting it. "They'll be back for more."

"That last guy was a nut."

The talker who wanted to kill someone left reluctantly when Nick decided he'd had enough to drink and was getting a crazy glint in his eye. After being told to leave, the talker took a long time to roll down his sleeves and fix the knot in his tie. He put on his jacket, winked at Margo and said, "Remember, Belize," before shuffling drunkenly out. Through the window Nick watched him stop and talk to a whore. A few seconds later, talker and whore were gone.

"They're all nuts," Margo said. "Why else would they come see me?" She fixed her hair in the mirror behind the bar and drew her fingers over her cheeks as if to smooth any wrinkles. "It's easy money. I'll say that for it."

Now Margo started to feel the strange emptiness that sometimes came over her when the night was nearing an end, and she couldn't picture what the coming day would be like. The urge to kiss Nick was strong tonight. She'd never done it before, although she often wanted to and nearly did once when he was resting after shadowboxing and his face looked especially sad and worried and vulnerable. She hadn't allowed a man to kiss her in a long time, and never a man who was paying.

She knew Paddy didn't want her and Nick to get friendly. Before long they'll be working their own little arrangement was his logic. When you're done working, you collect your money and go, Paddy told Margo when she first started at Blue Paradise. When he was around, that's what she did. There was no sense getting him angry. It was easy money here and she didn't want to jeopardize that.

✕

Paddy and Frank were shooting pool on a table warped and marked by spilled drinks.

"You wanna bet on the next game?" Frank said before shooting and missing on purpose.

Paddy watched Frank's ball roll wide of the pocket. He checked the clock. Five AM. He estimated Frank had enough alcohol in his system by now. "All right," he said.

Frank went over to the bar which Nick was wiping with a damp rag.

"You want another drink, Frank?" Nick asked.

"I'm not drinking anymore, Nick. I'm not drinking any less either. Yeah, I want another drink."

Nick poured him another shot of Jack Daniels.

"Just watch," Frank whispered. "Paddy's gonna

have to burn this place down and collect the insurance money when I'm through with him." He pushed a twenty across the bar to Nick. "That's from Jimmy and me."

Frank went back to the pool table. His knees popped when he crouched to rack. The spent end of his cigarette drooped and finally broke onto the triangle of balls. He blew the ashes away.

A shot glass anchored the pile of money they were playing for, keeping it from being blown away by the overhead fans. The game went quickly. When Frank sank the eight ball, he said, "Whaddaya say, big spender? Double or nothing for the next game?"

Without a word, Paddy walked to the register and punched the "No Sale" key. The cash drawer flew open into his stomach. It hurt but he didn't curse. The register was the one thing in Blue Paradise exempt from his curses. He took out fifty dollars and whispered into the drawer, "This is on temporary loan, that's all."

Nick came from behind the bar and sat with Jimmy who was leaning his chair back against the wall. Smoke curled ghost-like from the end of his Partagas cigar.

"Don't you ever play?" Nick asked. It occurred to him that he had never seen Jimmy play pool.

"I'm not a gambling man," Jimmy answered. "I only bet on things I can control. If I was good at pool, I'd play."

Frank broke. The balls scattered evenly, but none of them dropped. While Paddy prepared to shoot, Frank took a cocktail stirrer from the glass on the bar and chewed on it.

"Make your first shot a good one," he said. "It may be your last."

"Worry about your own shots," Paddy said, not looking up from the table.

Frank slipped the stirrer into his pocket and put a new one in his mouth.

Paddy clicked the cue ball lightly against the ten which hit a warp in the table and veered left of the pocket. He slammed the butt of his stick against the floor with frustration. Frank put another stirrer in his mouth.

"You know how much a box of those stirrers costs?" Paddy barked.

Frank ignored him and shot the three ball into the side pocket. Paddy glanced anxiously at the pile of money.

The traffic on 11th Avenue thickened as the sun approached, rising toward the never seen horizon behind the Midtown skyscrapers. The reflection of the _iner sign on the bar became less defined in the pre-dawn gloom. Outside the window, a whore got out of a car. She slung a small handbag over her shoulder, yawned and shut the car door. Nick wondered how long she would be around. How many more tricks before her trick was up.

Sometimes, in the early morning, when the regulars were gone, Nick would sit in the empty bar with only the tinny, electronic melody from the pinball machine breaking the silence. He would watch the girls drifting sleepily up and down 45th Street, finishing their shifts too. He recognized most of them night after night. Occasionally a new one would appear and become a regular. Soon she looked like she had always been there. One day, of course, she'd no longer be there, conveniently making a space for another new one. Death and rebirth. Nick watched the cycle played out like the pinball melody in the bar over and over again.

This morning the regulars were still here, as if none of them could bear to leave and face the heat alone. Jimmy's cigar added to the bluish haze congregating over the pool table. His red-rimmed eyes looked at Nick, trying to figure out something about him.

"A white kid in the fight game," he said. His voice sounded hoarse. "I remember when they were all white, Nick. Some of the guys from the neighborhood did pretty good. Nowadays, I don't know." Jimmy blew dual streams of smoke from his nostrils. "This city used to be white. Before you were born. There were different kinds of whites; Irish, Italians, Polacks, Jews. We hated each other, but at least we were kind of on the same side. The niggers, they stayed in their neighborhoods and left us alone. Now . . . now it's a different story. You gotta watch your back all the time."

With only the eight and cue balls remaining on the table, Frank poured another ounce of Jack Daniel's into his mouth and clamped down on another stirrer. Paddy shot for the corner pocket and missed. The cue ball stopped just short of scratching. Frank hunched over the table and missed too.

"That's one thing I like about Paddy's place," Jimmy said. "You don't get many niggers here. They're around but for some reason they don't come in here too much. You can drink in peace. It's not like I'm a racist or nothing. I just think people should act the way they're supposed to. If they act like niggers, though, then fuck 'em."

Nick went behind the bar to get a beer. He came back and noticed that Jimmy seemed a bit uneasy, pre-occupied.

"What's up, Jimmy?"

"You're favored to win, Nick," Jimmy said quietly.

"The fight? Yeah, I should."

"This Johnson any good?"

"He's fast and he's got a good right hand, but he's supposed to have a glass jaw. That's why I'm favored. If I keep the pressure on him and bang him hard to the body, then come upstairs in the later rounds, I'll be able to take him. I should be able to."

Jimmy relit his Partagas.

"Ten to one," he said, shaking the match out.

"Ten to one?"

"Those are the odds."

"I'm not favored by that much."

"We got a line on you," Jimmy said, meeting Nick's eyes with his own. "Those are the odds we set."

Nick looked confused. Jimmy explained: "Nick, I don't fix sewing machines for a living. Well, yeah, I do, but that's just a cover. I'm a bookmaker. I take bets on sporting events." Seeing that this did not clear Nick's confusion, Jimmy added," I thought you knew. I thought everyone knew. Anyway I'm telling you because you might be interested."

Nick drank some beer, stared at the pool table and wondered why Jimmy was discussing all this with him. He had always figured from the way Jimmy dressed and his expensive watches and rings that he had another source of income besides fixing sewing machines. He never gave it much thought though.

Jimmy opened his eyes and said, "Nick, you're a good guy. I hope you win if that's what you want."

"Thanks, Jimmy. I think I will."

"But what happens if you don't?"

Nick paused, unable to answer at first.

"I don't know. I'll get more fights. I'll keep bartending. Things won't be that different."

Jimmy closed his eyes and with them closed he said, "They could be different, Nick. Don't answer me yet, just listen to what I have to say."

And while Jimmy spoke, Nick had a difficulty hearing all of it once the shock from what he asked him to do set in.

×

Paddy and Frank decided to play one more game, doubling the stakes again. The eight ball stood alone on the table. The stick shook in Paddy's hand as he looked over at the pile of money, pumped three times and hit high on the cue ball, sending it to the eight which shot directly into the corner pocket. Paddy turned to Frank and smiled, glad he'd agreed to double the stakes. He could have won a hundred dollars. Now two hundred was his. But the cue ball kept rolling slowly, hit the warp and picked up speed. Paddy's smile disappeared when the ball reached the edge of the pocket and paused there briefly before dropping out of sight. He listened to the cue ball descend into the bowels of the table, not quite believing what he'd just seen. Frank took the stirrer from his mouth and grabbed the money from under the glass.

"What the hell ya think you're doing?" Paddy said. An angry crease ran from the top of his nose to the top of his forehead.

"Taking my money," Franks answered. "That's what the hell I'm doing!"

"Your money?"

"You scratched on the eight ball." Frank looked at Jimmy and Nick for support.

"I know damned well I scratched the eight ball," Paddy said. "But that still ain't your money."

"It is too! I beat you fair and square!"

"You had help, you sneaky bastard!" Paddy took a stirrer from the glass on the bar and held it up to Frank like evidence in a courtroom. "It's these stirrers you kept chewing and sticking in your pocket. Every time I was shooting you took one and chewed it and stuck it in your pocket. You think I'm stupid? You think I don't notice things?"

"You're saying I jinxed you with the magical cocktail stirrers?"

"Damned right, I am!" The vertical furrow on Paddy's forehead deepened. "I've known you for thirty years, Frank, and if I know one thing about you it's you'll do anything to win!"

Frank stared at Paddy in disbelief.

"You're not kidding, are you?"

"No, I'm not."

Frank hesitated while deciding what to do next. Then he crumpled the money into a ball and threw it at Paddy. It bounced off his chest and fell to the floor as separate wadded bills.

"Keep the godamned money!" he yelled. "I don't need it if you're gonna accuse me of cheatin' it out of ya! Go ahead, take it! Buy a new fuckin' seat for the can with it! I'm sick and tired of squatting over the piss stains anyway!"

They faced each other, both contemplating their next move. For a few moments it looked like they would fight. Paddy's jowls quaked with rage. Frank finally said, "C'mon, Jimmy, let's get the hell outta here."

Frank walked out. Jimmy pushed himself up from his chair and shrugged his shoulders at Paddy. He squished his cigar in the ashtray and leaned down to Nick.

"Think about it," he said with a pat on Nick's

shoulder. "Don't give me an answer now, just think about it."

The door shut behind Jimmy. Paddy had already started to pick the money up off the floor when the door opened and Frank walked back in. He dropped a handful of chewed-up stirrers on the bar.

"Keep these for good luck, ya hump," he said. "You'll need them." Before leaving again, Frank picked a stale potato chip from the bowl on the bar but put it back after holding it to his nose. "Hey, Paddy, why dontcha break the bank and buy a new bag of chips? These smell like farts like everything else around here."

Paddy waited until Frank was gone to continue gathering the money, carefully uncrumpling and smoothing each bill. He put them in his pocket, then reached over the bar and angled his glass under the tap. He took a sip of beer to calm his nerves and looked out the window at Frank and Jimmy walking away up 45th Street. Frank's hands were cutting the air in wild gestures.

"I've had enough of this small time shit," he said to Nick, but mainly to himself. "It's a waste."

Nick washed the rest of the glasses in the sink and put them on the drying rack. He grabbed his bag which was still damp from sweat-soaked gym clothes.

"I'll see you later, Paddy."

Paddy raised one finger but didn't answer. He barely noticed Nick leave. Outside, the heat of the new day was already building on the old heat of yesterday. Nick turned around, thinking he'd heard Paddy call to him. But Paddy was staring blankly through the window, his hand around his beer glass. A sorry sight,

Nick thought. He turned away from Paddy and Blue Paradise and realized that in some ways it was good to have a boss who was not a friend and never would be. One less burden. One less thing to think and worry about. He stepped off the curb toward home.

CHAPTER SEVEN

THE WALLS of Nick's apartment were bare except for the poster of a young Muhammad Ali standing over Sonny Liston. That and a two-year-old liquor store calendar with a different American landscape for each month. Nick used to look at the poster often and dream of fighting like Ali. He used to take the calendar off the wall, flip the pages and imagine he was walking through the fields and mountains in the pictures.

A passing siren faded into the jumble of city noises. Nick turned on his side. The sweat clinging to the small of his back cooled slightly. He looked out the window into the narrow courtyard used mainly as a garbage dump by the residents facing into it. Late nights and early mornings were often shattered by beer bottles thrown from the upper floors. When the wind blew down from above, the layer of paper bags and candy wrappers swirled like a mini-tornado.

Across the hall, his neighbor, William, was raging.

"I grew up in a shit neighborhood, and I have what you call street smarts!" he yelled. Silence while William listened to an imaginary response. "How could you be so fucking naive?" he continued. "Stupidity is the affliction of the twentieth century and you can't tell me that isn't true! You can't tell me that! You can't tell me anything, in fact!" William lowered his voice to a more intimate level and said, "You're not very street smart, are you?"

At first Nick assumed William's nightly tirades were directed at someone present, someone in particular. But William lived alone and had no telephone. He never had any visitors either. Still, Nick preferred William's bouts of anger to the depressing sounds of the elderly tenants in the building: their dry coughs, their sneezes, their fiddling with teapots. He'd hear them through the doors of their one-room apartments as he walked down the hall in the early mornings after work. He'd hear them on Christmas and Thanksgiving and New Year's Eve, unaware of or trying to forget the holiday.

But William's screams and hisses weren't the source of Nick's sleeplessness this morning. He was still thinking about what Jimmy had said last night and could hear his words more clearly now. "You got nothing to lose but your pride," Jimmy had said. "And that, you can recover."

It's not such a bad living, working the bar, Nick thought. The bills left on the mahogany each night add up. And with the occasional fight purse, it's not a bad living for a single guy. Nothing to speak of saved yet, Nick lamented, and there're certainly better ways, but there're worse too.

Nick remembered Jimmy lighting another cigar.

"This is chump change," he said as if he had read Nick's thoughts. "Making this kind of money is like taking half a shit. Turn it into something real." Jimmy watched Paddy and Frank play pool for a few moments, then said, "You spend your whole life looking for a way to get a little more. It seems like someone else always gets there first. You know, Nick, my ex-wife was a good cook. She used to make these little burritos and freeze 'em. I'd come home from work, stick them in the microwave and sit in front of the TV with a beer and eat 'em. So, one day I get this idea. Why not sell them? Sell them to supermarkets and pizza parlors and hot dog vendors. Hell, everyone loved them. All my friends did. We could make a killing."

Paddy shot. Jimmy watched the seven ball roll into the corner pocket and seemed to forget about the burritos.

"What ever happened with them?" Nick asked.

Jimmy waved his hand in front of his face.

"Nothing, that's what happened. Now you go to any supermarket and they got frozen burritos. They even got restaurants that sell only burritos. Everyone's eating the goddamned things." Jimmy looked at Nick again. "Listen, I got a sure thing with you. You got a sure thing with me. I been around a few years. Believe me, that don't happen too often."

A straight bet, no propositions, no speculation on knockouts or rounds. They were going to bet on Johnson, a ten to one underdog. The odds might go higher, Jimmy speculated, depending on the betting. "And of course, this is between you and me, Nick, no one else."

All Nick had to do was lose—decisively. Leave no doubt in the judges' minds. Don't fake a knockout. You'd need the referee, the fight doctor and even Leon in on it to pull off a fake knockout. Just let Johnson outpoint you, beat you to the punch. Let his jab past your gloves. "Bet everything you got," Jimmy said. "You can't lose. As long as you make it look real, that is."

Both fights Nick did lose were close ones. Both were the nearest thing to death without actually dying. But it was the sound of the ref's voice echoing across the half-empty arena, calling out the winner's name, that hurt more than all the punches combined. And for weeks afterward, whether he was lying in bed or standing behind the bar, Nick would see the entire fight in his head, each punch he could have landed, each one he could have avoided.

Jimmy didn't mention his mafia backers, but everyone knew that all the bookies in New York were backed by the mob. Nick figured that's who Jimmy was talking about when he said: "Don't worry about a thing. They won't suspect anything. People bet against the odds all the time. That's how you make the real money. This is boxing, Nick. Upsets happen."

Nick thought he was finished, but Jimmy continued: "Freedom," he said. "That's what money is. And freedom means telling the world to go fuck itself." He motioned his chin toward Paddy and whispered, "You wouldn't have to work for that fat prick no more."

No doubt the payoff would be good, and there were things Nick wanted. Although he couldn't think of any right now. A car maybe. What do you do with a car in the city? He could buy an apartment and some nice clothes. He could open his own place and spend the rest of his life like Paddy. If he got caught, he could go to jail.

The bottom line was he had no money to bet. In a way, that would make his decision easier. And the one

certain thing was he'd be throwing away his boxing career. He'd have to start from the bottom again, work his
way back up. That could take years, take him past his
prime and into danger of getting hurt like Uncle John.

As a kid, Nick used to watch John fight, covering
his face and peeking through his fingers whenever
blood started coming from his uncle's nose or mouth
or the ridge of his brow. You should stop fighting, his
friends used to tell him. John would only shrug his
shoulders. He continued fighting until he was thirty-
seven, until his short-term memory was almost gone,
until an illegal punch to the small of his back finally
forced him to retire.

But Nick never forgot that John was the only one
who could and did protect him from his father's belt
and fists. And he was the only one who ever patted
Nick on the head and pinched his cheek and took him
and his older brother, Tommy, to Yankee games in the
summer. He'd slip them a few bucks when Nick's
mother and father, John's brother, weren't looking—
more than a few if he'd just fought. "They were right,"
Nick felt like saying every time he went to visit him
now in his roach-infested apartment. "You should
have quit earlier."

Tommy left home first. "I'm gonna kill you one day!"
he yelled at his old man. The fist-fight that followed
lasted for over an hour, leaving both Nick's father and
brother bleeding and exhausted, temporarily beyond
any more hate for each other. The next morning Nick
woke early and found the bed on the other side of the
room was empty. Tommy was already on his way to
Boston where he stayed with friends before moving to
California a few months later.

The last time he returned to New York, he met Nick for a beer in Rudy's on Ninth Avenue. He looked different, sullen, like the old neighborhood was drowning him in the memories he'd run from. Nick couldn't put it into concrete terms, but he knew instinctually that Tommy had reached the age when unrealized dreams begin to die. He sensed he wasn't far behind. They drank a lot but said very little. They talked about sports and music and watched women strut past on the sidewalk. Tommy told Nick the weather was good out in California. "How's the old fucker?" he finally asked.

Nick rolled onto his back and tried to change his thoughts like a TV channel. He thought about Alice and realized that whenever he stopped fighting it, the idea of marrying her seemed like a good one. Some nights she would speak to him about marriage without mentioning it directly. As they lay in the dark, she'd describe a cute child she'd seen that day, or a romantic book she was reading. Nick liked coming to her apartment after work and telling her about the crazy guy who tried to steal his tips off the bar, or the drunk he had to escort out onto the sidewalk. Alice would listen and make him promise to be careful, then tell him about the man who died of cancer, how she made his wasted body look like he never had cancer at all.

Sometimes, while holding her head between his hands, Nick would have to hold back his tears. As they were about to breach the edges of his lids, he would smother her face with kisses until his lips ached and he forgot for the time being that his feelings for her might soften him and ruin his chances of becoming a good, if not a great fighter.

X

Thoughts of Alice intertwined with thoughts of Margo. Nick remembered that bitter cold morning last winter. He had just closed Blue Paradise when he heard a thin voice struggling through the wind that blew the stoplights like clock pendulums over the empty intersections. After making sure the door was locked, he turned around to find Margo standing only a few feet behind him, wearing stilletto heels, a pink, spandex mini-skirt, and a down waistcoat. Her red lipstick contrasted with her wind-chilled complexion.

She asked him if he wanted a date. Nick said no and kept walking, thinking how strange it sounded when a prostitute asked if he wanted a date, as if he was supposed to take her to dinner and a movie. The ones in the neighborhood that knew him didn't bother trying anymore. They only asked if they could use the bathroom in Blue Paradise. If Paddy was upstairs, Nick let them.

The relentless winter wind scooped the breath from Nick's mouth and left him gasping clouds of condensation. He walked to the corner of 38th Street, stopped and tucked his chin to his chest to inhale warmer air from inside his wool hunting jacket. Margo caught up to him and put her hand on his shoulder, light and tentative.

"You want me to go home with you?" she asked.

Up close, Nick could see that her face was surprisingly pretty, perfectly oval with long-lashed brown eyes that never seemed to blink. It had not yet become thick and spooky from years of nights spent on the sidewalk.

"It's a cold night, huh?" Nick said, immediately feeling stupid for stating the obvious, restraining the urge to ask her what she was still doing out at four in the morning when the other whores had gone for cover.

"I won't charge you," Margo said, her words barely audible above the wind-clattering "No Parking" sign.

"I don't want any."

Nick walked away, more slowly now. Margo's high heels clicked against the sidewalk behind him. When he reached his building, Nick's cold-stiff fingers struggled to turn the key. He pushed the door open and the less cold air inside the vestibule prickled his face. He held the door open until Margo rounded the corner of 11th Avenue and started down 26th Street toward him.

Upstairs in his apartment, Margo sat on the couch, crossed her legs and lit a cigarette. They studied each other, their eyes meeting for only a moment or two at a time. She shivered and Nick offered to make her a cup of coffee.

"You have a kind face," Margo said. "That's why I followed you."

Nick handed her a mug of coffee and tried to keep his eyes from roaming the contours of her body which was wrapped tightly in a mini-skirt and unseasonable halter top.

"Can I stay?" she asked again.

"No, you gotta go after you finish your coffee."

Icy air penetrated the crack in the window, tainting the weak heat struggling from the radiator. Margo drank the coffee slowly and inhaled her cigarette as if the smoke was warming her lungs. While the steady wind whistled against the edge of the building, she told Nick she was born in Casablanca. She told him she hadn't made much money that night.

There was nothing in the apartment she could take worth worrying about. But you don't let a whore stay, he thought to himself as he put a clean sheet on his bed and gave her an extra blanket. You don't let a whore stay, he repeated in his head even after Margo was asleep in his bed and he was lying on the couch in the dark, listening to her shallow breaths, smelling the too-flowery scent of her dime-store perfume.

Margo came to Blue Paradise the next night and started coming regularly after that, usually when Nick was closing and getting ready to jump rope and shadowbox. If he closed early, he'd wait for the sound of her fake diamond ring tapping against the window. His heart would race slightly when he saw her face lit red and blue by the neon beer signs. He'd let her in and then throw more punches, trying to concentrate on turning his fists over at the last possible moment.

At first Nick treated her as if she was just another customer even though he never charged her for drinks. She would sit at the table nearest the jukebox, sip a beer or gimlet and watch him shadowbox. She always played slow songs.

"Want to dance with me, Nick?" she asked one night.

"I'm all sweaty."

"That's alright. I don't mind sweat."

"Maybe tomorrow night."

She looked good dancing by herself: her thick, shapely legs, her breasts rounding the top of her bra, pushing against the inside of her blouse, her belly curving gently to her crotch. Nick liked what he saw, but couldn't bring himself to touch her. Too many other men already had. He had Alice to think about also. And when he stopped shadowboxing, he couldn't help knowing that Margo was still a whore.

She started coming to Blue Paradise earlier in the night and Paddy noticed that men liked talking to her.

They bought her drinks and soon she rarely had to pay for any. While they spoke, she listened, knowing how to nod even when she wasn't. She knew how to ask questions to keep them talking.

Paddy soon had Nick charging "extra" for the drinks the men bought her. You keep everything over the regular price of the drink, Paddy told Margo, aware that she could sell a lot of alcohol for him. The same men started coming back just to see her. Ten dollars for a drink and the undivided attention of a pretty woman. A bargain.

Nick sat up in bed, still tired but unable to quench his fatigue with sleep. He discovered his fear had grown overnight, become larger yet less focused. With the fight only a week and a half away, he tried but could no longer picture nor forecast it clearly. It wasn't losing a fair, real fight that scared him as much as it used to. What was it, then? Not throwing the fight convincingly? The realization that maybe he didn't want to win as badly as he once did? Nick put on his jeans and stuffed his shorts and handwraps into his canvas gym bag.

He got back into bed and threw a lazy jab toward the ceiling. The damp heat coming through the open window reminded him of the gym which was now part of another world, another reality. As he lay in bed, the leathery odor of gym sweat that always gave him a stab of anxiety came back to him. "You don't gotta fight, whiteboy." Nick could almost hear Leon's thick voice, clogged with the phlegm he never bothered to clear completely. "You got options. Great fighters don't got options." Fuck you, Leon! But Nick knew Leon might be right. He did have an option.

CHAPTER EIGHT

THE WAITRESS standing at the service bar answered Jerry's lustful stare with a frown before carrying her tray of drinks onto the casino floor. Jerry watched her weave among the gamblers, imagining her on top of him with passion, the kind that looks like pain, etched in her face. "Oh, yeah," he said aloud. He inhaled a sip of Seagrams.

The dealer was shooting cards out to a semi-circle of black jack players while, behind him, a stoic pit boss was overseeing his table and three others arranged in a square. The amount of Seagrams he had drunk was making it difficult for Jerry to focus on the dealer's face, but there was definitely something different about it, a certain degree of desperation in his eyes, the way he blew out his cheeks after taking deep breaths. He shifted his weight from one foot to the other and kept fidgeting with his apron.

Jerry was sure that reading faces was one of his few talents. Only the stone cold can keep their feelings a secret, he knew. But even the stone cold are human. Jerry remembered again what his father had said about dealers on that first trip to Atlantic City: "Who knows, maybe we'll find one who likes kids."

There were no clocks in the casino, but Jerry figured the dealer's shift could only last one or two more drinks. He buttoned his thrift shop blazer and checked his shoulders for dandruff. Appearance is everything. People don't see you, they see what you look like, especially at the top. Go to the ocean if you want to catch the big fish, he told himself. Well, that's exactly what I'm doing now, isn't it?

Jerry was happy to be finally following his own advice. He noticed that his money on the bar had diminished substantially in the past two hours. He downed the rest of his Seagrams. Its warmth spread through his body. Consider this an investment, he thought as he paid the bartender for another one.

The cocktail waitress returned with her tray empty and her tip cup full. Jerry caught her eye and smiled, pulling his lips tight and crooked over the top row of his teeth. The waitress looked away and said something to a large bartender who shot Jerry a mean look that made him decide he wouldn't smile at the waitresses or any other girls anymore.

On the floor, the dealer clapped his hands together, spread his fingers wide, and turned his palms up toward the camera hidden in the ceiling. He touched three fingers to his forehead in a sarcastic salute and said something to the pit boss before coming from behind his table and disappearing through a nondescript side door. Jerry drained his drink, crumpled his money into his pocket and made sure the bartender's back was turned before sliding off his stool and disappearing into the mass of gamblers.

Jerry figured he had at least ten minutes before the dealer would finish changing clothes and emerge from the employee exit on Pacific Avenue. He searched for the customer exit, but couldn't find it. The floor was jammed with gamblers, desperados playing black jack and roulette and craps, old ladies sitting at the slot machines with plastic change buckets cradled in their laps and their hands held eagerly under meager streams of dropping coinage. To regain his bearing, Jerry tried to find the bar again but it too was nowhere to be found. The lights and bells and screaming people and the continuous stream of quarters dropping in and out of the slot machines all around him only added to the confusion. Someone shouted, "Seven! Seven! Seven!" No one was smiling.

Jerry finally found the exit and stepped out into the ocean fog. By now his alcohol-induced calm was nearly gone. He stuck a cigarette in the corner of his mouth and his hands began to shake as he fished for the lighter in the pocket of his blazer. He got the cigarette lit and the first rush of nicotine settled his nerves a bit.

He crossed Pacific Avenue and waited directly across from the Caesar's Palace employee exit he had found earlier before going inside. Not many cars passed on the street and the only other people on the sidewalk was a gang of teenagers skulking by, silent and menacing. Jerry patted the zip stick in his pocket and wondered if it would work. He cupped his cigarette in his hand to keep the teenagers from seeing it. They'd want one if they saw it.

Someone came out of the exit. Jerry's breath caught in his throat until he realized it wasn't the one he was waiting for. His mind wandered again and he imagined that the fog thickening around him would soon fill his lungs until he suffocated.

The dealer eventually came out. He took off down Pacific Avenue, walking quickly past the quiet bars where the patrons drink more than talk, past pawn shops with cameras and jewelry in the windows, still open for gamblers willing to trade whatever they have left for a few more rolls of the dice. Bars and pawn shops. That's all there was except the Seven-Eleven where the teenagers had decided to stop and waste some more time.

Jerry tossed his cigarette butt into the gutter and was soon winded by his struggle to keep up with the dealer. Where's this fucker going? Jerry coughed and spat a gob of phlegm onto the sidewalk and was relieved when the dealer finally stopped and cupped his hand against the window of a bar with flickering red lightbulbs fringing a small marquee that read, "Curves" in black letters. Jerry watched him go into the bar, then leaned against a lamppost and decided to catch his breath and smoke another cigarette before joining him. No rush now. By the time he smoked the cigarette down to the filter, he still hadn't caught his breath. He shot the butt into the deserted street and went inside.

Rapidly flickering strobe lights made the dancers movements look robotic.

"That's five bucks," a slick-haired bouncer in a shiny, double-breasted suit said. It was more of an accusation than a request.

Jerry handed him the money and the bouncer gave him a threatening one-over. "Have a good time, fella." He folded Jerry's money around a wad of bills and shoved the wad back into his pocket.

The dealer was sitting alone at the bar, a bottle of Rolling Rock already in front of him. Even off from work, his shirt buttoned to the top and his sleeves were pinched tightly around his wrists by fake gold cuff links. His head was tilted up to the blonde on stage who rubbed her crotch against the brass pole that ran to the ceiling. The dealer handed her a dollar folded lengthwise. The blonde took it, said a distant thanks, then rubbed against the pole harder for a few moments. Jerry sat and ordered a Seagrams from the bartender whose tits were bigger than those of the two dancers on stage.

He put another cigarette between his lips and let it dangle unlit. While waiting for his drink, he noticed the stubble where the dancer in front of him had recently shaved her inner thighs. He searched for his lighter and, just as he was about to pull it out, dropped it back into his pocket and nudged the dealer's elbow instead.

"You got a light by any chance? I think I lost mine."

The dealer snapped out of his trance and turned to Jerry who immediately saw the same desperation he'd seen in the casino. With his hair neatly combed, a razor straight part on the side, and his pinched expression, he looked to Jerry like the kind of guy who breaks instead of bends, the kind of guy who hasn't taken a shit in a week. But also a guy willing to do almost anything if properly persuaded.

"Excuse me?" the dealer said.

"You got a light?" Jerry repeated. "I think I lost mine."

The dealer wasn't smoking, but he slid a stray book

of matches along the bar. Jerry lit his cigarette, shook the match out and watched the dancers going through their motions while trying to think of something else to say. Without knowing exactly where the words were coming from, he said, "We're the ones being exploited, not them."

"Who?" the dealer asked, confused.

"Us. You and me. We're the ones being used, not the dancers like everyone thinks."

"Yeah. Us," the dealer parroted wearily.

"Most people don't realize it, but we're really the victims in these bars," Jerry said. "Once you have a few drinks, you can't say no to these babes and they know it. The next thing you know, you're loaded and broke."

"That's the case everywhere. It's not just in these bars."

The girl in the sky blue thong bikini had a sixteen year-old face and a woman's body. She worked her way down the bar stools, from customer to customer. The dealer said no thank you to a lap dance. The girl did the same innocent eye-flutter for Jerry and said, "Hi, honey. You wanna private dance?"

"How much?"

"That's up to you."

"If it was up to me, it'd be free." Jerry glanced at the dealer to gauge his reaction. None. By the time he looked back to the girl, she was already standing in front of the man sitting on the next stool. "Cute one, isn't she?"

"She is," the dealer said.

"But I'm sick and tired of being taken for a ride all the time. I mean, all these girls see when they look at you is a big dollar sign. All that lovey-dovey shit is a scam. They're like all women, I guess. Wave a C-note under their noses and they love you. Whores."

"Everyone in this town's got their hand in your pocket. These girls, the casinos, everyone."

"Yeah, you got that right." Jerry snapped his fingers.

"You know, you look familiar to me. Where have I seen you before?"

"I don't know."

Jerry snapped his fingers again.

"I know. I saw you in Caesar's. You deal black jack there, right?" The dealer nodded reluctantly. Jerry lowered his voice to sound sad and a little defeated. "I just dropped two hundred playing craps there tonight. Maybe my luck would have been better if I'd gotten on your table."

"Maybe it would have," the dealer said.

Jerry was glad to see him grin.

"I'm Bill," Jerry said, not wanting to use his real name.

The dealer shook Jerry's weakly. "My name's Robert." He looked back at the blonde on stage.

"Robert, let me buy you a drink."

When the drinks came, Jerry put on a more cheery voice. "So you like dealing? Whenever my buddies and me play, I always deal because I'm the only one who can keep the cards from sticking together. I imagine it's a pretty good job, dealing."

"It's a shit job, Bill," Robert said without any hesitation. "It's Bill, right?" Jerry nodded.

"The highest paid factory job in America, Bill. That's what I call it."

Jerry's heart raced. A warm, cozy feeling returned.

"We're nothing but shit to the casinos," Robert said, starting to build steam. "We're expendable. There're no other jobs in this town and they know it. They blame us when the gamblers get lucky. If the casino doesn't make its quota, they take it out of our hides. You complain, you're fired. You smile at a customer, you're fired. You pick your nose, you're fired. They don't care. There's always someone willing to take your place."

Jerry sensed he was close and didn't want to blow it. He knew he had to have a strategy and would be able to think better without the music and the girls, who were starting to look damned good. He excused himself and went to the bathroom and stood full-bladdered at the urinal for nearly a minute before he could relax enough to pee. When he finished, he washed his hands carefully and ran them through his hair in front of the mirror. "Shit!" It was thinning in front and his eyes were dark and tired looking. His reflection seemed like nothing more than an acquaintance.

Jerry returned to the bar and ordered Robert another round.

"You have any idea how much money passes through my hands every night?" Robert said as if there had been no break in the conversation. "Believe me, there isn't a dealer alive who hasn't thought about it."

"Thought about what?"

Robert didn't answer. He put his hand over a quarter lying on the bar and contracted it slightly. The quarter disappeared into his palm. When Robert relaxed his hand, the quarter dropped with a ping onto the bar. He spun his stool around and leaned back. A different girl came over. This time Robert hooked a dollar in her garter and she moved between his parted knees and started to shimmy out of beat with the music thumping from the speakers. The girl licked her lips with counterfeit desire, then rubbed her round ass against his crotch. Robert let his hands rest on her hips while she earned her pay. When the minute was up, she stopped and walked off.

"You guys don't have a union?" Jerry asked, watching that great, round ass skip over him on its way to greener pastures.

Robert laughed.

"Union? There're better ways to screw those motherfuckers, believe me."

He spun his stool back to the bar and palmed the quarter again. Jerry expected him to say something else, but he continued to palm and drop the quarter with a concentration even the girls and the music couldn't disrupt.

The song ended and in the brief silence before the next one, Robert let the quarter rest and squinted hard at Jerry through the flickering lights. He took a long swallow of his new Rolling Rock, letting it flow freely into his mouth. A fresh wave of nervousness dampened Jerry's brow despite the air conditioning that prevented the dancers from sweating.

"So, what's your plan, Bob?" Jerry asked, pleased that the words came out smooth and casual.

Robert was neither surprised nor confused by the question but the silence between them would have been embarrassing at a cocktail party. Jerry steadied himself with a good pull of Seagrams.

"Who's asking?" Robert finally broke the silence.

Jerry smiled crookedly and said, "Just one guy in a bar asking another, that's all."

Robert's face and shoulders remained tight until Jerry added, "I wouldn't mind getting back that two hundred dollars I lost tonight, though."

Robert ordered another round. When the bartender was out of earshot, he said, "Chips are the best way."

"Chips, huh?"

Robert explained how they could do it. He told

Jerry about the apron the casinos make the dealers wear around their waists, supposedly to protect their pants, but really to prevent access to their pockets. The apron rubs against the table and has to be straightened frequently. That's the move. You adjust the apron. What they don't see is the palmed chip being dropped into the waistband of the pants beneath the apron. It's then guided by gravity down the shirt that's tucked into the underwear bag he'll be wearing; two pairs of underwear, the bottoms sewed together to form a pouch that holds the chips. He told Jerry he thought of sewing two aprons together, but decided on underwear. Not many pit bosses had the nerve to check there.

Jerry's job would be to cash the chips. Only once a week. More often and someone in the cashier cage might remember him and get suspicious. And the less they met, the better. Everything was going to be done carefully, well thought out. Of course, the split was going to be fifty-fifty.

They planned to meet again next week to iron out the details. Until then all Jerry had to do was get a mail box in New York under a fake name and maybe tell Big Bob to get someone else to watch his vans. A bus ride to Atlantic City and a trip to the cashier cage was going to be his job now. Jerry felt like celebrating a little, so he paid a girl to dance for him. She rubbed her body against his. Ah, the beauty of it! He gave her an extra two dollars for a kiss on the cheek. It felt good to be kissed by a girl on the cheek even if she was just a step above a whore.

The fog drifting across Pacific Avenue helped Jerry imagine he was already in heaven, a triumphant angel floating a foot above the pavement. The clock on the municipal building read three-thirty. Jerry stood on the deserted sidewalk, contented and tired. He took a crumpled bus schedule from the breast pocket of his blazer and studied the grid of times and destinations. The next bus to New York wasn't leaving until five AM.

He decided not to drink anymore. That would only cause his finely balanced high to crest and descend into drunkenness. So, he headed toward the water and, as he came closer, the waves grew louder and the smell of the ocean intensified. He climbed over the boardwalk railing and, after bracing himself for impact, dropped down to the beach. His skinny legs buckled beneath him and he fell back onto his ass. Still sitting, he took off his shoes and tried to remember the last time he'd felt sand beneath his bare feet. He stood and, too tired to run, he walked toward the white line of waves with his face pointed up to the sky. At the edge of the water he did a little victory dance. That gook bitch nearly screwed up his day, but things turned out okay after all.

Jerry considered taking off his khakis, then decided to just roll the legs to his knees and wade into the rushing foam. The cold water soon warmed around his calves. He splashed some into his face and onto his hair and opened his mouth to taste it. His body felt light, poised to float away.

For nearly half an hour he stood in the water watching the lights of the boats and ships cruising the dark horizon. He turned around and the casinos startled him as if they had not been there before. He walked up the gentle incline of the beach to where the hard, wet sand became dry and soft and squeaky. Jerry let his knees buckle and remained lying where he fell. Then he rolled onto his back and looked up at the stars and remembered what Robert had said about not being deceived by the fun and glitter of Atlantic City. It's a mean town, he'd said. It's only here to separate you from your money. But it can work both ways, they agreed. They agreed that's the way everything should work.

Jerry thought about that until he fell into a deep sleep. And while he slept, the sun slowly rose out of the Atlantic on its way toward the top of the sky. When he woke, he didn't care that he'd missed the five AM bus. He brushed the sand out of his hair and off of his clothes and went to a coffee shop on Pacific Avenue where he could cure his hangover with coffee and eggs while waiting for the noon bus back to New York.

CHAPTER NINE

Cars cut through rainbows of oil on 11th Avenue. Above them, the sky looked like it would smother the city if it came any lower.

"Maybe the rain will break it," Nick said to no one in particular. He stood in the doorway of Blue Paradise watching the fine drops float through the street lights, imagining the crowd at the fight screaming with each punch.

Stanley called for another beer. The regulars. They think they own you, Nick thought, slightly annoyed. They start expecting things, free drinks, like they deserve them, and you're doing them wrong if they don't get them. Serving a guy like Stanley every night for a living. Every fuckin' night, for the same two dollar tip. Nick walked to the end of the bar and ducked beneath it. He looked at Stanley's face and suddenly wanted to channel everything he was feeling into a punch, a straight right to his well-padded jaw. He tilted the tap forward and gave Stanley his beer.

"Thanks, Nick."

"No problem, Stanley."

No wonder no one else ever comes in here, Nick thought, remembering an incident that had occurred earlier in the evening. A kid wearing a college t-shirt had come in and ordered a beer. Nick poured it for him and, as soon as the kid began to drink, Jimmy started in on him: "Hey, there cupcake, where'd you go to school? Me, I went to college too. Fuck U. Every heard of it, creampuff? It was a good school. I got a real good education there."

The kid didn't respond and Nick thought that was the end of it, but Jimmy continued: "I'll bet you bang lots of co-eds, dont'cha, kid? The easy life. Mommy and daddy paying so you can bang cheerleaders. Well, how about I bang you, little girl? Whaddya come in here for, an assignment for your sociology class or was it urban studies? See how the other half lives."

The college kid left without saying a word. Half his beer and a dollar tip remained on the bar until Nick cleared it away.

"Why'd you do that, Jimmy?" he asked.

"Oh, c'mon, Nick, I was just having some fun. He left you a tip. He wasn't gonna have more than one anyway."

Nick willed his anger to mellow. Stanley, Jimmy, Paddy. What a bunch. He moved to the other end of the bar and checked on Margo who was talking to a man in ripped jeans and a Pittsburgh Steelers' cap. Nick guessed he was a construction worker or a truck driver. Not Margo's usual type of customer. His whiskey and soda was still nearly full and his hand was resting on her knee. Margo smiled nervously as the man stared into her with his shifty black, pin-point eyes. She leaned back as much as he leaned forward, then looked over at Nick whose reassuring wink dispelled most of the tension from her face.

Walter put down his Janet Frame novel and whispered the last line of the chapter to himself. He rubbed the sides of his mouth with his thumbs and whispered the line again. Next to him, Stanley was watching the Yankee game, his hand warming his new beer. Stanley unglued himself from the screen and eyed Dog who was sitting beneath the television.

"Don't you ever watch baseball, Dog?"

"It's just a game," Dog answered.

"It ain't just a game," Stanley snapped. "They're not just playing a game."

"That's what's sad about it," Walter said.

Stanley made a sucking sound against his teeth and said, "I don't wanna get into it with you, Mr. Professor." He looked to Nick for support. "Every time I say one fuckin' thing, he's gotta go make it bad. Now it's baseball. He's gotta make it bad."

"I hate to rain on your parade, Stanley," Walter stated calmly, as if talking to an unruly child. "But they're not out there for your entertainment. Everyone's making money from it except for schmucks like us. Do you agree, Nick?"

Nick didn't want to get involved. Tonight, just the effort of speaking was draining. And lately, ever since Jimmy's proposition, he was finding it hard to look people, even Walter, in the eye. It was as if everyone knew about it, could see right into him and hear his every thought.

"Yeah, I mean. You know. It's the national past-time," Nick said.

"That's exactly it," Walter concurred. "And the national pasttime in America is making money. Baseball is a perfect symbol for it. The players earn huge salaries. The owners rake it in. The stations and networks profit enormously. The beer, cigarette and car companies practically have a captive audience for their ads. Even the little billboards all over the stadium brainwash us into buying things we don't need. You're the smartest one, Dog. The safest place is under the TV where you can't see it."

A special news report interrupted Walter and the game. Nick turned up the volume so they could hear the newscaster urging viewers to spend as little time out of doors as possible. The prolonged heat and lack of wind was having an especially devastating effect on the lungs of the elderly and those with respiratory problems. And the rain was making it worse, bringing the pollution down to street level.

"How do you like that?" Stanley said when coverage of the game resumed. "You can't watch baseball or even breathe anymore without feeling bad."

Paddy never looked pleased when he came down from his apartment and saw only five people at the bar, especially five who were always there. He frowned first at the open door, then at the TV.

"Did you just see that special weather report, Nick?" he asked in a friendly way.

"Yeah, I saw it."

"You did see it?" Paddy cupped his hand behind his ear as if suddenly hard of hearing.

"I said I saw it."

"Did you hear it?"

"Of course I heard it. If I saw it, I heard it."

"Well, if you saw it and you heard it, why the fuck is the door still open?"

Paddy walked to the door and kicked the wooden wedge from under it. "You trying to let all that toxic shit in here?" he added as the wedge skittered and spun across the floor and the door swung shut. The TV became louder in the absence of street noise. Paddy pulled the cords on the overhead fans so they would wobble faster. He looked over at his patrons as if they were not worth even that meager effort, then sat at the bar next to Walter, ordered a beer from Nick and started watching the game.

The camera focused for a moment on George Steinbrenner, owner of the Yankees, sitting in his glass booth with two fingers pressed to his temple, peering down to the field like a cat stalking a mouse.

"Steinbrenner," Walter sniffed. "The epitome of the late twentieth-century American man. He's what I'm writing my novel about basically. He's a pig just like Donald Trump and Lee Iacocca, contemporary robber barons. At least the Rockefellers, the Morgans, the Carnegies, and the Fricks had the decency to give something back to society instead of just getting fat off it."

Stanley wasn't listening anymore. Paddy was, with sour contempt on his face.

"You know something, Walter?" Paddy said. "You oughta write a book called "The Adventures Of A Candy-Ass." At least you know something about that."

Back upstairs, Paddy wandered his apartment, not knowing what to do with himself. He peeked into the bedroom where his wife was sleeping, then went into the den and sat in his chair. His body forced old-smelling air out of the cracked vinyl upholstery that dug into his back. Sweat formed in the space between his back and his shirt. Tonight the apartment seemed to concentrate the heat from outside.

He thought of all the hot summers and the cold winters and the featureless springs and falls he'd spent here and downstairs at the bar his father opened when Paddy was six years old. The bar, it seemed to him, was a part of the family, a cranky grandparent he loved but didn't like, a legacy he was compelled to carry on. As soon as he was old enough to work it, he did. He took it over entirely when his mother and father could no longer run it. When they died, he might have moved from the city if he'd tried. No one was keeping him here anymore. But he had a living here, he'd argue in his head at night. Why risk that? And he had roots. So here he stayed.

Paddy looked up at the low ceiling, yellowed from water damage. Should have sold the damned building during the 80's. Can't give it away now. Some of the old-time places like his became unexpectedly popular during the free-spending 80's. Paddy had renamed it Blue Paradise to catch some of the cash. But business stayed the same. In fact, he was beginning to feel an intense frustration, even revulsion, whenever he went downstairs and saw the small amount of business he had, the same bunch sitting at his bar day after day, night after night.

Maybe Nick's the problem, Paddy reflected. Not a bad kid, but he needs a wake-up every once in a while. Thinks he can make it as a boxer. Who the fuck is he? He should concentrate on his bartending. So he's won a few fights. Just got lucky. He only got his shots because he's white. All those promoters see is green.

Paddy kept thinking. Maybe what Blue Paradise needs is a bartender who's hooked to the outside, who can draw in the right customers, people with cash, good-looking girls, businessmen from midtown. Nick's been hit in the head too many times to relate to those types. They want a bartender who can talk nice and remember jokes. The nickle and dimers from the neighborhood, them Nick can relate to. And who the fuck wants to drink in a place with those losers hanging around?

Paddy looked through the open window at the midtown skyscrapers, their top floors disappearing into the fog of heated pollution, only the airplane lights at the tops visible. He felt a vague satisfaction that maybe he was beginning to figure the world out, even if it was getting late for him to do anything about it. It's going to take something else, he thought. At this stage in my life it'll have to be something fast, something easy.

Paddy struggled to keep his eyes open as a wave of fatigue washed over him. The lottery numbers were going to be picked in an hour. He had to stay awake for that because he'd bought ten dollars worth of tickets this week. Twenty chances. He always bought that many when the jackpot went over eight million. He pulled the lottery stubs from his wallet. Certain things can't be changed. I was born in this apartment. That's one of them, he thought as he studied the computer printed numbers. But I don't have to die in it.

Paddy pushed himself out of the chair, walked to the window and poked his head out. Below him, on 11th Avenue, a few whores milled in imperfect circles. It made him feel a little better that they were out even in this weather. At least there're people in this city worse off than me.

Before closing, Nick stood again in the doorway and looked into the mist enshrouding 11th Avenue. He was glad Jimmy didn't come in tonight. He hadn't seen him since Thursday and, in that period of time, Jimmy had become more than just Jimmy, a Blue Paradise regular. Now he represented something slightly menacing. Of course, until he gave Jimmy the word, Nick knew his decision was neither final nor irreversible.

Excuses. Nick knew he used them far too often. In the gym, with Alice, here at Blue Paradise. He used them to avoid things such as where his relationship with Alice was going. Wait until after the fight, he'd tell himself and her before each one. He used excuses to avoid fights, real ones, street fights, bar fights. Afterwards he'd assure himself that walking away was the right thing to do. Afterwards, alone at the bar with his hands and knees still shaking, he'd drink vodka straight and warm to make them stop and to keep the vomit down in his stomach.

He never told anyone of his constant fears, not even Alice. He hadn't yet told her about throwing the fight either, and wasn't planning to. Why add to her worries? And Jerry. Sometimes, when they sat together in the van yard, Jerry would tell him that he had balls. "You were born with them, Nick," he'd say. Nick once replied that he only had balls when he had to have them, when there was no other choice. Nick wondered what Jerry was up to tonight. He remembered him saying something about going to Atlantic City to do some gambling.

Margo was washing and reapplying her makeup in the bathroom. She always came out smelling fresh and newly perfumed, her breath hinting mint from the small bottle of mouthwash she carried in her pocketbook. It gave Nick energy when she stayed and watched him shadowbox, knowing that she knew when his punches were flowing and had snap and when they didn't, that she knew when his feet were moving with balance and speed. It occurred to him that she, of all the people he knew, did not burden him at all. When she was around, he felt almost free.

Nick looked up, then down the avenue. Empty. He went back inside and sat at the bar and listened to the ice in the bin creak and shift as it melted. Paddy preferred to ice the beer. It's cheaper than buying a cooler.

Nick hadn't drank since last week with Jerry in La Cueva. He felt an almost physical need for one now, a tightness in his belly. He reached over the bar, took a bottle of Reingold from the ice and opened it. Foam spurted from the top. He took a sip and felt the beer filtering through his body. Just one.

The point was to be mean and hungry going into the ring. Even one beer could ruin that. No sex either. With Alice this wasn't much of a sacrifice, although his desire for Margo had been building steadily. He liked being with Margo. She made him forget about things, at least for a little while. He was probably going to throw the fight, take a dive in front of hundreds of people at the Paramount, in front of millions on TV. It was hard to forget that for very long. He took another swallow of beer and closed his eyes to sharpen the taste.

Margo came out of the bathroom. Her kiss left a red imprint on Nick's cheek. She let her tiny, sequined pocketbook fall from her shoulder onto the bar.

"Was that last guy alright?" Nick asked.

"He was a cheap bastard. He nursed his drinks like

they were made of gold. All he talked about was how unlucky he was to have such a big cock. He says the women are scared of it. He said he practically needs a blood transfusion to get the thing up, it's so big."

Nick handed Margo her money. She put the rolled up bills in her pocketbook without counting them.

"You want something to drink?" Nick asked.

Margo squenched her face with indecision.

"Could you make me one of those rum fruit drinks? The one with all the juices in it? It's not too much bother, is it, Nick?"

"No. It's no bother."

Nick went behind the bar and filled a glass with ice. He poured two fingers of Meyers rum and added equal parts of orange, grapefruit, pineapple, and cranberry juice. He took another bottle of Reingold from the bin. The cold glass felt good in his hand. He put the bottle back and came around to the other side with Margo's drink.

"You make the best drinks, Nick," she said after tasting it. "I don't know why you don't get a job at one of those fancy bars on the Upper East Side or someplace. I hear bartenders make all kinds of money in places like that."

"I probably should."

"Why dontcha? You been here long enough. No one ever comes in here."

"Some people come in," Nick said, trying not to sound defensive. "At least I know them. I can jump rope and do my shadowboxing here after closing."

"You can do that anywhere."

"I know. But the floor's good here. It's not too hard. It doesn't give me shin splints."

Nick didn't want to talk about it anymore because he knew Margo was right. He was relieved when she walked over to the jukebox and played "I Heard You're Getting Married" by Johnny Maestro and The Brooklyn Bridge. He listened to the lyrics, about unrequited love and yearning. While the song lasted, it gave his anxiety a concrete reason. Margo started swaying with the music while punching in more songs.

"Don't you want to dance, Nick? You're not sweaty yet."

"Not right now. I'm feeling kind of tired. Gotta save myself."

Margo lit a Marlboro and inhaled deeply before releasing the flame of her lighter. She put her pack of cigarettes on the bar and the lighter on top of it.

"Nick, did I ever tell you about the time when I was still hooking and this john had me pretend I was his wife?"

"No."

"You wanna hear about it?"

"Sure." But he didn't.

Margo smiled because she did want to tell Nick the story.

"This was about two years ago," she said, exhaling smoke. "I was on 27th Street between 11th and the highway, but closer to the highway. You know where I'm talking about?"

Nick pictured Margo standing on that dark, deserted side street.

"Yeah," he said. "I know where you're talking about."

"So this car pulls up, a big baby blue Oldsmobile or something. I don't know what it was. I don't know cars. Anyway, this guy rolls down the window on the passenger side and says 'You're the one I've been looking for. You're the one.' So he tells me to get in. Now, I'm no idiot, so I ask him if he's got any money. I mean

I've gotten into cars with jerks who want it all for nothing. Anyway, he flashes a stack of bills and says something like 'I'm willing to pay whatever it takes.' So I get in and he starts driving real fast like he's gotta take a pee or something and can't wait to get to the bathroom. When I asked him where we're goin', he didn't say, he just keeps driving around the block and back onto the highway. By now I'm a little scared. You know how many nuts are out there."

Nick stared out the window, listening. For a few moments he thought of Margo as a child in Casablanca and how the only thing foreign about her now was her looks. He imagined the two of them playing the roles of Humphrey Bogart and Ingrid Bergman in the movie he'd seen at least ten times.

"So, this guy takes me somewhere way the hell out in Jersey, some suburb about a half hour away. He didn't say anything to me the way most of them do, none of the usual bullshit about how this is their first time and how I seem like a nice girl and why the hell am I out on the street selling myself?"

"What did he look like?"

"A regular nine-to-fiver with a house and a dog and a wife and two bratty kids probably. The usual. I don't remember his face." Margo put her rum drink on the bar and pulled a wrinkle out of her stocking. For a second, with the cigarette hanging from her lips, she looked tired and older than she was. "So, he takes me to this school-yard, a high school, and parks the car. He tells me to get out and follow him. By now I'm getting scared again and I'm thinking this ain't worth it no matter how much money he's got. I didn't know if he wanted to kill me or tie me to one of them posts on the football field and leave me there. I didn't know. But, being way the hell out in Jersey, I had no choice, so I followed him until we got to this little hill that looked down on the school building. Then he tells me to take off my clothes and he starts telling me about how that was the exact spot where he and his wife did it for the first time when they were seniors."

Nick rubbed his eyes and kept them shut, picturing the scene inspite of his growing distaste.

"Anyway," Margo continued. "He told me he wanted to reenact the whole thing with me pretending to be his wife as a high school senior. Only this time he wanted me to do all the things his wife wouldn't."

"Let me guess. She doesn't go down on him."

"He also wanted me to grunt like some kind of animal and say things like 'Everytime you score a touchdown I want to devour your throbbing cock.' Run of the mill stuff, but most of these guys are starved for it. I didn't care. It's all the same to me. So, after we did all that, he made me cuddle up to him while he told me he was going to marry me after he got out of college. Then he paid me the three hundred dollars and drove me back to 27th Street. In a way it was kind of sweet that he wanted me to be his wife. No one ever wanted me to be his wife before."

"Real sweet of him," Nick said.

Margo's mouth turned down at the corners for a moment. A wet, dreaming look came into her dark, brown eyes. "Pretty soon I won't have to do this anymore," she said. "I mean, doing this here is better than hooking and all, but when I got enough money saved, I'm gonna open my own store or a restaurant or maybe a hair salon. I think I'd like doing people's hair. You can talk to them while you're doing it. I'm good at that."

"You'd have to learn how to cut hair first," Nick said, looking away from her because he could never look directly at her for very long, especially when she was telling him about turning tricks. He never asked her why she became a whore or much else about her past. She was born in Casablanca and came to America as a small child. That's all he knew. It was as if they had an unspoken agreement never to enter any deeper into that territory.

He looked at her again and couldn't help marveling at her face that always reminded him of a beautiful Indian squaw. It could be the face of a queen. Queen of the Nile. And the shape of her body. If only she wasn't . . . If only I could. Nick was almost thankful Alice didn't put him through this. It was comforting to know Alice didn't put him through this.

"You want to dance, Nick? I could put something real slow on."

Nick was still seeing her with the john in the school yard. Still, he wouldn't have minded dancing a slow one with her.

"No. I gotta shadowbox. I don't have much time before the fight." Nick considered running after shadowboxing despite the heat and pollution, despite the fact that if he accepted Jimmy's offer, he didn't need to shadowbox or run anymore.

"The fight's next Friday, right?"

"You coming?"

"Sure, I'm coming."

Nick wished she wasn't. He wished no one was. He got up to start his routine, moving around the bar, moving around her. Margo rocked her head from side to side and sang along with the Rolling Stones. Nick's legs were heavy at first. His fists felt slow. Margo stopped singing. She sat down and watched him work as Mick Jagger sang, *"The hand of fate is on me now . . ."*

CHAPTER TEN

NICK WASN'T SURPRISED to find Alice awake and standing in the dark at the entrance of her bedroom. She was wearing his favorite nightgown.

"Nick?" she whispered.

"It's me, sweety."

Nick went to her and held her face between his hands and kissed her, once on her lips, then on her nose and on each eyelid. He bit the round of flesh padding her cheekbone and handed her the bag of peaches he'd bought for her at the Korean market.

"They're nice and ripe, the way you like them."

"Thank you." Alice took the peaches. "How was your night?"

"Fine. Nothing special."

"I didn't know if you were coming."

Alice took Nick's hand and led him into the bedroom where her fan was pointed out the window, blowing the hot city air back to where it came from. Nick sat on the edge of the bed. He could remember only a few times when her room was neither hot nor cold.

"Are you tired?" Alice asked. She started to untie Nick's shoes.

"I'm always tired, lately."

Alice pulled off his shoes, then his socks. Nick reached down and guided her up to him.

"Get in bed, Alice." He kissed her forehead. "I'll undress myself."

Nick took off his t-shirt and, sitting in just his jeans, he stroked Alice's long, straight hair and cupped his hand over her damp forehead. The darkness thinned until he could see the blurry forms of her desk and bureau and the poster from the Metropolitan Museum of Art on the wall above it. He lay beside her and circled his arms over and beneath her. She moved closer and burrowed her head into his chest.

"Is everything okay?" Nick whispered into her ear.

Alice nodded and, before falling back to sleep, she asked him, "Is my weight crushing your arm?"

"It never does," Nick answered. "You don't always have to ask me that. It never does."

As always, Nick's thoughts ran unimpeded at night when nothing, including sleep, held them back. He was remembering his first date with Alice, two years ago at the Central Park Zoo. For only a dollar, they looked at the animals in their simulated habitats. After watching the polar bears suffer on the sun-baked rocks, they drank Cokes at the concession stand, feeling happy and calm amidst all the crying babies and hassled parents. Then they went inside the aquarium and watched the penguins shoot like styrofoam buoys through the water. Alice put her head on Nick's shoulder and said she was having the nicest time. "I am too," Nick said.

Alice's breathing deepened into gentle snores which stopped when Nick nudged her with his shoulder. It was true that she slept better when he was there. Nick once asked her about when he wasn't. She told him she slept, just not as well.

One night, while watching her sleep, tears came to Nick's eyes. He sniffled quietly to keep from waking her and tried to remember when that had happened before. Since then, it happened often and he was sure it was because he loved her, only not the way she wanted him to.

Nick kissed her temple again and sat up on the edge of the bed. "I'm going to watch some TV," he whispered. He shut the bedroom door behind him and felt around on the couch for the remote, then turned on the TV. Flickering blue filled the room and Nick flipped through the channels, through the sitcom reruns, infomercials selling exercise equipment, bikini movies and a nude talk show. He stopped at a war movie in which three American soldiers were ducking the bullets and shrapnel shredding the palm trees above them. Two of the soldiers scrambled out of the foxhole and belly-crawled into the open to save a fourth soldier who had been shot and was screaming, "I'm a dead man! Get back in the hole! I'm a dead man!" His buddies wouldn't listen, and one took a bullet in the center of his forehead, leaving the other to drag the wounded soldier back to the foxhole where he lay broken and bleeding and safe for the time being. Nick turned to another channel and when he came back to the movie, the soldier who had been wounded was now staring unblinking up at the tropical sky that didn't give a shit that he was dead.

The movie reminded Nick of the Vietnam veteran who used to come to Blue Paradise last summer, a small, wiry guy with long, grey hair, a matching goatee, and a nervous intensity that said he trusted very few people and none completely. He wore a chain around his neck with an M-16 bullet where his dog tag used to be. "This was the last bullet left in my last clip in the last firefight I was in before coming home," he would explain to anyone who asked. Stanley once asked him if he ever took the chain off. The veteran looked at Stanley for a few moments. His face became hard and mean. "No one'll ever take this off me," he said, forcing the words through his colorless lips. "Wanna try?"

"You ever hear of the Sullivan Law?" the veteran once asked Nick. "In World War II there were five brothers named Sullivan who were drafted into the navy and served on the same battleship. Their ship was in a big fight in the South Pacific. It got hit by a Japanese torpedo and went down. All five Sullivan brothers died. Every fuckin' one. After that, they passed a law so brothers can't serve together. My older brother was drafted into the army first," he said sadly, in a way that made Nick want to ask him if his brother was dead. "He wigged out in basic down at Parris Island. Lost his fuckin' mind. He had a breakdown, he was so fuckin' scared of going to 'Nam. After two weeks, they sent him home and took me instead." The veteran stopped talking. He seemed to be swallowing a ball of anger. Then he said, "I don't begrudge my brother for making me go. He didn't do it on purpose. In a way it was a good thing I went. Now there's nothing that can get to me. You come home and none of this kids' stuff can touch you anymore. It's like taking a walk in the woods."

One hot, humid night, the veteran was drinking heavily. Someone in the bar complained about the heat and the veteran said, "You ever been down in a VC tunnel only an inch wider than your shoulders and the only sound is the sweat dripping off your chin? Have you? Huh? Have you?" No one answered. He didn't expect an answer. "When you come back to the surface and it's a hundred and ten but you're still alive because you were lucky enough not to find any slant-eyed gooks down there, you think that it's never felt so cool. You meet buck-tooth Charlie down there, now that's hot. You don't and it's cool. That's what heat is all about. Not this panty-waist pussy shit."

The veteran stopped coming in after a few months and Nick didn't think of him again until one night when Walter happened to be in an especially pensive mood. "You know what's wrong with the current generation, Nick?" he said. "There's no longer any rite of passage. Other generations had World War One, the Depression, World War Two, Korea, and then Vietnam. Today there's no longer any test to pass. How do we know now who's a man or a woman as opposed to who's still a boy or girl?" Walter drank from his third port. "We have young people in this country who think they're mature only by virtue of the number of years they've lived or because they make a certain amount of money and drive a sports car and eat at fancy restaurants."

"What does make you a man?" Nick asked, hoping Walter would have an answer, one he could understand.

"I don't know, Nick," Walter said. "I guess there's no one thing that makes a someone a man." He pinched his chin between his thumb and index finger. "I suppose being responsible for someone other than ones' self. Maybe going through a horrible experience and staying alive and relatively intact." Walter thought deeply for a few more moments. "Having the courage to pursue a dream. Very few people have the courage to do that."

The war movie ended and Nick absently flipped the channels thinking that, besides a few hard fights, he hadn't yet gone through anything tough. Working the bar was boring, not tough. The sex phone commercials he was barely watching started to seem more lonely now. The studio audience listening to the man in the plaid blazer tell them that they too can become millionaires seemed more pathetic. Nick pushed the "Off" button and the TV screen shrank into a white dot that lingered before finally disappearing. He put the remote down on the couch and folded his arms behind his head and shut his tired eyes. Through the thin, plasterboard wall, he could hear Alice turn in her sleep and the drops falling from the kitchen sink faucet sparking through the early morning darkness.

The tightness in the pit of his stomach was getting tighter and more painful each day. Nick was glad Alice didn't keep any alcohol in the apartment because he would be drinking it now if she did. He went back into her room, kissed her cheek and cupped her forehead. The rhythm of her breathing broke. She turned her head suddenly and looked up at him.

"I'm going to take a walk," Nick whispered.

"Why?"

"I can't sleep."

Worry spread across Alice's face.

"Where are you going to walk? It's dangerous,

Nick. You should stay here." She reached out and held his arm just above his wrist. "Are you coming back?"

"Of course, I'm coming back." Silence. "I'm just taking a walk. I'm not going anywhere."

"There's something wrong, Nick."

"There's nothing wrong, baby." Nick felt her grip tighten and considered not going. "I just got a lot on my mind, that's all."

"It's the fight, isn't it? I wish you wouldn't fight. All it does is make you miserable."

Nick was going to tell her not to worry about him fighting anymore. He was going to tell her that this would be his last one, but the words stuck in his throat.

"I'll be back soon." He stood. "Go to sleep. I'll be back soon."

Nick forced a cough and his Uncle John slowly turned around from the window he was looking out of.

"Nicholas. I didn't hear you come in."

"Hi, Uncle John. I came in quietly."

"Did you win the fight?"

"It's next week."

Nick bent down and kissed his uncle's cheek.

"How you feelin', Uncle John?"

"I feel fine," John lied. "I always feel fine."

"That's good."

Nick took a chair from the round, oak table he'd known since childhood. He sat and looked out the window at the deserted street below.

"Why don't you use the fan I bought you?" He said, noticing the beads of sweat clinging to John's forehead. "It's like an oven in here."

"Once you get used to a fan, you need it all the time," John said. "It's better not to get used to it."

For the few minutes that they didn't speak, it

seemed like John forgot Nick was there. Then he put his hand, arthritic and misshapen by years in the ring, on Nick's knee.

"Thanks for buying me the fan," he said. "One of these days I'm gonna need it."

There were things Nick had planned to say tonight. Now, he couldn't find the words.

"So, you feelin' okay, Uncle John?" he asked. "You have everything you need?"

"Yeah, I got everything I need. Cecilia, the lady down the hall, she takes good care of me. She buys food for me, she cashes my check, she brings me my mail. I think she wants something in return."

"Why don't you give it to her?"

"Naw, I can't give her that."

They laughed and when their laughter stopped, they were silent again until Nick said, "I'm sorry I didn't come to see you last week."

John smiled. "I know what it's like, Nicholas. When you got a fight coming up, you don't think about nothing else. You don't want to be near no one because you're feeling mean and you don't want to give that to someone who don't deserve it. You want something to eat or drink?"

"No, I'm okay."

"Well, I'm gonna get some water."

"I'll get it."

"Stay here. I can get my own water."

John's body tensed and the muscles on his arms that Nick used to hang from like a jungle gym strained as he turned his wheelchair around and wheeled over to the refrigerator. He returned with the water, his face flush from the effort. His hand shook when he held the water to his lips. He finished drinking and pulled the cold glass across his forehead.

"So, who's this guy you're fighting again?"

"Johnson. Leroy Johnson."

"Leroy Johnson. Well, you do like I told you. Stick him with your jab. You got a good jab. Don't stand toe to toe like I used to. You do that and you'll end up in a wheelchair like me. Just score points. Don't worry about the knockout and you'll win."

"I should."

"Whaddya mean, you should ?"

"Even the great ones lose, you know."

"Marciano never lost," John said sharply. "The only thing that beat him was an airplane crash." He looked at Nick and shook his head. "Now you're talking like your father. You talk like that and you're gonna lose for sure. You might as well not show up for the fight."

Nick looked out the window. Instead of seeing the building across the street, he was seeing his father at the end of his life, after all the anger had drained out of him. It was at a barbeque in Brooklyn. Everyone was laughing and drinking beer. Nick's father, his hair nearly white, his body thin and wasted by cancer, stood off to the side by himself, leaning against the cedar fence. It was then that Nick knew his father had given up and it would be only a matter of time before he died. At the funeral, after the casket had been lowered into the earth, John gave Nick a strong hug. "He was a good man, my brother was," he said. "But he wasn't a fighter."

John put his hand on Nick's knee again, bringing him back to the present. Seeing his uncle sitting next to him now in his wheelchair convinced him that throwing the fight was the right thing to do. Take the dive, take the money, get it over and done with. He knew it would kill John if he found out where the money he was going to be given came from, but it was for his own good.

"The heat's gonna break soon, Nicholas," John said. "Any day now."

"Yeah, I think it will."

✕

The streets were still empty when Nick left John's apartment. The muggy air had cooled a little but was poised to begin heating again in a few hours. Nick looked east and saw the first light of the approaching sun. He walked over to 10th Avenue, up to 27th Street, then west across 11th Avenue and between the brick-windowed warehouses that loomed dark and battered on either side of him. Behind him, a delivery truck stopped briefly at a newsstand to hurl a bundle of papers before speeding away. Nick stepped off the sidewalk to avoid the used condoms and green-capped crack vials, then continued in the street toward the lights perched on the New Jersey side of the river.

His heels scraping the street echoed off the walls of the warehouses. Between the echoes, Nick heard the music. He stopped walking to hear it better, the unseen trumpet, playing long, soulful notes that seemed to be speaking to him, another language, but one he could understand. The music jumped back and forth across the street, buzzing Nick's ears like a mosquito. He searched the edges of the warehouse roofs for the player, glad he was out there with him this morning.

When he reached the Westside Highway, Nick could no longer hear the trumpet. He turned around and looked back up the empty street and remembered that this was where the john from New Jersey had picked up Margo. There were no whores or johns out now. Yet Nick almost wished there were to keep him company. At times like this, he often imagined he was the only one left in the city, like the "Twilight Zone" episode he'd seen as a kid. The prospect of such complete aloneness ran a chill the length of his spine.

He started walking uptown without any destination in mind, crossing the streets that ended at the highway after their journey across the island from the East River. At 45th Street, the grey hull of the Intrepid Air and Space Museum curved like a giant wave out of the water, dwarfing the Circle Line boats docked a hundred yards away. Nick stopped and sat on a cinderblock wall and leaned back against a chain-link fence that enclosed a parking lot full of construction vehicles. The bow of the Intrepid threatened to slice him in two if the highway had not been there to prevent it. That's one proud ship, he thought.

The new sunlight coming from the east set fire to the windows of the buildings on the Jersey side of the river. Nick thought of the people living in those building and how each apartment contained its own story. He thought of Alice sleeping alone, waiting for him and he longed to be with her now, with his arms around her waist. When he got back, he would apologize for leaving and kiss the back of her neck while her body curled into his like two matching spoons.

He crossed the highway and walked south along the river that looked calm but had strong currents swirling beneath the surface. By the time he reached 25th Street, the heat had risen, making him want to jump in and swim. He hadn't been swimming in years and wondered where the river would take him if he floated on his back and let it.

Alice woke when Nick lay beside her.

"You're back," she said. "Are you going to sleep now?"

"Yeah. I'm sorry I left."

"That's okay." Alice smiled and put her head on Nick's chest and listened to his heart beating fast. She said, "I was thinking about the time we were in that Japanese restaurant with the goldfish pool and someone put one of the goldfish in a glass of beer. Do you remember that?"

"I don't think so."

"Well, you took the goldfish and put it back in its pool. That was nice. It would have died in the beer if you hadn't saved it."

Nick vaguely remembered the incident.

"Alice?" he said.

"Yes."

"Did you fix any stiffs today?"

"An old man. It wasn't sad because he was an old man."

"That's good." Nick was silent as he thought of Alice working on the dead man, making him look good and almost alive. He wished she could tell him if the man died happy and satisfied with his life, or whether he took secrets he was ashamed of to the grave with him.

"Hey, Alice?"

"Yes, honey?"

"Do you think he was a good man, the old man?"

"A lot of people came to the funeral. That says something about him."

Nick was silent again, wondering how many people would come to his funeral if he died tomorrow. Then, instead of saying what he wanted to say, telling Alice everything he no longer wanted to keep inside, he said, "Alice, why do you think they made the Intrepid into a museum?"

Alice yawned.

"It probably got too old to do anything else."

Alice rolled on her side and molded her body into Nick's. He kissed the back of her neck.

"I guess you're right," he said, knowing that he wasn't going to tell her anything this morning. "That's some ship, though. It must have been something in its day."

CHAPTER ELEVEN

Grains of sand rubbed between Jerry's toes as he walked out of the Port Authority bus terminal and between the honking cars on 8th Avenue. He bought a flask bottle of Seagrams Seven in the liquor store on 42nd Street. On the sidewalk outside, he cracked the seal and let gravity pull the smooth rye whiskey into his mouth.

The alcohol heated his empty stomach and dulled his persistent hangover. Besides being tired from not sleeping very deeply on the beach in Atlantic City, the girls in "Curves" had made him horny as all hell. Wanting it so bad, not knowing when or if he'll ever get any, kept him awake and uneasy the whole ride back.

Now, with Times Square buzzing all around him, Atlantic City seemed like a distant dream. But it did happen. There was sand between his toes. And Jerry knew his meeting with Robert had been as real as the people passing him on the sidewalk and the bite of the Seagrams hitting the back of his throat.

The sign in the window of the peep show next to the liquor store read: "OUR GIRLS ARE WORKING THEIR WAY THROUGH COLLEGE." The ticker on the Show World awning across the avenue repeated: "THIS WEEK THE FABULOUS ANGEL, PER-FORMING LIVE ON STAGE" over and over. The electronic words caught Jerry's eye and he remem-bered being in there late one drunken night.

He stuck the half-full bottle in his back pocket, dodged across the 8th Avenue traffic and stood outside Show World looking up at the poster of Angel, her ripe lips parted just a little, her nipples and crotch obscured by black censor bars. Jerry recognized her from the hardcore magazines he sometimes read at work. An-gel. Can't be her real name. Sexy bitch, that's for sure. He took another nip of Seagrams and slipped inside.

The man at the door took Jerry's dollar in exchange for four octagonal tokens with the crude figure of a dancing woman surrounded by musical notes on one side and "The Worlds Greatest Show Place" written on the other. Daytime quickly disappeared as Jerry walked past him and down a corridor lined by orange booths and exploding strobe lights that echoed the music beating out of hidden speakers. The blinking bulbs strung along the ceiling reflected off miniature mosaic mirrors fitted together in the form of impossi-bly big-titted women.

Muffled moans and screams of ecstasy came from every direction. Rising crescendos of Yes! Yes! Yes! were punctuated by tokens jingling into slots and channel buttons being pressed hard and often from inside the video booths where men watched movies while jerking off. This combination of sound and light made Jerry uneasy. He reached into his pocket and took hold of his zipstick and hoped there would be no need to use it in here. There were worse, more shameful things than getting killed in a porn palace, but he couldn't think of any right now.

A gravelly voice boomed through the PA: *"C'mon gentlemen, up the stairway to heaven! See the multiorgasmic Angel perform live for you! For only ten dollars, who knows, maybe you'll get in on the action!"* Jerry studied the movie posters on the door of each booth. The tokens became moist in his palm.

He climbed the stairs to the second floor where women in skimpy lingerie stood in the doorways of private fantasy booths, batting their painted eyelids at him. One with enormous breasts held firmly in place by her bra, reached out and touched Jerry's arm and said, "Why dontcha come talk to me, handsome?"

"How much?"

"A five-dollar token gets you two and a half minutes. That don't include my tip. All my men tip me well," she purred.

Jerry imagined standing in the booth, watching her undress through the thick glass that would be separating them. He wouldn't be able to touch her which was okay. The way she looked, it was better that way.

The woman sucked her teeth with disdain when Jerry said, "I'll think about it," and continued walking past her and her colleagues who leaned in the doorways of their booths, boring their lifeless eyes into him.

Jerry ducked into a booth to escape the attention he imagined was focused solely on him. He shut the door and hunched his already narrow shoulders together to avoid touching the walls. Disinfectant shot up his nostrils, forcing him to take only shallow breaths. He slipped a token into the slot. The overhead light immediately disappeared and the square, metal blind in front of him went up slowly.

He expected a video, but through the window, in the middle of a round, unelevated stage, stood a real woman, naked except for spike-heeled shoes. She had an alcohol and drug-ravaged face. She walked slow and lazy and hip-swaying, one foot directly in front of the other, like no one had ever told her she was ugly. She grabbed onto a pole that ran from the floor to the ceiling, leaned back and let the weight of her ass swing her around in a circle. Then she toured the perimeter of her enclosed stage, making sure the faces surrounding her saw the bills in her hand when she came over to give a closer look.

She stopped and gyrated her hips and pelvis for the unseen man in the booth next to Jerry. Jerry heard the man say, "Yeah, baby" and the woman say, "You want it?" She thrust her crotch forward, then drew it back and around until it returned to the forward position. The man's hand reached through the glass-less window and handed her a five-dollar bill. She took it, turned around, bent over and looked at him upside-down between her legs. The man reached out again and grabbed her birthmarked ass and squeezed and kneaded it for all his money was worth.

"Fellas, buy your tickets now on the third floor!" the PA voice was saying as Jerry emerged from the booth. *"It's almost show time and Angel wants to see you as much as you wanna see her! Who knows, for only ten dollars, maybe you can get in on the action!"*

Jerry stepped into a another booth, into the smell of

barely diluted ammonia. He put a token in the slot and a man taking a woman from behind appeared on the tv screen, his balls slapping against her ass at even, mechanical intervals, like a wind-up toy. Jerry pressed the glowing red button and the next channel revealed an orgy of tangled limbs, slurping mouths and closeups of women's faces laced with cum. Jerry spent his last two tokens on this channel and when the screen went blank and the lights went on, he searched his pockets for another one, then left the booth and noticed a short Puerto Rican man in an orange Show World apron immediately go in and start swabbing the walls and the floor with a mop.

Jerry checked his pocket. Only seventeen dollars left. Don't spend it, he told himself. Chico was supposed to pay up tonight. But he never pays on time. Just go back to the van yard, jerk off, take a shower in the garage, get some sleep. Don't let them get you. That's what they do here. They make you crazy so you'll do anything for it. They take your money and you leave broke with nothing but your dick in your hand. Any idiot can see that. The voice on the PA said: *"Gentlemen, Angel's waiting for you upstairs on the third floor! You don't want to disappoint her now, do you?"*

"Live Nude Girls" was written in green lights on each step leading up to the third floor. Jerry took them two at a time. At the top of the stairs, he handed the man in the box office his ten-dollar bill. The man straightened and smoothed it and held it up to the light before giving Jerry a ticket stub and motioning him through the turnstile with a backward jerk of his thumb.

The walls of the hallway Jerry followed were black except for the clusters of mosaic mirrors. His eyes adjusted to the dark as he made his way to a room at the end where ten men in movie theater chairs stared at an empty stage. No one sat next to or looked at anyone else. The occasional dry cough made the hushed room seem even quieter. A man in the back row was hunched forward with only his bald head visible above the seat in front of him. Jerry took the seat on the end of the second row, closest to the exit.

While waiting, he savored more Seagrams and let his eyes close, then forced them open, not wanting to fall asleep here amongst these perverts. There were more coughs and a sneeze. A man in a business suit was eating his dinner; a sandwich and a Snickers bar. Jerry's unshaven reflection in the mirror behind the stage looked worse then the one in the bathroom in Atlantic City. His hair was tangled and uneven and the shadows nestling in the hollows of his face were darker. Sleeping on the beach will do that to you, he thought.

The lights finally dimmed and the audience stopped coughing and brushing their feet against the floor. It was like everyone was holding their breath with anticipation. The music started, a disco hit from the Seventies and the voice on the PA said: *"And now gents, before the main event, we're gonna get you nice and warm. Hot's more like it. So loosen your collars and your wallets and give a big hand for New York's own MO-N-N-IQUE!"*

Monique was tall and black. She skipped down the aisle like a little girl, patting the head of a man asleep in his seat and wagging her tongue at another before mounting the stage where she danced three songs, keeping her silk robe and lingerie on for the first, taking them off during the second, dancing naked and masturbating during the third.

Jerry watched her closely, concentrating first on her tits, then her ass, then her legs and her crotch. She greased a shiny silver dildo with vaseline, laid on her back, brought her knees to her chest and proceeded to push and pull it in and out of her vagina. Jerry watched intently and imagined mounting her and making her fake moans real.

By the third song, Jerry's mind began to wander until an unexpected wave of depression hit him hard and sudden, grabbing him by the throat and pressing him down into his seat. This time it had a specific cause at least. Jerry hoped to cure it by thinking back to its origins—Lucille Sarducci.

Jerry never told Nick what had happened with her. He never told anyone, in fact, and didn't like to think about it often. Maybe things would be different now if he had listened to his own advice, accepted the fact that she was out of his league. It all happened during the summer, the summer Jerry wished he could erase, the one after sophomore year during the week Nick was with his family at the cabin they'd rented on the lake.

At school, Lucille was one of the pretty girls, tall with dark, wavy hair that looked good whether she kept it in a bun or a pony-tail or natural. Her eyes sparkled when she laughed. And those legs. The memory of them was still sharp in Jerry's mind. That summer, she worked the counter at Ed's Deli on 24th and 9th. Jerry was cutting plywood with his father in Mackenzie's Lumber Yard. Everyday he'd scrub himself clean, slap on some Old Spice to cover the smell of sawdust and sweat, then head to Ed's to buy his lunch. He usually went back later, for a soda or a candy bar he never bothered to eat.

To his surprise, Lucille said yes when he finally

gathered enough courage to ask her out. Jerry saw very little of the movie they went to. He was too busy thinking of things to say to her afterwards. Lucille paid close attention and laughed at all the funny parts. Toward the end of the movie, Jerry put his hand on the back of her seat and almost touched her far shoulder before returning it to his lap.

They went out again, for coffee, and again a few days later for drinks at Rudy's, the only bar that wouldn't ID them. Next week, over plates of spaghetti and veal parmagian at Alfonse's, she told Jerry that he was sensitive and kind and not after sex like the other boys. You think I'm sensitive? Jerry asked, embarrassed because no one had ever said anything like that to him before, and ashamed because he hoped to prove her wrong soon.

As September approached, Jerry began to think it wasn't just the summer that was almost over. He knew the weekend Lucille's parents went out to Long Island was when he had to make his move. He persuaded Lucille to have him over, order in Chinese, watch movies on TV. He brought a six-pack of beer and a bottle of scotch with him. She drank two beers and Jerry drank the rest along with three scotches on ice which made him feel good and relaxed, but not drunk. When the ten o'clock movie ended, Lucille seemed anxious. You should probably go now, she told him.

Go now? Why? Jerry knew this was the chance and he didn't want to blow it. After tonight he planned on knowing exactly what the other guys were talking about when they talked about sex. He could finally do some talking of his own. He was persistent. Lucille refused. He kissed her long and hard until she gave in.

Afterward. There was no afterward, actually. Something has to happen for there to be an afterward. Lu-

cille was kind and gentle about Jerry's failure to perform. She kissed Jerry's cheek and told him not to
worry. She told him how much she liked being in bed
with him, how that was the important part. But he
didn't hear her. Her voice had become just a series of
muffled sounds.

It didn't happen, he tried to convince himself as he
lay in bed next to her. It couldn't have. He wished it
was a nightmare, but knew he had been awake the
whole time. Must have been the alcohol. He'd heard
alcohol can do that to a man. But the room was spin-
ning with disbelief, not drunkenness. Jerry never felt
so sober in his life.

He got out of bed and started to dress. Lucille asked
him where he was going. Jerry couldn't bring himself
to look her in the eye or even say her name. All he said
was that he was sorry and had to go. Then he was on
the street, not knowing what time it was except that it
was the middle of the night. He walked in a trance until morning.

Jerry didn't go to Ed's Deli for the rest of the summer. He walked the other way when he saw Lucille on
the street. She tried to call him twice. Both times Jerry
told his mother to say he wasn't home. His shame became anger, at Lucille, at all women.

He kept working instead of going back to school in
the fall. No point in going back if he wasn't going to
use a diploma for anything, he reasoned. And he did-
n't want to have to see Lucille every day either. A few
times he waited across the street from school for her.
But she always came out surrounded by classmates
and he'd go home and say the things he was going to
tell her to the walls of his room instead.

He had another sexual opportunity not long afterward, with the older woman he met one night in Irish

Eyes. When Jerry realized she wanted to take him home, he started drinking heavily to calm his nerves. In her studio apartment on 51st Street, she grabbed and caressed his balls until he achieved an erection. That's good. Everything's fine. Stay that way. And it did until he started thinking about what had happened with Lucille. The woman unzipped his fly, took out his penis and put it in her mouth. Jerry's heartbeat quickened and sweat dampened his upper lip. He leaned back against the refrigerator, unable to feel himself anymore. He didn't dare look down.

"Aren't you scared, bringing a stranger like me to your apartment?" he asked her, his voice shaking.

The woman took Jerry's flaccid penis out of her mouth.

"You don't scare me," she said, holding back a laugh. "You don't scare me at all."

Monique finished her set. Jerry watched her picking stray dollars off the stage and thought that maybe Lucille would be his now if things had gone differently that night. A bad start, that's all. Another try, another chance, and I might have gotten it right. He knew she had been willing to try it again. She said that being together was the most important thing. And she did call twice afterward. Jerry sank deeper into his seat. What's the use thinking about it? Thinking about it only makes it worse.

After Monique, a stripper named Candy with thin, bleached-blonde hair, teased high off her head took the stage. She danced hard, but no one tipped, so she stopped after only one song and sat with her back against the mirror to make the audience feel guilty or at least sorry for her.

The lights stayed off after Candy put on her clothes and nearly tripped descending from the stage. The booing died down and it became quiet as the audience again concentrated on looking at the empty stage and not at each other. Jerry noticed the bald man in the back row still busy abusing himself in his seat. Ten long minutes passed before the PA popped with static, ending the uncomfortable wait: *"All right, gentlemen, the time has finally come! So, put your peckers back in, get your dollars out, and give a warm welcome to the fabulous and famous woman of your wet dreams, A-N-N-N-GEL!"*

The music started again; hard rock with a heavy bass that vibrated the room. The song was half over before Angel came strutting down the aisle like she owned it. Her energy filled the room and made her seem larger than she was. She mounted the stage and moved around it like the music was trapped inside her body and trying to get out. Jerry leaned forward and followed her around the stage with his eyes. Lucille and the woman from Irish Eyes disappeared, replaced by Angel who smiled directly at him, giving him a surprisingly substantial erection.

When the second song started, Angel was already naked except for white garters circling each of her muscular thighs. She jumped down from the stage and into the lap of a man in the front row. She ran her long, brown fingers through the man's hair and pretended to scratch his cheeks with passion, then climbed back on the stage and was showered with dollars that flew through the air and landed at her feet. She kicked them with contempt, like pieces of garbage.

Some of the men came to the edge of the stage, holding dollars out to Angel so she could squeeze her breasts around their outstretched hands and then pull back with the money trapped in her cleavage. Jerry went to the stage, folded his dollar lengthwise and waited until Angel came over to him. Angel licked her lips and narrowed her eyes and thrust her large chest forward. Jerry's knees started to tremble as her warm, firm flesh swallowed his hand. He let go reluctantly and Angel bit her lower lip, rolled her eyes in mock ecstasy, and gyrated her hips faster. Jerry sat down, hoping no one had noticed his hard-on.

The bald man walked toward the stage, tentative and humble, like a pauper approaching a king's throne. He opened his wallet and offered it to Angel who reached in, removed all the bills and tucked them into her garter. The man leaned forward and Angel shined his hairless pate with her breasts. He straightened up and his face became lost in her cleavage. The loud, smothered sucking noises that he made sounded like he was suffocating. He took a deep breath when he emerged and blew a kiss off his palm. Angel blew one back and kept blowing until the man indicated with a backward jerk of his head that it had reached him. Angel danced to the other side of the stage and the bald man returned to his seat with a smile stretched across his face.

After the show, most of the audience lined up in the hallway outside to have their pictures taken with Angel. One by one they handed the photographer ten dollars and Angel, still covered with a light sweat, sat on their laps and puckering her lips for the camera. "What's your name?" she'd ask each man, then say something like, "Oh, I have a friend named John" while writing "Dear John, Make me cum! Love, Angel" on his picture.

"Where are you performing next?" someone in line asked.

Angel thought for a moment.

"In Phoenix next week. You gonna come see me?"

"I'll buy my plane ticket tomorrow."

The PA said: *"Gentlemen, for twenty dollars, enjoy your own session with Angel in her private fantasy booth! Twenty dollars for fifteen minutes! You can't beat that!"*

"Anyone here waiting for a session with Angel?" the photographer, who was clearly drunk, asked.

The bald man raised his hand with twenty dollars clutched in it.

Jerry reached into his pocket and remembered he only had five dollars left. They got you, he thought, hook, line and sinker. But he couldn't take his eyes off Angel. The sight of her made him feel light-headed and tingly. With her he'd have no problem, he was sure. It would be different than the Korean whorehouse. For twenty dollars he could talk to her alone and tell her what he needed. She'd help him if he asked her. He could see that from the way she talked to the men and signed each picture individually.

And soon he'd be making real money in Atlantic City. I'll treat her like a queen with some of that money. All she'll have to do is what comes naturally. Jerry tried to catch Angel's eye before leaving, but she was too busy posing and signing pictures. "I'll see you soon, Angel," he said softly before walking to the end of the hall and pushing through the turnstile.

CHAPTER TWELVE

Nick walked east on 26th Street, imagining the sidewalk turned upside-down with all the used condoms still clinging to it. Most of the condoms were white or transparent, but some had lipstick marks around the part that looked like a rubberband. An old one crunched under Nick's shoe. The girls did well tonight, he thought. Real well.

In the office shack, Jerry was reading the brittle and yellowed pages of a Louis L'Amour western. A woman's ass smiled from the cover of the Hustler magazine on the floor. Nick poked his head in the door, nearly jolting the book from Jerry's hand.

"Fuckin' A, Nick! You gotta stop scaring the shit outta me like that!" Jerry coughed fitfully and took a deep breath to reinflate his lungs. "Why don't you try knocking once in a while? That's what most people do."

Nick picked up the Hustler and sat on the cot next to Jerry.

"What's going on, Jerry?"

"You should have seen it," Jerry said. "The money the girls made tonight. There was practically a traffic jam." Jerry pointed out the door to the corner of 26th and 11th at a whore whose breasts were shaped like Casava melons. "Take a look at those. One of hers is as big as your whole fuckin' head. And they're real. One hundred percent."

"How can tell the which ones are real from all the way over here?"

"I can tell."

Jerry marked his page with a Chinese takeout menu.

"So how was business tonight?" Nick asked.

"Big Bob did pretty good. Tons of Yuppies breaking their leases and moving out of their apartments." Jerry bit a grimy hangnail from the side of his index finger and blew it off the end of his tongue. "I didn't make dick, though. Chico's was supposed to pay me tonight. The greasy 'rican never showed up. I think he's using someone else to run his shit. I know that black sonofabitch working the deadman over at Mendon Vans would sell his balls for a dollar. Chico told me he doesn't need as many vans anymore, but I think he's just using me once in a while as a backup in case Mendon falls through."

Jerry lit a cigarette and held the pack out to Nick who ignored it and leaned back against the wall which gave a little under his weight. He rested his feet on the edge of the two-drawer filing cabinet where the receipts were kept and wondered why he'd even bothered to come see Jerry tonight.

"What's it about?" Nick asked, noticing the lean, tough-looking cowboy on the cover of Jerry's book.

"It sucks," Jerry said, holding the book pinched between his thumb and index finger like a piece of excrement. "It's about some jerkoff in a white hat who goes around saving ranchers from this gang of even bigger jerkoffs in black hats. They're all a bunch of morons except for the cows they're fighting over. The cows are smarter than any of them. I like reading the letters in Hustler better. At least they're real."

Jerry tossed the book against the wall. It chipped a patch of the cheap, green paint before falling to the floor.

"So how was Blue Paradise tonight? Same bunch of world beaters?"

"Yeah, same bunch."

"That's too bad. Want some Seagrams? I don't think Barbara'll mind."

Nick looked up at the Snap-On Tools calender. Miss April's static beauty beamed down at him, her mindless gaze locked on his.

"You should change months already, Jerry? It's almost July for crissakes."

"Don't worry. I plan to. Miss July's name is Carrie. She'll make you forget all about Barbara. Miss May and June weren't even worth bothering with."

"Let's take a look at Carrie."

"Not yet. Her time will come. I just hope she isn't such a hard-ass about the booze like Barbara. I hate drinking in front of a woman who doesn't want me to drink."

Jerry opened the bottom drawer of the cabinet, pulled the hanging files forward, and took out the bottle of Seagrams. He twisted the top off and sucked in a large sip before passing it to Nick who did the same.

"You know, Jerry," Nick said after swallowing. "I was looking at all these used condoms on the way over here and I started thinking about how many lives are lying out there on the sidewalk. There could be some real geniuses in those condoms that never got a shot. Maybe another Einstein or Muhammad Ali."

Jerry looked at Nick out of the corner of his eye to see if he was serious.

"They got a shot alright," he said. "That's about all they got."

"Yeah, they got a shot," Nick agreed. "What I'm saying is they never got a chance. It sounds crazy, but I feel kind of sorry for those poor bastards, drying up and crunching under someone's heel."

Jerry lit another cigarette, drew in some smoke and exhaled slowly. He took two more hits from the bottle.

"Don't lose any sleep over it," he said. "I don't think any Noble Prize winners are going to waste. The world's probably better off with them ending up right where they started."

Waste. The word made Nick sad for a moment. It sounded so hopeless, so final.

"You're probably right," he said. "But you never know. Let's say a genius comes along once every few million sperm. There must be thousands of millions of sperms out there tonight. And this is only 26th Street. What about all the other streets around here?"

"There's one thing you forget, Nick. All those thousands of millions of sperms are produced by only a few schmucks from Jersey. So don't worry about it."

Nick laughed and felt a little embarrassed for bringing it up in the first place. He should have known better than to attempt any serious conversation with Jerry because serious conversation with Jerry almost always degenerated into the usual bullshitting. It occurred to him that ninety percent of his friendship with Jerry was just that: bullshitting. The other ten percent was spent drinking and watching whores turn tricks. They rarely said anything to each other that meant much. But Nick knew their friendship was real, that he would do anything for Jerry and Jerry would do as much as he could in return. Still, he sometimes wondered how well they did know each other, whether he knew what was going on inside Jerry's head, or his own head for that matter.

The clock hanging on the wall read four-thirty. It had been a routine night at Blue Paradise, routine but tiring. Nick's legs and feet still ached from standing for nine hours. As usual, Stanley got drunk and then angry. He left and came back again for one more beer before leaving for good. Walter drank three ports and completed the *New York Times* crossword puzzle. Taking a break from the puzzle, he looked up at the coverage of the Fifth Avenue Rape case on the eleven o'clock news and said, "They're trying the case on the TV. That's what they're doing."

And Jimmy was there. He didn't say much. Most of the time he watched Frank and Paddy play pool, occasionally giving Nick a few long stares that Nick couldn't return fully. Once, when their eyes met, Jimmy nodded in a knowing way. As he was leaving, he said, "Rest up for that fight, Nick."

The city was silent except for the drone of the postal trucks and the haunting sound of a barge horn on the river. Nick hated this kind of silence.

"So, how'd it go in Atlantic City?" he asked Jerry.

"Atlantic City? It went alright."

Nick waited for Jerry to say more. He didn't. "Did you win anything?"

"A few dollars. I pretty much broke even."

Jerry stood and went to the doorway and stared out into the night that was nothing more than a day that had died. He pulled a long drag on his cigarette and the ash steadily worked its way down to the filter. Most of the whores were gone now, including the big one with the real tits. Everyone has to rest, even the queen of the whores, he thought, taking more Seagrams, then more smoke into his mouth. Behind him, he heard Nick flipping through the Hustler.

"It's a mean town, you know, Nick."

"Which town?"

"Atlantic City. Any town that's only there to separate you from your money, is mean."

"I know that. Everyone knows that."

"But no one does anything about it."

"What are you supposed to do? You go down there and lose. You try to win it back and maybe you do, but most of the time you lose even more. Everyone knows the score with Atlantic City."

"They're a bunch of robbers, the casinos."

"And who are you, Robin Hood?"

Jerry grinned but he wasn't in the mood to laugh.

"Maybe I am. What would you say if I was?"

"I'd say your chicken legs wouldn't look good in tights."

"You can joke, Nick, but there's lots of money down there. I intend on getting some of it."

"You better start taking card lessons."

Jerry grinned again and swallowed the impulse to tell Nick about his meeting with Robert. He counted to ten in his head to control the urge to tell him about their plan to cash in stolen chips. Nick would undoubtably give his old honesty speech about how you should be able to look yourself in the mirror. That might make him think twice about doing it and Jerry didn't want to think twice. That honesty thing is a load of crap anyway. The world doesn't work that way and it never did, Nick. You're born, you die, and you do the best you can for yourself in between. There's no heaven. There's no hell. Here and now is all there is. Maybe I am Robin Hood, taking from the rich casinos and giving to me: the poor. Maybe I'll give some to you, Nick, if you don't mind taking stolen money. After all, your boxing career might not pan out. Would you take it, I wonder?

It dawned on Jerry that he needed Nick for this. He needed protection and an extra pair of eyes. But mainly, he needed Nick to help cash the chips. Doing it himself every week would only draw suspicion from the cashier cage. He also needed the company. It would be comforting to have Nick there with him.

Nick barely paid attention to the fleshy pages he was turning. It was quiet again and he didn't feel like breaking the silence this time. Arguing took too much energy, especially with Jerry who never won, but never let anyone else win either. He looked at Jerry's back, his almost non-existent shoulders high and tight with tension. Jerry came back inside and sat on the cot next to Nick. He looked up at Barbara and held the Seagram's bottle toward her as if offering her a sip.

"She's a beauty, isn't she, Nick?"

"She's a photograph, Jerry."

"She's beautiful anyway."

"She's a calendar, Jerry."

"You know what Walter would say?" Jerry said. "He'd say Barbara's a tool Snap-On's using to make us spend money with our cocks instead of our heads. He'd say she's a tool to make our tools make us buy their tools."

Nick closed the Hustler and looked up at Barbara and the money-earning smile frozen on her face.

"He'd be right," Nick said, "Hard-ons are what make the world go around when it comes down to it."

"Well, there's more to life than having a hard-on all the time," Jerry said, an edge in his voice. "We'd both be a lot better off if we spent our energy constructively rather than just trying to get hard-ons."

The fullness at the back of Jerry's mouth returned, like something was going to vomit out of him. Telling Nick about Lucille and the lady at Irish Eyes and the Korean whorehouse might be the cure, just telling him, getting it out in the open and over with. He could tell Nick about his plan with Angel and Nick could share that burden and, with the burden lightened, it might go away. He could also tell Nick about Atlantic City, ask him to help, take half the money and half the risk. Jerry wondered if Nick would turn down such easy money. Then his lips were moving and what came out was, "So, you ready for the fight, Nick?"

Nick dropped the Hustler to the floor and looked at the clock on the wall again. 4:45. Alice was waiting for him and he wished more than ever that he'd gone straight to her instead of stopping here. Being around Jerry was making him increasingly uncomfortable. How could he keep telling him that renting his employer's vans to drug dealers was dishonest when he was going to throw a fight on national TV? And Jerry would know he threw the fight. Of all the people in the world, including Leon, Jerry would know.

"I'm as ready as I'll ever be," Nick said. The phrase; "Doing the wrong thing for the right reason," popped into his head.

"You going to Alice's tonight?" Jerry asked.

"I don't know. Maybe not."

"If I were you, I would. She's a nice girl."

"I know she is."

Then Nick wished he had said he was definitely not going to see Alice. He wished Jerry had not asked him about her and hoped he wouldn't ask his usual questions about their sex life, questions that made him wonder if Jerry had ever had a sex life of his own. And whenever Jerry asked about Alice, it always reminded Nick of Margo because the sex with Alice he sometimes described was really the sex he would have with Margo. Suddenly the shack seemed smaller, like the walls were closing in. Nick stood and threw some punches.

"Listen, Jerry," he said, doubling a jab. "Things could be changing pretty soon. My life might be a lot different."

"You're right about that."

"Whaddaya mean, I'm right about that?"

"What I meant as in what way. That's all I meant."

Nick started throwing punches faster. He lobbed a few down at Jerry.

"For one, I might be breaking up with Alice."

"Breaking up?"

"I don't know. Maybe. I love her. I'm pretty sure of that. I just don't think I'm gonna want to marry her. If I'm not gonna marry her, I'm wasting her time."

"She wants to marry you, though, right?"

"I think she does. She talks about kids a lot. Sometimes I wonder if she really knows me. She thinks I'm some kind of great guy who always does the right thing. But we hardly ever see each other except at four in the morning when she's half asleep. How do you get to know someone you only see half asleep at four in the morning?"

"I don't know how the hell you live that way," Jerry said. "Always doing the right thing."

Nick stopped punching.

"Maybe I won't anymore. Take Blue Paradise, for instance. You know how much bigger my tips would be if I gave away more of Paddy's booze? He's treats me like shit either way, so why am I looking out for him instead of myself? It's not getting me anywhere."

Nick walked outside to escape the shrinking shack. He kicked a pebble across the lot. The pebble bounced under a van and pinged off the gas tank. Across 11th Avenue, trucks continued to drive into the postal plant like bees entering a hive. Jerry came out with the bottle in his hand. His eyes were beginning to glaze and his right lid was twitching it's rapid half-blink.

"Did you ever fill out that application for the Post Office?" Nick asked.

Jerry's mouth angled to repress a laugh. Post Office. He tried to imagine sorting letters in some cavernous mail room or wheeling a canvas cart through the streets where everyone would see his skinny legs in those dorky blue shorts. The Postal Service. Twenty bills a years. Two week vacations in the Poconos or some other place cheap and boring.

"No, I haven't filled it out yet," Jerry said, his voice thin and distant. "I've been meaning to."

Nick got up on his toes and circled Jerry who put up his hands as if on cue.

"What's that about Johnson's overhand right you were telling me?" Jerry said, flinching each time Nick's fist connected with his palm.

Nick saw Johnson's right hand dropping out of the darkness beyond the ring lights. He could almost feel it landing on the bridge of his nose, sending him to the canvas.

"He's has this overhand right that comes from way up where most fighters don't expect it." Nick demonstrated the punch. "It's supposed to be hard to see because it comes down at a sharp angle."

"But since you know about it, it'll be no problem."

The corners of Nick's mouth pulled down.

"That's supposed to be his only good punch and I hear he has a weak chin, but you can never tell what's going to happen in the ring. That's the thing about boxing, you can never tell." Nick crouched and spun a flurry of upper-cuts a few inches from Jerry's stomach. Eager to change the subject, he said, "So, what do you think about the Fifth Avenue Rape case? You think those kids did it?"

"Sure they did it. They found sperm and threads from one of their T-shirts on the lady. Those niggers are guilty as sin."

"You think so?"

"I know so."

Jerry expected Nick to agree readily and was surprised that he didn't.

"What do you think?"

Nick shook his head.

"I don't know. Things aren't always what they appear to be." He boxed Jerry's hands for another minute, then stopped and wiped away the sweat stinging his eyes. "Listen, I gotta get going."

"You just got here." Jerry's face became anxious and his right eye twitched faster.

"I better get some rest. I'm supposed to spar this guy from Gleason's Gym today. Leon says he's going to tear me a new asshole." Nick couldn't tell if it was tears or just a heavier glaze forming in Jerry's eyes. He considered staying a while longer and said, "Listen, Jerry, if you need help with something, just ask me."

"I don't need any help," Jerry answered quickly, too quickly, Nick thought. "What would I need help for?"

"I don't know. I'm just sayin' if you ever need anything, let me know."

"All right. If I do need help, which I don't, I'll let you know."

Nick started walking away. He turned around when he was halfway to the gate and looked back at Jerry who was holding his bottle of Seagrams down along his leg. Jerry waved with his free hand. Nick waved back and when he got to the gate, he heard Jerry call to him.

"Hey, Nick?"

Nick stopped. He didn't expect to escape this easily. He never did.

"Whaddya want, Jerry?"

Jerry took a swig of Seagrams to bolster his courage, then said, "I do need your help with something."

CHAPTER THIRTEEN

The fighter from Gleason's Gym didn't tear Nick a new asshole, but his left cheekbone felt tender and sore as hell now. "My grandma could fight better'n that!" Leon yelled when Nick came out of the ring after four rounds of sparring. "And my grandma couldn't fight fo' shit!"

From the corner of 42nd Street and 11th Avenue, Blue Paradise, dwarfed by the UPS building next to it, looked like a brick discarded on a construction site. Only the front window disrupted its plain facade. As always, the sight of it gave Nick a twinge of anxiety and made him wonder if tonight the baseball bat he kept behind the bar would be enough.

Leon always said great boxers think the entire fight through, plan it in their heads before stepping into the ring. Nick knew he'd have to do the same thing, only plan his defeat instead of his victory.

Nick's entrance into Blue Paradise caused Gracie to look at the clock over the register and Jimmy to stop talking to Frank. His eyes rested briefly on Nick's damaged cheekbone. Returning his attention to Frank, he said, "It's a dog. Any moron can see that."

"What kind of dog?" Frank said. "It don't look like any dog I ever seen. I heard of stupid names for dogs, but Spuds? Don't you think Spot would be better?"

"They call it Spuds because they make beer out of potatoes and they call potatoes spuds! "

"They make vodka from potatoes, not beer," Frank corrected.

"Look," Jimmy said more calmly, feeling silly for having lost his cool over something like the new beer sign Paddy had bought from a second-hand junk dealer down on the Bowery. "I didn't name the dog and I didn't make him look like he does. The god-damned Budweiser company did and from what I hear, all the yuppie bastards think he's the messiah or something."

"But what if someone orders a Bud?" Frank said. "Why the hell did Paddy get a Budweiser sign if he doesn't even serve the beer?"

Jimmy looked at Nick's cheekbone again and seemed to forget about Spuds Mackenzie and Budweiser. He fell into deep thought for a few moments, then said, "Hey, Nick, did I ever tell you about the woman with the crocodile eyes?"

"I don't think so," Nick said, relieved that Jimmy had snapped out of his unsettling trance.

"You know what crocodile eyes are, dontcha, Walter?" Jimmy asked.

Walter had finished the Janet Frame novel and was

now reading one called *The Fifth Business* by Robertson Davies.

"Crocodile eyes? I don't think I've ever heard that term," he said.

"You might have seen them before. Men can have them too, you know." Jimmy winked at Frank.

Walter didn't answer. He went back to his book, but Nick could tell he wasn't reading.

"Anyway," Jimmy continued. "This woman was giving me a blow job not long ago. Not a bad blow job. She used her teeth a little too much, but not bad."

"What woman was this?" Nick asked.

"Some bimbo." Jimmy waved his hand dismissively. "It doesn't matter. So, she's giving me a blow job and then right in the middle of it she starts looking up at me and I could swear her eyes looked just like crocodile eyes. You know how crocodile's eyes look when that's all you see sticking out of the water? So, she looks up at me and takes my cock out of her mouth and says, 'As a woman I have the right not to suck your penis.' Can you believe that? I looked down at her, now I'm just about to break out laughing, and I said, 'As a man my right to have you suck my penis overrules your right as a woman not to suck my penis.' I tell ya, she didn't know what the hell to say to that, so she stopped her lip and finished what she started."

"I know what I would have said," Gracie said, but she didn't say it because Harvey, the bus driver, was at the bar tonight. Harvey only came to Blue Paradise once or twice a week when he was ahead of schedule and had time to kill. Harvey's face used to be lean and handsome but had filled out considerably over the years. The bus drivers cap he always wore had gradually taken the place of his hair. Gracie turned to him and smiled and said, "Harvey, hon, you want another beer before I do the register?"

"No thanks, Gracie." Harvey checked his watch. "I should be going soon."

"Harvey's the only gentleman in the world," Gracie said to Nick as if Harvey had already left. "He's quiet, not like these two idiots." She jerked her thumb over her shoulder at Jimmy and Frank.

Gracie cashed out the register and left a two hundred dollar bank which Nick counted twice because he trusted neither Gracie nor his counting ability. By the time he finished, Gracie was already on the other side of the bar next to Harvey, a cold bottle of Reingold cupped in her hand.

"You going to see Mr. Handsome tonight?" Nick asked her, not caring whether Gracie was going to see Mr. Handsome, but knowing it was in his best interest to remain on friendly terms with her. The last time they argued, about who was supposed to polish the liquor bottles, she made sure three rolls of dimes were broken in the register the next day when they changed shifts. Nick had to count fifteen dollars worth of dimes while Gracie sat on the other side of the bar, drinking beer with a satisfied smirk on her face.

"Mr. Handsome and me had a disagreement," Gracie said, straining to sound sophisticated for Harvey. "I'm choosing not to see him tonight." She looked at Harvey quickly to see if he was listening. "Sometimes I think me and him are not—what's the word I'm looking for?—comparable for each other." Gracie drank some beer straight from the bottle, then asked Nick for a glass.

Paddy came downstairs and winched like he had just been dropped into a sewer. He walked to the bar in his shiny black shoes, stiff and squeaky from rarely being worn. He seemed uncomfortable and out of his element dressed in his yellow polo shirt, blue blazer and khakis.

"Nick, you're lettin' Harvey here go dry," he said, spotting Harvey's empty mug. "Get the man another beer."

"No thanks, Paddy." Harvey looked at his watch again and checked it against the clock over the register. "I have to get going. Thanks anyway."

"Don't thank me, Harvey. I would have charged you."

Paddy went behind the bar and searched the bottles until he found the Glenlivet single malt scotch. He poured a large shot and drank it in one swallow. "Ah! Good stuff." He pulled down on his lapels and brushed some dandruff from his shoulders.

"What the fuck are you guys doing here?" he said, noticing Frank and Jimmy for the first time.

"Whaddya mean, what the fuck are we doing here?" Frank put his hands up like he was catching a beach ball.

"I told you two I have business to attend to tonight."

"Oh, what kind of business?" Frank asked as if he didn't remember.

"Not that it's any of your concern, but I'm gonna do a little research on other bars and see if I can make some changes around here. I should start by getting new regulars."

Paddy started toward the door, then reversed direction and drank another shot of Glenlivet. He put his hand on Nick's shoulder, pulled him close and whispered, "Frank and Jimmy pay for their drinks tonight. They only drink free when I'm here, understand? And I don't want any whores using the bathrooms unless you charge them the three dollars."

"Don't worry about it, Paddy."

"I do worry about it. It's my fuckin' bar, so I do worry about it." His index finger was three inches from Nick's face. "And speaking of whores, where the hell is Margo? She's supposed to be here by now."

"I don't know where she is."

As soon as Paddy left, Frank said, "Now doesn't he look like a prize horse's ass?" Frank was looking through the Spuds MacKenzie sign in the window at Paddy walking toward the heart of the city in his new shoes, heading into the distant jungle of skyscrapers that shimmered in the late day heat like a mirage he could never possibly reach. "He puts on his blue jacket and his nice pants that don't fit him anymore. He'll get plastered as usual and he won't remember a god-damned thing in the morning."

Harvey stood and said goodbye to Gracie and Nick.

"Someday you're gonna have to let me drive your bus, Harvey," Gracie said.

"Oh, I can't do that."

"You can do anything you want, Harvey." Gracie's smile was more a leer than a smile. It disappeared as soon as Harvey left. Outside, his bus produced a steamy, mechanical fart before pulling away from the curb.

"Hey, Nick, can I get a beer?" Frank said.

"I gotta charge you, Frank."

"You gotta charge me? Jimmy too?"

Nick nodded and shrugged. "Paddy said so."

Frank and Jimmy looked at each other, their amazement quickly giving way to indignation. Frank shook his head a couple of times. "Nick, do me and Jimmy a favor," he said. "You tell Paddy when you see him that we tried real hard to think of a word to describe him, but 'cocksucker' was all we could come up with. Do me a favor, Nick, deliver that message."

A man with a three-day growth and a tattered and unseasonable overcoat walked into Blue Paradise, asked to use the bathroom and grunted thanks when Nick pointed to the back. Watching the man amble past, Nick wondered if Paddy's new rule for charging whores to use the bathroom applied to bums as well.

He continued turning the top shelf bottles so their labels faced forward and decided to polish them later when the bar would be empty and he'd need the distraction. Ten minutes passed before Nick remembered the bum had not come out yet. He waited another two minutes, then went into the bathroom where chemical smoke, not the familiar, earthy-stale cigarette smoke wafted from the stall. The man's legs were visible beneath the stall door, standing, not sitting.

"You almost done in there?" Nick said, trying to keep his voice calm and even. You never know what an addict will do. They're like animals when cornered. He'd seen that before.

"Out in a second," the man answered, his voice thick and phlegmy. Something dropped to the floor and an empty crack vial rolled out from under the stall toward the sink. It stopped in a seam between two tiles. Nick picked it up and examined the residue of white dust coating the inside. He pulled on the stall door and was surprised to find it unlocked. The man's eyes opened wide at being discovered. He dropped the glass pipe he was smoking. The pipe shattered. Instinctively, Nick checked to see if the man had any weapons before rushing him and taking his collar in his fist. "You're gonna leave quietly now."

Up close, the man's eyes were big but lifeless, his black pupils dilated to the size of marbles. For a moment Nick's attention was captivated by his reflection, a miniature version of himself, looking out from the man's depthless eyes. "Do it somewhere else," Nick said. The man didn't respond. He held Nick in his mirror eyes until Nick let go of his collar. The man left.

Jimmy was telling another story when Nick returned to the bar. It didn't matter whether the story was entirely true or not, or true at all. Listening to Jimmy and taking a double shot of Absolut helped steady his trembling knees.

". . . and this beautiful woman was sitting at the bar by herself," Jimmy was saying. "So this guy's thinking, what the fuck? A good-looking chick by herself. He moves down next to her and they start talking and he buys her a few drinks and everything's going great. The next thing he knows, she has her hand on his knee and it's climbing up his leg and he's getting a stiff one like any guy would. So he excuses himself and goes to the bathroom to rearrange himself. When he comes back he takes a sip of his beer and it tastes a little different but he don't take much notice because all he's thinking about is getting this chick into the sack. To make a long story short, she ends up taking him back to her place and, just as they're getting into it, he starts feeling kind of weak and dizzy. That was the last thing he remembered." Jimmy's voice became deadpan. "When he woke up he wasn't in her apartment anymore. He was lying in a back alley near the Hudson River. It was morning—three days later. The poor guy feels a pain in his side. He pulls up his shirt and sees this red gash that'd been stitched up, a real messy job.

So he goes to the doctor." Jimmy paused to add dramatic tension. "It turns out one of his kidneys is missing. Turns out there's a racket that sells stolen kidneys on the black market and they got one of his."

Jimmy waited for a reaction. No one said anything.

"What was the guy's name?" Nick finally asked.

"What was his name? Joe something. I don't remember. I knew him a long time ago."

"Sounds like a morality tale to me," Walter offered.

"A morality tale?" Anger spread across Jimmy's face. "The poor fucker can barely take a piss now and you're calling it a morality tale? You let your guard down with women and they steal your kidney! That's the only moral of that story!"

Two beers and the heat were boosting Gracie's temper as well.

"Ya know, smart guy," she said to Jimmy. "If it wasn't for a woman, none of youse would have kidney's to begin with. Ever think of that?"

Jimmy pretended to think about it, then said, "Now correct me if I'm wrong, because I've been known to be wrong once in a while, but besides the Immaculate Conception, I think there's always been a man involved in creating a human being with kidneys."

No one acknowledged Stanley when he walked in. Nick brought him a beer.

"You men are so scared of women," Gracie said. "You're all a bunch of chickenshits! That's what you are!"

"Can you blame us?" Jimmy shot back. "You go around stealing our kidneys!"

"The real problem is women don't know how to be women anymore," Frank said. "You ever try holding a door for one? They look at you like you just grabbed their ass."

"You may as well grab their ass," Jimmy said. "As long as you're gonna take shit you may as well get something for it."

Walter finished his glass of port and reluctantly marked his page with a cocktail napkin.

"Nick, can you bring me another Sandeman, please?" he said.

Nick brought his port. Walter took a small sip and swished it around in his mouth while waiting for Jimmy and Frank to stop talking. When they did, he said, "What's happened is our society has become so complex and automated that there's very little need for the sexes to be different. That's why there's so much tension these days. Machines and computers have made muscle and courage and other traditional forms of masculinity almost obsolete."

"Whaddaya saying, that women never had muscle and courage?" Gracie asked indignantly.

"What I'm saying is men are traditionally the providers and protectors. They had to use muscle and courage to accomplish that. Now it's possible for women to provide just as easily. You don't need to be tough or courageous to be an accountant or a scientist. You don't have to be a skillful hunter to go to the supermarket." Walter knew he was on a pretty good roll. Why stop now? "So, you see, it's not really the man's fault he acts the way he does. What most women don't understand is men have a much different sexuality that stems back to prehistoric days when it was necessary for a man to spread his seed amongst as many women as possible in order to insure that the species would survive. The rate of infant mortality was so high men had to play a numbers game. The reason why women don't have such an urgent sex drive is because they had to try to keep one man so they could raise a family that would survive."

Gracie's lips were pressed together hard, making them almost colorless since most of her lipstick had been washed away by the beer. She started to say something but Walter cut her off before she could.

"I think what may eventually happen," he continued, "is the human race will evolve into one sex that reproduces artificially."

"That's the most ridiculous thing I ever heard," Stanley said. "How can men and women become the same thing? Like one day I'm going to have tits and start wearing dresses?"

"It would take millions of years, Stanley," Walter said with a hint of condescension. "It wouldn't happen over night."

Satisfied that he'd made his point, Walter opened his book again. Before starting to read, it occurred to him, as it had many times before, that Blue Paradise is not the best place to read and certainly not the best place to discuss ideas. No one here could stimulate him intellectually or even keep up, not that it bothered him very much. And he was well aware that the time he spent drinking port should be spent trying to write. But the port here is cheap and, what the hell, he'd made his point for the night, a good one no matter who understood it.

Gracie tipped back the rest of her third beer, slid off her stool and steadied herself against the bar. Her face looked bloated and sunburned despite the fact she rarely spent much time outdoors.

"You know, you and your big words don't fool me, Walter," she said, jabbing her finger in his direction. "You're as much of a pig as Jimmy and Frank."

"What about me?" Stanley asked, laughing.

"You? You're just stupid," Gracie answered. She left before Stanley or anyone else could return her insults.

"The big-titted dingbat strikes again," Jimmy said.

✕

Jimmy didn't leave with Frank tonight. And when Stanley and Dog and Walter left, no one else remained in the bar, just him and Nick. Nick noticed Jimmy's mood had changed, become somber again, as if all his arguing about beer signs and women a few hours earlier had been an act, a cover for what was really going on inside his head.

"You want to play a game of pool, Nick?" Jimmy asked, studying the bubbles rising to the top of his beer.

"I thought you never played pool."

"When I got nothing else to do, I'll play a game."

Nick racked and Jimmy broke. The balls scattered evenly across the table but none of them dropped.

"You want to play eight ball, Jimmy?"

Jimmy lit his cigar. The match flame leapt with each turn and puff.

"Eight ball's fine," he said.

They played without talking and Jimmy didn't pay much attention to his shots or care very much that Nick won easily. He racked for the next game and as Nick pumped the cue to break, Jimmy said, "So, what's it gonna be, Nick?"

The breath caught in Nick's throat. He was expecting this but it startled him anyway. Before he could answer, Jimmy held his index finger to his lips, walked over to the door and shut it. He looked around the bar to make sure no one was hiding in the corners, then up at the ceiling as if Paddy's wife had her ear to the floor. "Don't say anything," he said quietly. "Nod or shake your head, but don't say anything. I don't want to take no chances."

They stood facing each other. In any other circumstance Nick would have been embarrassed, staring into another man's eyes for so long without blinking or looking away. He knew that whatever he did now, nod or shake, would be final. If he gave his word, then went back on it, he would be crossing not only Jimmy but his mafia backers as well. He did have an out, though, a shake of his head. But if he didn't take it, he was in, in all the way.

No use thinking it all through again, the pros and the cons. He'd already done that, over and over. Ten to one odds. Ten grand plus a dive would equal one hundred thousand dollars. Simple arithmetic. And even though his mind was cloudy and muddled now, Nick knew he'd already decided and his decision was the right one. The wrong one for the right reason. That's it.

"A nod or a shake, Nick," Jimmy repeated, still staring into Nick's eyes. "Remember, once we're gonna do it, we're gonna do it." Jimmy looked away for a moment, then back at Nick. "You're a good guy and I like you, Nick, but you give me the word and then change your mind and there's nothing I can do to help you."

Nick remained frozen, thinking about this. Suddenly, the muscles in his neck loosened and, unable to think about it any more, he nodded.

"You give me your money any time before Friday, Nick. The sooner the better."

"Okay."

"You want to play the second game?" Jimmy asked.

"No. Do you?"

"All right, then. So, we're not playing anymore."

Jimmy left without finishing his beer. Nick locked the door and while cleaning the bar, he didn't think about the fight because it was over now as far as he was concerned. Instead, he thought about Uncle John and Alice and Jerry. He thought about Jimmy, how he didn't seem to be the same person he once knew. He thought about Margo too and wondered why she didn't show up tonight. And he saw his reflection in the mirror behind the bottles, the same reflection he'd seen in the crackhead's eyes.

CHAPTER FOURTEEN

NICK'S FOOTSTEPS played a steady rhythm against the pavement, every other one pounding pain into his right knee. This morning the punches he threw into the steamy air ahead of him were tight and slow. He sucked hard to fill his lungs and wondered if he should be listening to the TV reports advising against strenuous outdoor activity.

Despite the loneliness, early morning was his favorite time, when the streets were quiet and empty and he could think. He ran the same route he always did, zig-zagging between 11th Avenue and the highway, from 45th to 26th Street. It goes faster when every block, every doorway, every sectioned view of the river at the end of each block is familiar. He started slowly from Blue Paradise, jogging down 11th Avenue to 44th Street, west to the highway, down to 43rd, back over to 11th.

Now that he no longer had to think about the fight, Nick thought mainly about Alice, about taking her away when it was over, maybe to the country for a few days. They could stay in one of those inns she often talked about and eat a breakfast of freshly baked muffins downstairs in the morning. He could do that. He could also end it. After the fight. That would be the time to do it if he was going to. Lose the fight, take the money he was going to make, pack up and leave for good.

But it hurt, almost physically, to imagine Alice alone, the years passing, her growing older and more lonely. She'll find someone else. Probably. Eventually. What if she doesn't? Nick remembered the party, thrown by an artist friend of Walter's in a loft down in Soho. He and Alice spent most of the party sitting on the couch rather than risking conversation with Walter's intellectual friends. Nick nursed foreign beers from the bottle and Alice sipped a glass of white wine and nervously nibbled the cheese and olives on the glass coffee table in front of them.

A man dressed in a T-shirt and a checkered blazer, sat next to them and asked a lot of questions and listened carefully to the answers. He became even more interested when he learned of Nick's boxing and Alice's job as a mortician. When he stood to get another drink, Alice noticed a cocktail napkin taped to his back, "I'M AN IDIOT SAVANT!" written on it in bold, hand-drawn letters.

Nick looked around at the other guests but no one there seemed the type to do something like that. Alice followed the man to the bar, touched his back and said, "I think I'll have some more wine. It's very good wine." She returned to the couch with her glass refilled and the napkin note crumpled in her hand. Nick took the napkin and put it in his pocket, then held onto her hand for the rest of the night. You won't make her happy, he thought, pushing his tired legs a little harder. She thinks you'll make her happy, but you know damned well you won't.

Nick tried to breath only through his nose, like when he was really training, for a real fight. Keep the mouth shut. If it's open you'll be swallowing your teeth. One good punch and they'll be bouncing off the back of your throat. His lungs labored to filter oxygen from the hot, wet air that he gulped as if it was water. And without making a conscious decision to, he stopped running and bent over until his breathing slowed and evened. He had never before allowed himself to stop like this.

When his breath returned, Nick started moving in a circle, throwing three jabs, a right, a left hook, and an upper-cut. The flurry exhausted him. He shook his arms loose and ran again until he reached 33rd Street where he slowed to a walk. Stop once and you'll stop every time, he had always told himself. He knew it was true now.

Trucks and buses were lined along both sides of 33rd Street, from 11th Avenue to the highway. At the end of the line, in the truck nearest the avenue, a driver sat with his hands clasped behind his head, staring straight ahead at the back of the truck in front of him. A whore's head bobbed up and down in his lap, in and out of view, her cheeks sucked hollowed with the effort. Nick stood against the wall in the shadow and watched what seemed like a movie, two-dimensional and unreal.

It didn't take long for the whore to finish the job. She opened the window and a condom splatted onto the sidewalk. She rinsed her mouth from a bottle of water and spit a milky stream before jumping down from the truck and wobbling for a moment on her high heels.

Her features were not yet visible but the outline of her body, unconcealed by her tight, pink dress, looked familiar to Nick: her rounded hips, the way they swayed when she walked. She slung her pocketbook over her shoulder and adjusted the strap of her bra, then walked toward Nick, trapping him in the shadow. She stopped to remove her shoe and shake a pebble out of it. She continued walking and when she passed beneath the streetlamp, Nick could see that it was Margo. She saw him too.

"Nick!" Her voice sounded different, harder, outside of Blue Paradise. "It's late to be hanging around, isn't it?"

"I was doing some roadwork," Nick said, still startled, not knowing how else to respond.

"They say you shouldn't be running in this weather."

"They're probably right."

Neither knew what to say next.

"You weren't at Blue Paradise tonight," Nick said.

"How long have you been standing here?"

"Just a few seconds."

Margo's face went blank in an effort to conceal her disappointment.

"Hot night, isn't it? Everything's so damned sweaty," She said. She looked at her watch. "Four-thirty already. Time flies when your having fun, doesn't it?" She forced a short laugh and put up her hands. "C'mon, Nick, gimme a few punches."

No. It's gonna hurt."

"I can take it. It'll help you get ready for your fight."

Margo kept her hands up and waited for Nick's punches, her pocketbook hanging from the crook of her elbow, a determined look on her face.

"All right. A few punches."

Nick got up on his toes and moved around her, throwing three lefts lightly. Pop! Pop! Pop! The punches felt good and natural now, no longer heavy and forced.

"It doesn't hurt?" he asked.

"It feels good."

Nick threw more jabs, then a right. Margo tucked her lower lip between her teeth and let her hands absorb the blows, enjoying the pain inflicted by Nick's hard knuckles. Aware that he was hurting her, Nick moved away and boxed the air. He crouched and spun a volley of uppercuts into the belly of an invisible opponent who became Leroy Johnson for a few seconds.

"You look good, Nick," Margo said, rubbing her palms together.

Nick stopped boxing.

"You think so?"

"You always look good."

"Don't say that. Everyone has their bad days."

They started walking and Nick was glad Margo had given him an excuse not to finish his run. He had planned to visit Jerry before going to see Alice tonight, but now, as they headed south on the deserted avenue, both knowing but neither saying where they were going, he felt released of both obligations.

"Do you think this heat will ever end?" Margo said, breaking the expectant silence hanging in the air between them.

"It'll end soon."

The starless sky hung lower than Nick had ever seen it, making the dark buildings on either side of the avenue appear higher in contrast. At the corner of 27th Street they stopped and Nick looked at Margo and saw her servicing the truck driver, cleaning out her mouth, jumping down to the sidewalk.

"You live around here, right, Nick?"

"About a block away."

"I haven't been to your place in a long time.

There was a bottle of Gordon's in Nick's freezer. The ice in the glass cracked when he poured the slightly syrupy vodka over it. He handed the drink to Margo who was sitting on the new old couch he found on the sidewalk one night on his way home from work. Before taking a sip, Margo drew an "M" in the condensation on the side of the glass.

"Ahhh, that's good." She leaned back and let her body go limp. She pushed a few strands of hair from her forehead, drank more vodka and waved her hand in front of her face to create a breeze.

"Don't you have a fan, Nick?"

"No." Nick sat on the couch next to her. "I bought one but I gave it to my uncle.

"How can you sleep without a fan?"

"You get used to it."

"I guess you can get used to anything."

The quiet that always seemed thicker and purer at night was beginning to effect Margo, make her edgy. But the vodka helped to dull the reality of knowing Nick had seen her and what she was doing in the truck.

"Don't you have a radio or something, Nick?"

"I had one but it broke. I haven't bothered getting a new one yet."

"You live a pretty simple life, don't you?" Margo

said, looking around Nick's apartment, at the nearly bare walls, at the chair and small wooden table, the only other furnishings besides the couch and Nick's bed in the other room. She focused briefly on the calender with the pictures of landscapes she thought were too perfect to be beautiful.

"The less you have, the less you need," Nick said. "That's the way I see it."

Margo swallowed more cold vodka.

"God, this feels good. Aren't you having any, Nick?"

"I never drink before a fight."

The sound of the ice knocking together in Margo's glass and the savoring way she brought it to her lips made Nick want a drink badly. He couldn't drink in front of her, though. He never drank before a fight and Margo might think it unusual if he did. He didn't want anyone thinking anything was unusual. He refilled Margo's glass.

"You were going to see Alice tonight, weren't you?" Margo said.

"I was thinking about it."

"So, why didn't you? You could've told me you were going to see her."

"I would have if I wanted to. She'd be asleep anyway. It's hard to talk much to someone who's half asleep. I go over there and lie awake in bed for hours while she sleeps."

"You don't talk?"

"We talk some. I tell her about my night and she tells me about the body she worked on that day." Nick breathed Margo's scent deep into his lungs. "She worries about me fighting. She wants me to quit before I get hurt. I tell ya, Margo, she's probably right. Sometimes I don't even care whether I win or lose this fight.

I just want it to be over. Maybe I'll lose it so I won't have to fight anymore."

"What would you do then?"

"I don't know, go someplace maybe. You wanna come with me?" Nick knew he shouldn't have said that.

"Sure. I could earn a living anywhere." Margo laughed and stirred her drink with her index finger. For a while they listened to the humming of the refrigerator, disrupted only by the squealing brakes of a garbage truck making its way along 26th Street.

"So, what do you do during the day?" Nick asked. He'd never seen Margo in the daylight.

"Sleep mostly. Sometimes I just walk around." Margo drank some vodka. "The other day I was walking past the schoolyard where I went when I was a kid after coming over from Casablanca. The same swing set's still there, you know. I sat on it and nobody was there and all these memories came back to me, one after another. All the faces and the names and the teachers. It was like it was really happening in front of my eyes. I even saw myself. It was strange seeing myself. It was like I was watching an old home movie or something. I had my hair in pigtails and I was wearing a pink sun dress and saddle shoes. I looked so cute, Nick."

"I bet you did."

Margo wiped a tear from the corner of her eye and said, "It seemed like I was a totally different person then, like that little girl was going to grow up to be someone else, not me. I wish I could have gone over to her and told her how to do it differently. It wouldn't be so hard. All I'd have to do is tell her and everything'd be all right." Margo swallowed a large sip of vodka. "Do you remember what it was like being a kid, Nick?"

"Not really. I remember how I kept waiting to be an adult so I wouldn't have to take shit from my father anymore. I used to think that one morning I was just going to wake up and be one. Now I think you don't ever really grow up, you just grow older."

Margo went into the bathroom. A minute later, the toilet flushed followed by water running in the sink. The water stopped and Margo came out with her mascara smudged under her eyes, like shiners, Nick thought. Her shoes were in her hand and her legs looked less shapely but more natural without them on. Nick tried not to look at her legs for long.

Margo sat and leaned against him. She touched the side of his neck and licked the end of her finger.

"You taste salty, Nick."

"I should take a shower. I probably smell."

"I like the way you smell. I don't like the way most men smell."

With her face closer to his, Nick could see the tracks the tears had cut through her mascara. He saw her in the cab of the truck again and this made his heartbeat quicken.

"Sometimes I get so scared, Nick." Margo's voice sounded smaller now. "Do you ever get scared?"

"Scared of what?"

"I don't know, just scared. Scared that you're gonna die or something."

"I'm not scared of dying."

Margo rested her head on Nick's shoulder. It had never been there before. She pressed closer, making the heat nearly unbearable. Her tears started to flow, dropping onto Nick's shoulder, soaking through his T-shirt. He wanted to kiss her, but knew where her lips had been, that they could never be completely clean. He put his arm along the couch behind her and Margo sniffled into his chest. She looked up at him. The rims of her eyes were swollen.

"I'm sorry, Nick. I didn't mean to cry. I usually don't cry."

"That's okay. I don't mind."

"You never cry, do you?"

"I cry. Sometimes I do. I have nothing to cry about right now."

"Everyone has something to cry about."

She put her head back on Nick's chest. Through the window, the first weak light was beginning to reveal the bricks of the building across the courtyard. Nick put his hand on Margo's head and ran his fingers through her hair until he was touching her bare neck. She moaned softly as Nick continued to stroke her hair, letting it glide between his fingers.

"Margo," Nick whispered. "I'm gonna take a shower."

He got up and went into the bathroom. Before closing the door, he looked back and saw her watching him. He stepped under the hot water and adjusted it until it ran cold and icy.

After showering and drying, he combed his hair in the mirror and came out with a towel wrapped around his waist. Margo's glass was empty now except for two chunks of ice, the edges rounded by the heat. Her eyes struggled to stay open.

"Want some more vodka?" Nick said.

"No. I had enough for one night."

"Are you hungry? I could go out and get us something. There's not much in the fridge."

"You saw me in the truck tonight," Margo said, her voice wavering with fatigue.

Nick considered lying then said, "Yeah, I saw you. You sure you don't want something to eat?"

"I wish you hadn't seen me."

"I wish I hadn't seen you either."

Nick went into his room and put on a pair of jeans. When he came out, Margo was stretched lengthwise on the couch.

"I'm not gonna judge you, Margo," he said, standing over her. "I'm not gonna judge anyone."

Margo smiled and closed her eyes.

"I'm so tired, Nick," she said. "Can I sleep on the couch tonight? I don't feel like going back out there."

Nick bent down, took Margo's hand and pulled her to her feet. He held onto her hand the way he'd held Alice's hand at the party and felt almost the same way inside. They stood close to each other, nearly touching.

"You don't have to sleep on the couch," Nick said before leading her into the bedroom.

C H A P T E R   F I F T E E N

WEAK AIR-CONDITIONING blew against Jerry's cheek, reminding him that he had to keep a cool head, think things through before he got to Atlantic City. Can't be nervous or scared. People can sense fear like dogs and horses.

He pushed the recline button on his armrest, leaned his seat back and watched Manhattan's distant skyline shimmering through the soft, early evening sky. He was beginning to enjoy this ride, even look forward to it. For three hours he could relax while the Grayline bus took him further from the city and closer to his destiny.

The bus descended onto the swampland flats and Jerry squinted into the sun glaring its last effort behind the tangle of factories and oil tanks from which black and grey tornados of chemical smoke stretched toward the sky, separated from their stacks by an invisible layer of pure heat. The smell of burning rubber filled the bus at the same place it always did. In a mile the smell was gone.

The sun dropped out of sight and the remaining light intensified to orange and red, turning dirty ponds on either side of the turnpike into pools of molten metal. As the bus pushed further south into New Jersey, the light gave way to darkness that settled over the swamps which gradually evolved into low, dense woods. Jerry stared into the woods, imagining they held secrets only those brave enough to venture in would ever know. He looked away from the window, at Nick sitting in the seat next to him. He nudged Nick awake with his elbow and said, "I'm glad you're coming, Nick."

"This is fuckin' crazy," Nick said, annoyed at being awoken. "I must be crazy.'

"You're not crazy. You're finally using the old noodle. I know it feels strange for you to do that."

"Just once, Jerry. This is it."

"Sure, sure, just once."

But Jerry knew Nick would never be satisfied with just once when he saw how easy it was going to be.

Jerry dozed off as well, until a hoarse, monotone voice brought him back from his dream of the Korean whorehouse and the shrieking laughter he couldn't escape. Relieved to be awake and still on the bus with Nick, he rubbed his eyes clear and listened to the man sitting in front of him explain how to beat the roulette wheel. He wanted to wake Nick again so he too could hear the man's theory, but decided to let him continue sleeping.

Casino billboards grew alongside the road with increasing frequency. The woods gave way to fields of seagrass as if in anticipation of the spot-lit casinos which appeared in the distance, partially obscured by fog rolling in off the Atlantic. The bus exited the highway and was soon crossing a dark tenement neighborhood. It stopped at a traffic light next to a liquor store with a flashing neon sign advertising Trump Castle's "Slotzilla" on its side.

The light turned green and the bus drove a few more dismal blocks before pulling under a vaulted concrete canopy at the Atlantic City Terminal. The few passengers who came for purposes other than gambling retrieved their bags from the overhead racks and filed off the bus, the defeat in their faces contrasting sharply with the eager hope molding those of the passengers who came to gamble. When the last one was off the bus, the driver closed the door and quickly backed out of the terminal as if glad to be rid of them.

The bus stopped next and finally in the Caesar's Palace parking lot. Jerry and Nick let the remaining passengers off first. To kill time they bought a pack of cigarettes in a deli, then walked Pacific Avenue past the casinos built one after another along the ocean, past the prostitutes huddled together on the corners, seemingly more interested in their conversations than attracting customers.

They walked as far as "Curves" and considered going in before turning around and coming back to Caesar's and heading to the bar where, according to the plan, they sat separately. Nick ordered seltzer with lime and Jerry ordered a beer and looked out at the huge room packed with gamblers sitting at blackjack tables, in front of one-armed bandits, screaming for luck at the craps tables.

This time Robert was dealing Black Jack at a different table. Jerry noticed the same things about him, though, his shifty eyes, the way he looked at his watch while his players placed bets, or at the cocktail waitresses balancing trays of drinks. Jerry noticed him adjust his apron a few times too.

Jerry wondered how closely Robert was being watched by the surveillance globe bubbling from the ceiling over his head, if his watcher could see him palming chips. He didn't watch Robert for long for fear that his attention might somehow guide the suspicion of the large pitboss standing behind him with his arms folded across his barrel chest.

A man in a green sweatsuit and new white sneakers was rolling for nine at a craps table on the other side of the floor. The bleach blonde with him pushed out her small, hard breasts against her low-cut black dress. The heavy-set man standing at the side of the table never removed the fat cigar from his mouth as he yelled, "It's all you, shooter! It's all you, shooter!"

The frenetic pace at the craps table was making Jerry tense, reminding him of his own situation. He wanted a Seagrams to help relax but stuck to beer, knowing that drinking the hard stuff would make him want it too badly. He'd only blow it by wanting it too badly. He looked down the bar at Nick. Their eyes met for a moment before they both looked away.

The girl had a wholesome, milk-fed kind of beauty; brown hair in a bob that framed her round face and narrow but full-lipped mouth. The fatigue pulling at the corners of her eyes was still a few years away from becoming permanent. She sat at the bar with an unlit cigarette held between her first two fingers. She searched her bag for matches. Jerry found some in his jacket pocket.

"Need a light?"

"Yeah, thanks."

A chip of burning sulfur stuck to the end of Jerry's index finger when he lit the match. He gritted his teeth against the pain as the girl leaned her cigarette into the flame which he also used to light his own before cooling his finger against the side of his beer. The girl tilted her head back and exhaled a long stream.

"Feels good to finally sit down," she said.

"Were you gambling?" Jerry asked.

"No. Working." She gestured with her cigarette at the mass of gamblers that looked like a colony of ants. "Serving drinks to this bunch."

Jerry recognized her as one of the cocktail waitresses he'd been watching and said, "I wouldn't want your job."

"I don't think you'd look too good in the uniform." Her slightly gruff laugh didn't match her delicate appearance. Jerry pictured himself in the skimpy uniform she'd been wearing earlier and laughed too.

"I don't think I could walk in them high heels either," he said.

"I could teach you how to do that. It's not hard."

She ordered a rum and coke from the bartender who asked how her shift was. She told him it was the same as always. Jerry pushed his last twenty across the bar and bought her drink before realizing he could have saved his money. She probably drank for free here.

"What's your name?"

"Jerry."

"Thanks for the drink, Jerry. I'm Susan."

They shook hands. Hers was small and felt fragile.

"So, it's tough work serving drinks to gamblers?" Jerry asked.

"It's fine if you don't mind getting your ass patted a hundred times a night." Susan crushed her cigarette in the ashtray. "The money's not bad, though."

Susan looked at the TV above the bar and Jerry searched for something else to say, wishing he was a better conversationalist, particularly with women. He remembered Nick once telling him that people like to talk about themselves. He'd learned that bartending. All you have to do is ask them questions to keep a conversation going.

"How long have you been working here?" Jerry asked.

"Three years. It pays the bills." Susan's eyes went back to the "Cheers" rerun on the TV. "I love this show. That Rhea Perlman is a riot. If I could land my dream role, it would be one like that."

"You ever do any acting?" Jerry was surprised and pleased at how easy the questions were coming to him.

"I was in Guys and Dolls a couple of years ago. They put it on at the Community Theater here. I've been told I'm good. What I really want is to go to New York and try my luck there. You have to go to New York to make it big in theater. I figure I can get a waiting job there. I know I can wait tables. That's one thing I know I can do."

Jerry watched her mouth as she spoke. He knew it was a crazy idea, but when he had enough money from cashing chips he decided he'd ask her if she wanted to come live with him in New York. He'd have to get an apartment first. Other than that, it didn't seem so crazy really.

"You're not gambling?" Susan asked, looking at Jerry's right eye, making him wonder if it was twitching.

"I always stop while my streak's still going." Jerry gestured to the gamblers on the floor. "There're losers because they don't know when to quit. Me, I lost a lot of money before I finally learned that."

"The good ones don't drink while they gamble either," Susan said. "The ones that get drunk are the ones that lose big. That's what I'm here for." She smiled mischievously. "I see it every night."

"I'm sure you do."

"So, what do you do, Jerry?"

Jerry sipped his beer to give himself time to think.

"I own a restaurant in Manhattan."

What was left of the fatigue in Susan's eyes disappeared.

"Wow! What kind of place is it?"

Jerry immediately regretted having said it. He certainly hadn't planned to. Susan was waiting for his answer with an innocent kind of expectancy that made him forget what they were talking about for a moment.

"It's real nice place," he said, picking up his broken train of thought. He looked down the bar and saw his lie mirrored in Nick's honest face. He looked back at Susan and said, "It's a tough business, the restaurant business. You got all kinds of things to deal with. I'm thinking about getting out. It's no easy buck, you know."

"I guess nothing is."

"I don't know about that."

The beer was having a slow, smoothing effect on Jerry tonight, like driving a long, gradual curve instead of the sharp turn Seagrams usually took him on. He checked his watch, glanced over to where Robert was still shooting out cards to the players, then looked away from Robert and told Susan a few of the bad jokes he usually couldn't remember.

"Do you get any celebrities in your restaurant?" Susan asked between laughing at his jokes.

"Sometimes. As a matter of fact, Spuds MacKenzie hangs there. Mostly in the window."

Susan stopped laughing and said, "No, really, which celebrities do you get?"

"Not many. Alec Baldwin from time to time. Mickey Rourke when he's in town. John Kennedy Jr. comes in because no one bothers him there."

Jerry resisted a strong urge to pull Susan close, to taste her lips and stop her from asking any more questions. When she asked if he needed any waitresses, Jerry changed the subject to what he would do when he hit it really big at the tables.

"Maybe you and I'll go down to Mexico for a while."

"Isn't the water bad there?"

"You'll get used to it."

"I'd have to get my shifts here covered."

Jerry smoothed his hair with his hand and said with impeccable timing, "You won't have to worry about covering any shifts."

Nick drank his second seltzer and watched the man in green sweats win big and then lose it all. He stood alone at the empty table now. Gone was the cigar smoker and his other fans, cheering and slapping his back, actually loving him like a brother, like a hero, for a while. The man walked away from the table with his head down, his blonde girlfriend following him from a safe distance in case he turned to vent his despair on her. Nick felt no pity whatsoever for him. That's what happens when you let chance do your bidding instead of taking things into your own hands, he thought. Now when the hell is Jerry gonna finish with that broad?

The beer gave Jerry enough courage to tell Susan he liked the way she looked in her uniform.

"It brings the customers in," Susan said. "I bet your waitresses don't dress like that."

"Maybe they should."

"I'd probably bring lots of customers into your restaurant. Some guys come here just to see me. They don't even gamble."

"I don't blame them."

"Maybe I could come work for you. I'd love to meet John John Kennedy. Is he nice?"

"Yeah, he's real nice. Right now I got a full staff," Jerry said, ashamed that his lie was now snowballing into new ones. "But I'll keep you in mind."

Susan smiled gratefully.

"That would be a dream. You don't know how happy that would make me." She took some money from her purse. "Let me buy you a drink this time."

She's probably playing me for a sucker. With that in mind, Jerry no longer felt bad about lying to her. Maybe she isn't yanking my chain. She probably is, though. No one ever plays you straight. All that laughing and smiling and eyelash batting. He noted how she had moved closer and started laughing at every stupid joke as soon as he told her he owned a restaurant in New York. He checked his watch again, twelve o'-clock already, then looked over at Robert's table, empty now and roped off. He scanned the floor, his eye darting from table to table, unable to find Robert.

"Is something wrong?" Susan asked.

Jerry didn't answer or look at her.

"Is something wrong?" She asked again.

"Nothing's wrong," Jerry answered, angry with her

now for causing him to miss Robert, annoyed with Nick for not noticing and telling him even though that would be a violation of their rule not to speak in the casino or anywhere else in Atlantic City.

"Are you sure nothing's wrong?

"Yeah, I'm sure. Listen, I gotta get going."

"You're not going to have a drink?"

"No, I gotta get going."

"Well, why don't I give you my number then?" Susan asked hopefully.

She borrowed a pen from the bartender and wrote her telephone number on a scrap of paper she found in her pocketbook. As Jerry read it, his anger softened somewhat and he felt mean and low for suspecting she had motives for being friendly. Now he didn't want to leave her. If he didn't have to go meet Robert he might just stay here at the bar and feed her some more harmless lies. Not knowing exactly how to say goodbye, he stood and held out his hand. Susan shook it, leaned over and kissed him quickly on the lips. Jerry felt a stirring in his groin. He carefully folded the paper with her number and pushed it deep in his breast pocket.

The barmaid at "Curves" slapped the change on the bar. Jerry counted it, the last of his cash, and wished he'd brought his flask so he could order a Coke and spice it in the bathroom like Dog did. The fact that Robert wasn't there yet was making him nervous. Probably still changing out of his uniform, he figured. Should be here any minute if he hasn't chickened out.

Still following the plan, Nick had tailed Jerry to "Curves" and taken a seat on the opposite side of the circular bar. Jerry decided if Robert didn't show by the time he drank the rest of his money, they would leave, let it go and not think twice about it. Like he always told Nick; you have to know how to walk away from a deal. Can't put all your eggs in one basket. At least there were other eggs, like the vans, and more importantly, what he'd found in one of them the other night. But the thought of putting that to use scared him enough to relegate it to ace-in-the-hole status, a last resort if his less risky ideas fail.

A hand fell on his shoulder.

"Sorry I'm late," Robert said. "I got lectured by the floor manager for yawning too much. You're supposed to make the gamblers think you're having as much fun as they are."

Robert remained standing, as if waiting for Jerry to invite him to sit.

"All that fun can tire you out," Jerry said. "Want a drink?"

"Rolling Rock."

Robert sat and smiled up at the girl on stage who said, "How's tricks?" before dancing to the other side.

"Can we start a tab?" Jerry asked the barmaid when she came to take their order. He hoped to run up a big one and melt away before it came time to settle. He knew he'd never be back in this bar. For now on his trips to Atlantic City would be strictly business. Besides, the girls in New York bars are hotter.

"We don't run tabs here," the barmaid replied.

"All right, gimme two Rolling Rocks, then."

The barmaid brought their beer and counted the remainder of Jerry's bills. "I need two more dollars," she said.

Jerry made a show of reaching for his empty pocket and was relieved when Robert handed her the two dollars. They drank and watched the girls dance, both keenly aware of the others presence. On the other side of the bar, Nick sipped his seltzer, wondering what the hell he was doing here. Fuckin' Jerry. Always trying to drag me down to his low-life level.

Jerry's beer quickly reached the bottom of his mug. Robert's mug was still nearly full and he didn't offer to buy Jerry another. Instead, he went to the bathroom and took longer than a man's piss should. While waiting for Robert to return, Jerry gave Nick the okay sign, then watched the blue and white lights flash off the girls' bodies and tried to think of a smooth, matter-of-fact way to bring up the obvious purpose of this meeting. Robert came back with a drop of water clinging to his chin and one hanging from his left earlobe.

"They don't let you piss at Caesars," Robert said. "You can't even go into the bathroom after your shift. They think you'll pull a fast one on them."

"I guess they have their reasons," Jerry said.

Instead of agreeing, Robert shook his head and muttered, "Bastards."

A girl in a string bikini offered a lap dance to Jerry.

"So, let's talk business," Jerry said, swallowing his longing for a lap dance, immediately wishing his voice had sounded more casual.

The girl frowned at being ignored and moved on.

"That's what we're here for," Robert replied, happy Jerry was the one who'd finally said it. He took a look around the bar as if still expecting his supervisor to walk in. "Did you get a mail box?"

Jerry nodded and handed him a slip of paper with the mailbox address written on it. Robert put the paper in his wallet without reading it.

"I can contact you now if I need to," he said. "Besides that, you and I aren't going to have much to do with each other after tonight." Robert took two small keys from his pocket. One of them had black plastic coating the top. He held them below the level of the bar. "Take one."

Jerry took the one without the plastic.

"This is the key to locker number twenty-four in the Atlantic City bus station," Robert whispered so low Jerry could barely hear him above the music. "I had a copy made. I checked them out. They both work."

Robert waited for any questions Jerry might have. Jerry had none.

"Every Monday you go to locker twenty-four. It's in the back row, so it's hidden. There'll be a gym bag in it with the chips, not a lot of chips because the casino might get suspicious and start remembering you if there's a lot each week. You take them to Caesars and cash them at the cage. Wait until night time when it's busy and you'll be just another face in the crowd. Then you come back and leave my half of the money in the bag in the locker. I'll pick it up every Tuesday morning using my key."

"Sounds good," Jerry said, keeping his face deadpan to conceal his excitement. This guy isn't bad to work with. At least he has a brain. It's nice not having to do all the thinking all the time, he thought, shooting a quick look at Nick who was chewing an ice cube and intently watching the girls on stage.

With nothing left to discuss, they pretended to study the dancers on stage as well. The DJ played "You Really Got Me" by the Kinks. The girls had a hard time finding the rhythm but Robert was glad to hear the familiar sound of Ray Davies' voice after all the throbbing disco music. He listened to the lyrics and watched Jerry out of the corner of his eye, trying to pinpoint what it was about him he didn't trust entirely: his jerky movements, his twitching right eye, his fast, nervous way of talking. But it was a good plan and not many people would be willing to be part of it. Or desperate enough. Maybe that was it. Desperation, whether his own or someone elses, always made Robert uneasy.

Jerry waited for him to say more. He didn't. That's it? It seemed so easy. Too easy. If it sounds too good to be true, it probably is, right? He searched for a catch, a setup and considered pulling out or even trying to do it alone at another casino now that he had the idea and knew the procedure. He could find a way to steal chips himself, from other gamblers when they weren't looking or got too drunk to notice. He pondered different percentages in his head. If only he didn't need Robert, he and Nick could keep a hundred percent instead of fifty. He looked at his watch and remembered that the next bus would be leaving for New York in twenty minutes. No reason to stay longer than that.

Jerry downed the last inch of his beer and said, "I better get going. I have to work tonight at the—"

"I don't want to know," Robert cut him off. He softened his voice. "Sorry. The less we know about each other, the better. That's all."

Realizing Robert was right, Jerry said, "I guess I won't be seeing you, then."

"If all goes well, you won't."

Jerry offered his hand and Robert gripped it with very little strength or effort.

"Be careful out there," Jerry said.

"I'm always careful."

"That's good. So am I."

✕

Jerry and Nick walked out of the Port Authority and into the city canyons still shrouded by early morning darkness. They turned up 8th Avenue, populated mostly by hollow-eyed junkies and scared runaways acting brave. Passing Show World, they stopped and looked up at the poster of Angel, her hungry eyes squinting pleasure down at them, her pink tongue wetting her upper lip.

"You don't go in these places anymore, do ya?" Nick said.

"Me, naw. Nothing but a bunch of perves in there."

But truth be told, Jerry wished Nick wasn't there and he had the money to go in and see Angel right now. That's exactly what he would do. He remembered Susan's number in his jacket and a pang of hope replaced his empty longing. Maybe if things worked with her, he wouldn't need to bother with Angel. Who was Angel anyway? A porn star. Just a notch or two above a whore. She'd probably give me some kind of disease. And Susan would certainly be a lot cheaper.

He decided he'd call Susan tomorrow and ask her if she wanted to have dinner next Monday after they cashed their first batch of chips. Of course, he'd have to think his way out of being a restaurant owner before she uncovered that lie. Shouldn't be too difficult. He could sell the business or have it burn down. Would she still like him if his restaurant burned down? Probably not, the bitch. Nonetheless, he took the scrap of paper with her phone number from his jacket and put it in the front pocket of his jeans where it would be safer.

"It went good tonight, Nick."

"Yeah, whatever. What are you gonna do now?"

"I don't know. Maybe I'll just wander around."

"Get some sleep. That's what you need."

"I'm not tired."

"Well, I'm bushed. I'm gonna hit the sack."

"You're supposed to be the one in shape, Nick, not me. How come you're always tired?

Nick shrugged.

"Maybe I'm getting old. Maybe I don't have it anymore."

"Don't worry, Nick. Pretty soon you won't have to have it anymore."

"For once in your life, you might be right."

Nick left Jerry on the corner of 42nd Street. After watching him walk away, Jerry turned west and passed the church directly across the street from the old McGraw-Hill building. He wished the church was open now so he could go in and sit for a while in one of the pews. Unlike the previous block that was lit with miles of neon, this end of 42nd Street was dark and menacing.

Jerry crossed 9th Avenue and continued past the parking garage, deserted except for the resting cars. As the river drew him further west, worry began to creep into the corners of his mind. What if Robert didn't come through? What if he got cold feet or decided to get someone else to cash the chips? What he'd told Nick about walking away from a deal didn't seem as easy to do now. A chill shook his body, but the heat returned like a fever, hotter than before.

The New Jersey lights visible on the other side of the river were not as sharp as they should have been and they seemed further away than they actually were. Jerry walked toward them and when he got to 10th Avenue, he knew exactly what he wanted to do.

When he came to the highway, he crossed it without having to avoid any cars. And luckily there were no people at the edge of the river. Jerry climbed the cyclone fence. On the other side, he took off his jacket and shirt and shoes. In just his pants, he walked out onto the short and mostly rotted wooden pier. At the end, he stood looking down at the black, chopping water while waiting for his nerve to come.

CHAPTER SIXTEEN

THE FANS in Blue Paradise hung motionless from the ceiling. Paddy blamed Nick.

"You're supposed to turn the fuckin' things off at the end of the night!"

"It's not my fault the wiring burned out."

Two weeks of shallow, un-airconditioned sleep was pulling on Frank and Walter and Stanley's faces.

"Why dont'cha get them fixed?" Jimmy said.

"It costs too much to get them fixed," Paddy replied. "Why do you care? You got air conditioning."

"We'll go someplace else to drink, then," Frank said.

"Good. Go someplace else."

"No one's going to come in here without fans," Walter said. "It's bad for your business not to mention our health."

"Summer'll be over in two months," Paddy coun-

196

tered, tired and clearly wanting to end the discussion. "It's Nick's fault anyway."

No one wanted to argue about it any more. Arguing about the heat was only making it hotter.

✕

"You don't know what "thoink" means?" Jimmy asked Frank as they watched Paddy haul himself around the pool table, warming up before challenging Frank to play.

Frank said "thoink" to himself.

"No, I dunno . . . thoink?"

Jimmy gave him a few more seconds to think about it, then said, "It's the noise your hard-on makes when you hit a woman across the face with it."

"Why the hell would you hit a woman with your hard-on?" Frank was genuinely puzzled. "You could hurt yourself."

Walter's sour expression matched the way he was feeling. He was trying to read and not listen to Frank and Jimmy but wasn't having much luck. Nor was he able to savor each mouthful of port as he usually did. Every few minutes he picked up his book, read a few sentences, then put it face-down on the bar again. Unable to concentrate, he listened to Jimmy telling Frank: "So she says 'Kiss me where it stinks.' She's trying to be cute, ya see. So I say 'Babe, do I really have to drive you all the way out to Jersey to kiss you?'"

On the TV, the newscaster was reporting the latest about the Fifth Avenue Rape case. It turns out one of the suspects was abused as a child, subjected to forced enemas on a regular basis.

"Who gives a shit?" Stanley said.

"He obviously did," Walter said. No one understood his joke.

"He'll be getting a few forced enemas when he goes to jail," Jimmy said. "Ah, he won't be going to jail. Those fuckers won't be going anywhere. That slick defense lawyer'll tell the jury that because they're black in a white society they had no choice but to fuck some rich lady up the ass."

"There's some truth to that," Walter said. "Most of these kids have nothing to lose. They grow up in the slums with no sense of hope. They watch television and see the things they can't have."

"Why don't they try working for them?" Jimmy grumbled.

"Good jobs aren't easy to come by if you don't have an education. The only ones they can get are at Mc-Donalds, if that. Most people won't hire poor black— I mean African-American—kids."

"Because they're little fuckers, that's why," Jimmy said.

"That's a constructive way of looking at it," Walter said, sarcastically.

"How else am I supposed to look at it? These people are running wild in the streets and intellectual assholes like you are saying we should take it lying down because their great great grandfathers were slaves. That jury won't convict them because they're scared of a race riot. But that's what all the niggers want, an excuse to burn down their own fuckin' neighborhoods."

"Don't get me wrong," Walter said. "I'm not saying they should get off scot free. If they are guilty, they should go to jail. But that's just taking care of the symptom, not the problem. We need to build more schools and housing and put money into job training and education. That's the only way to improve the situation."

"Yeah, more of our tax dollars going to support

people who don't know how to do anything but hold their hands out for more," Jimmy said. "We build them schools and houses and what do they do? They spray grafitti on the walls and shit in the halls and piss in the elevators."

"That's exactly what I'm saying," Walter said. "We have to do more than just give them material things. Until we help them help themselves, we're never going to solve the problem."

"They're never gonna help themselves. They been here for three hundred years. What the fuck are they waiting for? Look at the Koreans. They come over here and in a couple of years they got their own stores. They work their asses off and have to watch these animals steal from them every day. Then the niggers complain that the Koreans are rude to them. What the fuck do they expect? They should open their own stores but they're too fuckin' lazy."

"You're failing to take into account that they were the only group brought to America by force and made to work as slaves," Walter explained patiently. "Many of them had their families torn apart in the process."

"Yeah, yeah, yeah, I heard all that liberal crap before. Believe me, the Irish and the Italians and practically everyone else didn't exactly have it easy when they came over either, but they're doing pretty good now. They're not running around mugging people."

The heat was making each word an effort. With his energy draining away fast, Walter summoned his strength for a final closing statement, one that would make his point clean and clear, allow him to go home and write without thinking of things he should have said. He held up his book of short stories by Somerset Maugham and tapped his index finger on the cover.

"Your problem, Jimmy, is you never read. The only

information you ever get about the world is from the damned TV and the scandal sheets you call newspapers. Don't you think they want people to hate each other? That's what sells newspapers and air time. Do you have any idea how much money the media is making off this Fifth Avenue rape case?"

"I don't give a shit how much money they're making. The fact remains that a bunch of spooks broke into a lady's apartment and raped her. The papers don't lie. They don't make stories up."

"Innocent until proven guilty," Walter said. "Isn't that in the Constitution somewhere?"

"It don't matter what it says in the Constitution," Jimmy countered, barely giving Walter time to finish his sentence. "The Constitution was written two hundred years ago when people still knew how to behave."

Walter turned away from Jimmy. Before starting to read again, he said, "All I can say is we reap what we sow. As Malcolm X once said, 'The chickens come home to roost.' And they certainly have."

"What the hell do chickens have to do with it?" Stanley asked.

"Niggers eat a lot of chicken, Stanley," Jimmy explained with a grin. "That's what chickens have to do with it. It's just that these coons are starting to choke on the fuckin' bones."

The story Walter had been reading was about a small group of people stranded on a rain-soaked Pacific Island. The words were hardly making sense to him anymore. He'd made his point about the media and thought that would be it. But Jimmy's chicken comment bothered him. One comic note like that can steal an entire carefully constructed argument. Walter closed the book and frowned into his glass.

"Nick, there's sediment in my port. You know I don't like any sediment."

Nick put the glass he was drying back on the shelf and held Walter's port up to the cash register light.

"Sorry, Walter. I didn't know the bottle was getting that low."

Nick dumped the remains in the sink, rinsed it out and refilled it from a new bottle.

"That's alright, Nick. I'm sorry I snapped at you. I don't know what the hell's wrong with me lately."

"Bad day at work?"

Walter closed his eyes and nodded.

"I can't even begin to tell you. A bunch of prima donnas I have to wait on every day. They all think you're their personal slave, not their waiter." Walter fanned his face with his book. "I come home lately and I'm so wound up I can barely even write a sentence. I mean, I do write, just not as well or as much as I want to. Then I come here to unwind and I'm confronted by this collection of idiocy."

If Jimmy's ears could have perked like a dog's, they would have.

"You wouldn't happen to be talking about us, would ya, Walter?" he said.

"I was talking to Nick about my job."

"Yeah, I know," Jimmy said with menace creeping into his voice. "But it wasn't just your job you were talking about, was it? If it wasn't so hot, I'd come over there and bitch-slap you."

Walter didn't respond to this.

"Why don't you say it again, Walter?" Jimmy persisted. "If you're gonna say something once, you should have the guts to say it again."

Walter continued staring straight ahead into the bar mirror. Nick noticed a trace of fear in his eyes and said, "He didn't say anything about anyone, Jimmy."

"No, that's fine, Nick," Walter said. He turned to Jimmy and tried to affect complete contempt. "What I said, Jimmy, was that the patrons of this bar are a collection of idiots. Look at you, having a word for the sound your penis makes when you hit a woman's face with it. We have Stanley who believes everything he sees on that idiot box over the bar. There's Paddy and Frank whose friendship is based on trying to cheat each other out of as much money as possible. And you, Mr. Rabid Racist, would probably like to see every African-American in this city exterminated. Besides Nick, the only one in here I have any respect for is Dog. He at least has the sense to keep his mouth shut." Walter raised his glass to Dog. "Here's to you, Dog. You're probably smarter than the rest of them put together."

Jimmy's face had darkened to a light purple.

"And who the fuck are you to judge us?" he said, pointing his finger at Walter. "As far as I can see it, you're nothing more than a guy who complains about everything but doesn't do shit about anything. You know what you are, Walter? You're a waiter who knows a few big words but doesn't have any balls."

"I'd hold my tongue if I were you, Jimmy," Walter said, sharply. "At least I make an honest living."

"What the fuck's that supposed to mean?" Jimmy shot a quick glance at Nick.

"Let's just say you're a good American doing what Americans do best; you make money any way you can."

"How is fixing sewing machines dishonest?"

"Fixing sewing machines!" Walter put his forehead on the bar in frustration. He raised it back up. "Who are you trying to kid, Jimmy? Everyone here knows you're a bookie! You make odds and take money on illegal bets!"

Jimmy got to his feet, his fists clenched at his sides. Frank and Paddy stopped playing pool but made no move to calm or restrain him.

"You know, Walter, what you need is to learn a lesson in reality, the way you sit there talking shit every night!" Jimmy shook his fist toward Walter. "This is what the world is about after all your intellectual horseshit is washed away! You got one race against another! You make your money any way you can and try to get the fuck out before it's too late! And when I come in here I don't want to hear some hard-on like you telling me I'm an idiot for seeing things the way they really are in this crazy fucked-up city!"

Jimmy took another step toward Walter but stopped when he saw Nick grab the edge of the bar, poised to vault over it. His fist unclenched and his jaw loosened, allowing the blood trapped in his face to drain.

"Why don't you get down off your cross, Walter. Someone else needs the wood," he said calmly before going back to his stool and sitting.

The port Walter brought to his lips now chopped in his glass like the ocean on a windy day. His stomach was too unsettled to accept anything else into it so he put the glass back down on the bar without taking a sip.

"Unfortunately there are a lot of people who think, or I should say, don't think, just like you, Jimmy." Walter's words came out of his mouth halting and unsteady. He spoke as if obligated to by some personal dare to himself. "You don't even realize they've got you in their hip pocket. You're too bloody stupid to know it."

"Are you gonna shut the fuck up now, Walter?" Semi-circular patches of sweat beneath Paddy's arms were spreading toward the middle of his chest. Before taking his next shot, he added, "None of your babbling makes any sense to me."

"None of it makes sense to any of you," Walter lamented. "I could explain it until the cows come home, but it still wouldn't make sense to you."

No one responded to this. Jimmy sat smoking his Partagas, oblivious to Walter, as if he had suddenly disappeared. There was no longer any need to take offense at or defend himself against the insults. Walter was now nothing more to him than a small dog that barks a lot, but is completely harmless and inconsequential.

The bar became quiet, as if Walter and Jimmy's argument had used up the remaining air in it. Paddy racked the balls slowly, two at a time. Frank had won the first two games and they were preparing to play the third, double or nothing. Walter left abruptly, without saying goodbye to anyone except Nick. When he was gone, Frank asked Paddy whether he thought Walter was a faggot or not.

"I don't know. Probably."

"Jimmy and me think he probably is too."

Nick was about to disagree. But he didn't say anything because he wasn't entirely sure. Frank broke. None of the balls dropped.

"I had a hard day today too, Nick," Stanley said.

Nick cringed. The last thing he wanted to do was listen to anyone, particularly Stanley.

"The bums I work with, they sit around all day

drinking beer and then they take the credit for the work I do."

"That doesn't sound right," Nick said, distracted, his attention numbed by boredom.

"You're damned right it's not right. Just today I spent my lunch hour polishing hinges. You know how hard it is to take the paint off brass hinges and get them looking shiny as new? It takes about twenty minutes to get each one clean. I been spending my lunch hours for the past week shining them and when I finally finished today, Joe Schlanta tells the boss that he did half of them."

"Did he?"

"He did two."

"Why didn't you tell the boss that?"

"Why bother? He wouldn't believe me anyway. He always believes Joe Schlanta, that cocksucker."

"Who's the cocksucker, Joe Schlanta or your boss?"

"They're both cocksuckers."

Nick found some more dirty glasses. After washing them, he moved to the end of the bar and looked out the window at the light-speckled skyscrapers. He wondered if all the lives those building contained seemed as important and urgent to the people living them as his did to him right now. He thought about Atlantic City and the nerve butterflies fluttered in his stomach.

"I tell ya," Stanley said. "Sometimes life really stinks."

"You shouldn't think that way," Nick said without caring very much that Stanley's life stank. "You gotta make the most of life because it's short, you know."

"Yeah, then why is mine taking so long?"

Nick checked the clock. Only eleven o'clock.

"It's late, Stanley," he said, suddenly taken by a strong urge to be somewhere outside the window, anywhere but behind the bar. "Your cat's probably getting hungry."

Stanley frowned at his watch.

"Thanks for reminding me, Nick. I'd have another beer with you but I better get home and feed her. The damned thing, all it does is eat and sleep. I wish I could live like her. Sorry I gotta go so soon, Nick."

"I don't mind, Stanley."

Tonight Margo drank her water gimlet on the rocks. The man who wanted to kill someone had been in earlier and had stayed for almost an hour, fine-tuning his plans to take Margo to Belize after the deed was done. Nick overheard him say to her: "Killing isn't a sin if it's done for the right reasons. Read the Bible. Read the Koran. There's righteous killing in both of those books."

"I'm not very religious," Margo said.

"Well, you should be. You're a ship without a moral rudder if you don't have religion."

Margo's next customer never took his eyes off of her except to blink. He even watched her over the rim of his Campari and soda while he drank. Although slightly unnerved, Margo was happy that at least she didn't have to hold up her end of the conversation. She just stared back at the man with the love in her eyes he insisted on.

"It's the rarest, most beautiful thing in the world," he said to her in his high, womanish voice. "Words don't mean much. They're the cheapest things in the world." He placed his hand over his heart. "Love doesn't come from the mouth. It comes from the heart."

When the talker left, Margo blew out her cheeks with relief and said to Nick, "Maybe I'll have a real drink next time."

For most of the night they had been avoiding each other. But since Paddy and Frank were concentrating on their game, Nick took the opportunity to say, "How you doing tonight, Margo?"

"Besides the heat, I'm okay." Margo blew down at her chest to dry the moisture collecting in her cleavage. "How 'bout you?"

"I'm okay too, I guess." Nick sensed something was on her mind. They hadn't spoken much since the night Margo came to his apartment. "Did you want to talk about something?"

"That would be nice."

"Okay, we'll talk." Nick looked over at Paddy who missed his shot and cursed. "Best not to talk with him here," he said.

"If you don't want to talk, Nick, we don't have to."

"No, I want to. It's just better not to do it with Paddy here. Why don't we do it later? It can wait until later, can't it?"

"Yeah, it can wait."

Paddy came over for a refill of beer. Nick poured it down the side of the glass to prevent a head from forming.

✕

The alcohol wouldn't let Frank quit when he should have. And Paddy was being smart tonight, keeping the bottle of Jack Daniel's on the side of the pool table.

"Save yourself the trip to the bar, Frank. Help yourself. My liquor is your liquor."

Swollen red capillaries etched Frank's eyeballs and he nearly fell backward as he racked the balls. He challenged Paddy to the last game, double or nothing again, winner take all. They played and Paddy won easily, mercilessly cleaning Frank out of a hundred dollars. Before going upstairs with a satisfied grin on his face, he told Nick to polish the brass foot rail with Noxon.

Jimmy left with his arm around Frank's shoulder to keep him from collapsing. "I'll see ya, Nick," he said, winking and rubbing the thumb and index finger of his free hand together before helping Frank out the door.

Three-thirty. Alone with only Margo in Blue Paradise, Nick busied himself by wiping the bar with Murphy oil and Turtle Wax to remove the condensation rings left by the bottoms of highballs and beer bottles. Where Dog sat, there was never any rings to clean since he always kept his drink on a cocktail napkin. Tonight he only said two things and one of them was, "People are like rats in a barrel. We shouldn't think we're anything more than that." He had said it so softly that only Nick heard him.

Nick knew Margo was waiting for him to speak about it first but he didn't know where to begin. And if he did begin, he wouldn't know where to end. The sex had been even more intense and animalistic than what he often imagined it would be. After leading Margo into his bedroom, there was no gentle kissing, no slow seduction. They both were naked without consciously undressing. Then Nick was on top of her and inside of her; his teeth clamped over Margo's throat, his tongue tasting the salt on her skin.

Afterward, he lay next to her, breathing hard, his blood pumping waves through his temples. Margo put her head on his chest and told him how great it had been. A deep fatigue suddenly came over Nick, followed by an intense melancholy that made him want to roll over and sleep instead of hold her. It was too hot to hold her and he had no urge to anyway, not like he did with Alice. Margo asked him if he minded if she stayed the night. Nick said he didn't. He turned on his side, facing away from her, and spent the next two hours thinking about Alice and what had just happened, trying to fall asleep so he wouldn't have to think about it anymore.

It seemed more like a dream now than reality. Remembering it made Nick's breath shallow.

"You don't have to be so nervous," Margo said, looking at Nick in a penetrating way that was having the opposite effect on him.

"I'm not nervous," he said. "Why would I be nervous?"

"I don't know. You look it. All I wanted to tell you was I had a good time the other night. It was nice being with you."

"So did I. I did. Really."

"Good, I'm glad." Margo hesitated, then said, "Maybe we can do it again sometime."

A lump of sadness caught in Nick's throat, similar to but not the same as a lump formed by fear.

"Listen, Margo. I don't know if that's such a good idea. I have a girlfriend. We have to be careful, you know."

"About what? No one here'll find out."

"It's not that."

"What is it then?"

Margo waited for Nick's answer.

"Well, I mean, you have been with a few other-"

Nick stopped in mid-sentence when Margo got up

and walked over to the jukebox.

"You have any quarters?" she asked over her shoulder.

Nick brought her four and Margo played some slow songs that moved her body in a sensuous way and took her mind far from Blue Paradise. The third song was "Silver Threads and Golden Needles" by Linda Ronstadt. As it played, Margo motioned Nick to come to her. He did and rested his hands on either side of her waist. She reached up and clasped her fingers around the back of his neck and he looked down at the smooth ridge where her throat met her collarbone.

"What was it we were talking about?" Nick said.

"I don't remember."

They danced slowly, barely moving. And Nick was glad not to have to shadowbox or run tonight. He pulled her closer and enjoyed the feel of her body against his. The lump in his throat melted away. He knew it would return but for now it felt good that it was gone.

CHAPTER SEVENTEEN

JERRY FOUND HIMSELF bent in half, looking down at the gray-black tarmac while pain spread from his stomach and into his chest. He caught enough of his breath to say, "I don't know what the fuck you're talking about, you slimy Rican." The same fist slammed into him again.

There weren't many condoms on the sidewalk tonight and only a few of the remaining whores looked familiar to Nick whose knees ached from a run that consisted mainly of walking. He coughed, a futile attempt to expel the impurities the TV weatherman had once again warned were invading his lungs at an alarming rate.

For a change, he looked forward to lounging in the

beach chair, shutting his brain off while listening to Jerry talk about the whores on the corner or some crazy new idea. Sometimes, in theory at least, they actually made sense. Like Atlantic City. As long as you didn't think too much about it.

Jerry took a knee direct to the balls. It forced a gasp from his lungs that Nick could hear breaking the early morning quiet. He quickened his pace and when he got to the entrance of the van yard, he saw a blue Chevy parked in front of the office shack, the engine still running, its headlights throwing elongated shadows of the three men who had Jerry surrounded and trapped against the side of the office shack.

The biggest one, standing only a few inches from Jerry said, "Why dontcha make it easy on yo' self?" He followed a punch to Jerry's stomach with a shot to his face that knocked Jerry's head back like he had no muscles in his neck. Nick came from behind. The big one heard him, turned and said, "We ain't rentin' no vans tonight." Jerry took advantage of the distraction to wipe his blood-covered mouth and nose.

Three against two was not good odds, Nick figured, especially since the wall of the office shack was the only thing keeping Jerry on his feet. He wanted to say something like, "If you fuckers want to die, you came to the right place!" When he opened his mouth, "What's the problem here?" came out in a voice that sounded far away, like it hadn't been used it in years.

The big one pulled the corners of his mouth downward into an angry, reverse smile. He jerked his thumb at Nick and said to Jerry, "Who the fuck is dis guy?"

Jerry didn't answer, so Nick said, "Why don'tcha leave him alone and get the hell outta here?" His voice had regained some of its strength but he knew words weren't going to make them leave. It doesn't work that way in real life.

Their eyes locked on each other and neither wanted to blink or look away first. Nick tried to ignore the drops of sweat tickling his forehead and coming to rest on his lashes. His perspective pulled away, allowing him to watch the scene from a movie-like distance.

"This ain't none of your business, muthafucka!" The big one said. "Unless you wanna make it your business, I'd keep movin'."

"Fuck 'im up, Juan," the pockmarked one said.

"This whiteboy think he's Clint Eastwood or some shit," the one with the goatee said.

The stream of blood flowing from Jerry's nose had joined the one from his mouth to form a liquid beard.

"You okay, Jerry?" Nick asked, wary of any sudden movement from Juan.

"Never felt better," Jerry said, his words slurring through thickening lips. "Like a million bucks."

"That's what happens when you fuck with Chico," Juan said, confirming Nick's suspicion that Jerry's business arrangement with Chico would eventually result in something like this. Now look at him. Drops of blood were falling from Jerry's chin into a small puddle on the pavement. He leaned over and vomited a thin stream of bile.

"Fuckin' pig," the goatee said.

Juan's fist came fast but Nick ducked beneath it and countered with a straight left that landed squarely. His companions moved closer and Nick knew he had to put Juan away quickly or have to deal with the three of them at once. Juan lunged again, swinging a wild arc that Nick slipped before crashing his fist into his nose, buckling his knees. After a moment's delay, he fell hard to the tarmac.

Taking no chances, Nick stayed up on his toes. He could practically feel the blood rushing through his veins. He hoped they would leave now but also that Juan would attack again so he could hit him again, harder.

Juan rose to his feet, slowly. Instead of rushing Nick, he brushed the dirt and black tar grit off his T-shirt. Now he too had a mustache and beard of blood that made him look comically evil instead of pathetic like Jerry. Nick kept his hands up and his elbows tucked to his ribs, ready to block and counter another attack. None came.

"Let's go," Juan said to his partners who stood watching stunned, frozen like mannequins. He turned to Nick and said, "This ain't the end of it."

The three of them got in the Chevy and Juan drove out of the yard. At the corner of 10th Avenue, he ran the red light.

The sky above them had lightened to royal blue. Jerry wiped his face with a wet rag. A small amount of new blood still leaked from his nose. Some had dried and hardened into dark boogers on the rims of his nostrils.

"You shouldn't have done that," Nick said.

"When I see an opportunity, I take it." Jerry winced as he dabbed his split lip with the rag. "I can't help it. It's my instinct."

"There's something called the survival instinct too, you know."

"Sometimes it pays off."

"When?"

Jerry touched his lip more gently.

"What would you've done?" he asked, trying to switch the spotlight of judgment onto Nick.

"If I found a pound of Chico's cocaine while I was parking one of the vans?"

"If a pound of cocaine they forgot fell from under the dashboard to your feet, like God dropped it from the heavens?"

"I would've shoved it right back where it came from, for crissakes! In the first place I wouldn't be renting vans that don't belong to me to dealers so they can spread drugs all over the city. The more I think about it, the more I think you got what you deserve." Nick looked away from Jerry. The smug expression on his damaged face was beginning to annoy him. "I don't know why I even bother to save your ass all the time. I'm probably not helping you any in the long run."

"It's worth a lot of money, Nick. That could help me in the long run."

"So, you're not gonna give it back?"

"Of course not."

"And you're planning on being a drug dealer now?"

"Only if I have to. It's what I call my ace in the hole for when times get tough. Besides, if I give it back now, they'll know I was lying. Then I'm really a dead man."

Jerry smiled through his broken lips, satisfied with his ability to think a situation through.

"I don't know what you're smiling about," Nick said. "They'll be back. They said they would. Next time he'll bring a knife or a gun and I probably won't be here to help you."

"I'll be alright."

"If you're lucky the worst that'll happen is you lose Chico's business."

"He's already using Mendon most of the time anyway." Jerry waved his hand to dismiss Chico's importance. "Pretty soon I won't need him anyway. You'll see. We won't need any of this shit pretty soon."

The gathering heat was keeping pace with the increasing activity at the US Postal plant across 11th Avenue. Sitting in their nylon beach chairs, Nick and Jerry watched the mail trucks drive into the huge building at steady intervals, up the entrance ramp and out the exit on the other side. To Nick it was comforting that no matter what happened, short of nuclear war or Sunday, those trucks would always be driving in and out of that monstrous building.

"Why don't you fill out that post office application I gave you?" Nick said. "Get yourself a real job, for crissakes."

"The Postal Service," Jerry said dully.

"The pay's not bad. You get good vacation time and a pension."

"Yeah. After twenty years," Jerry said with even less enthusiasm. He touched his nose which had swollen in proportion to his lips, giving him a clown-like appearance. Nick looked at him and tried not to laugh. Getting beaten was nothing to laugh at.

"You'll be back to normal in a couple of weeks," he said.

"Yeah, back to just looking ugly."

Susan! Damn! Jerry hadn't thought about her until now. Suddenly it occurred to him that he couldn't see her looking like this. And his heart sank even further when he realized that after what happened last night, it would be impossible to even call her. He remembered standing on the pier looking down at the Hudson River until he finally found the nerve to step off of it. The warm air rushing past his ears quickly became water that was colder than he had expected. After what seemed like forever, his head broke the surface and he smelled the layer of oil floating like a skin on top of the water. For a second or two it was tremen-

dously peaceful, until the swirling river begin to pull at
him. Jerry thrashed his arms in frantic semi-circles,
and as the grip of the murky night water tightened, he
remembered that he didn't know how to swim. He
also remembered that Susan's number was in his
pocket.

Of course, none of this would be a problem if it
wasn't for Chico. If he hadn't gotten beaten up, he
could just go see Susan at Caesar's Palace on Monday,
looking normal if not exactly handsome. The pain so-
lidified and settled deeper into Jerry's skull and stomach. His anger shifted from Chico to Juan to himself,
then to Chico again. Yeah, I took the cocaine, but find-
ers keepers. That's the way it works. A drug dealer
should know that. Anyone would have done the same
thing, kept it—except Nick, maybe. Jerry got up and
stretched his aching limbs.

"You want some, Nick?"

"No . . . Yeah, I'll have a sip."

Jerry shuffled like an old man into the shack and
searched in the back of the small closet where he now
kept his Seagram's so no one would discover it in the
filing cabinet. He found the bottle, held it up to the
dirt-crusted halo light attached to the ceiling. No crabs
yet. Through the bottle, Miss April's gaze met his.

"I fucked up," Jerry said to her. "Do you still love
me? You do? Even looking like this? Good." He
toasted the bottle to the calender and drank a long
one, until his throat closed with emotion. "Here's to
you, Barbara," he said. "You never let me down."

Jerry came back outside and sat in the Disney World
chair and felt like he would never get up again even
though the Seagram's had dulled some of the pain
coursing through his body.

"I should put some ice on my face, huh?"

"Too late," Nick said. "It's already swollen."

Nick looked at his hands and noticed that some of his knuckles were cut. He pulled off pieces of broken skin and hoped Juan didn't have any diseases. Could have broke my hand on his thick skull. No payday if that had happened. They wouldn't let me in the ring with a broken paw. You can't lose a fight if you can't get in the ring.

Jerry sucked on the bottle and handed it toward Nick.

"Just one sip," Nick said, taking some of the rye into his mouth and hesitating before swallowing. He felt disgusted with himself for drinking. Normally, if it was going to be a real fight, he would be home in bed by now. Suddenly he didn't want to be there at the van yard anymore, drinking the deceptively smooth rye or listening to Jerry justify keeping the cocaine. But it was more than that making him yearn for escape. How can I sit here telling Jerry what's right and what's wrong. Who the hell am I to make that judgment anymore now that I'm participating in the Atlantic City scheme. But I have to, Nick rationalized, after telling Jimmy yes and setting the whole thing in motion. And if I'm gonna take a dive, I should at least have some money to do it with.

The beach chair creaked and more nylon fibers snapped as Nick pushed his body out of it. He stood and looked down at Jerry's misshapened face.

"So, we're going back down to old A. C. Monday," Jerry said. "Easy money. Easy fuckin' money."

"Rub some salt water on your cuts," Nick said. "It'll toughen them up."

"Salt water'll sting, won't it?"

"You're scared of a little sting?"

"Will it make them heal faster?"

"No."

Before Nick could leave, Jerry said, "Hey, Nick, I went swimming last night, in the river at 42nd Street."

"You can't swim in that water."

"I know. It was so damned hot, though. I had to cool off. Maybe the heat's making me crazy."

Nick was impatient to go. Alice was expecting him in her half sleep.

"It was great at first," Jerry said. "Until I forgot how to swim. Can you believe that? They say swimming's like riding a bike. I guess they were wrong."

"You're lucky you didn't drown."

"I almost did. Someone heard me yelling and called the police. They threw one of those styrofoam life preservers and pulled me out. It felt good, though."

"What? Nearly drowning?"

"No. Just being in the water. Before I started to sink, it was like nobody on the land could touch me."

"You're a nut, Jerry."

Nick turned toward 26th Street and said, "I'll see you later." He was nearly at the gate when Jerry called after him.

"Don't forget Atlantic City!" Jerry yelled. "Mucho dinero!"

"Yeah, mucho dinero," Nick replied half-heartedly.

"Hey, Nick, good punching! You punch like you did tonight and that Rodney Johnson don't stand a chance!"

"It's Leroy Johnson!"

Nick wanted to come back and sit down again. There was a lot more he wanted to tell Jerry, mainly not to be so sure about anyone's chances. He felt like telling him not to place any bets either, but he kept walking and didn't tell him anything.

X

The humidity made the lock stick. Nick turned the key harder and when he was inside the apartment, he heard the door to Alice's bedroom open.

"Nick?"

"It's me, baby."

Alice came to him. Nick tried to kiss her lips but she turned her head away. She never let him kiss her lips after she'd been sleeping and her mouth tasted of morning breath. Nick kissed her forehead instead. Alice led him into the bedroom and got back in bed still holding onto his hand.

"How was your day?" Nick asked, sitting on the edge of the bed, using his free hand to untie his double-knotted laces.

"Fine. Mr. McElroy says he's going to give me a raise as soon as business picks up."

"As soon as more people start dying?"

Alice punched Nick in the side.

"Oh, Nick, stop that. As long as people have to die, they may as well come here where they'll be taken care of. Anyway, if I get a raise I was thinking of getting a bigger apartment so maybe you can move in. What do you think? We can share the rent."

"I don't know Alice. That's a big step, isn't it?"

Nick had an itch on his other arm but didn't want to pull his hand from hers to scratch it. Her fingers found the cuts on his knuckles.

"Nick, what happened?"

"Nothing. I hit the bags too hard today." Nick pulled his hand away and scratched his arm. "The heat and humidity is softening my skin."

Alice didn't believe him. She knew his skin had toughened from years of hitting the bags and wouldn't cut from an ordinary workout. What she didn't know was he hadn't been to the gym in three days. She kissed his palm and gently caressed his knuckles with her fingertips.

"Do they hurt?"

"No."

"Good."

Nick peeled off his T-shirt and hung it on the doorknob. He took a shower and as he dried his hair with the towel, Alice said, "I'm thinking of asking Mr. McElroy if he can put me on nights."

Nick stopped toweling his hair.

"Why do you want to work nights?"

"Do you think I should ask him? I mean, would you want me to?"

Nick started arranging his wet hair with his fingers.

"I don't want you to do it on account of me, Alice."

"Why else would I do it?" Alice said, her voice tinged with irritation. "The only time we ever see each other is in the dark. I want to see what you look like. I want to be able to do things together like other people."

"What do other people do?" Nick said, immediately wishing he hadn't said that.

"I don't know." Alice's voice sharpened, then became exasperated. "Have dinner together, take walks, I don't know. Everyday things."

"Baby, let me fight this fight first. Let me just get it over with. Then we can worry about us."

Nick sat and tried to cup her forehead but Alice turned her head away and moved to the far side of the bed. Nick tried to think of something to make her feel better, to make himself feel better. He couldn't think of anything, though. He lay down next to her and was soon listening to the even rhythm of her breath. "I care about you," he whispered to the back of her sleeping head. Then, without waking her, he dressed and tip-toed out of her room and shut the door quietly behind him.

John was at his window, looking out of it. He wasn't surprised or startled when Nick let himself into the apartment and pulled a chair beside him. He put his hand on the back of Nick's head and patted it a couple of times.

"Couldn't sleep again, huh, Nick? I couldn't sleep either."

Nick almost asked him about the fan again, but decided not to. He'd get the same answer.

"Is it the heat, Nick?"

"Yeah, it's the heat. I can't sleep in the heat."

John's eyes were narrowed with fatigue. He took short, hollow breaths. Nick wanted to ask him if he was okay, if he needed anything, but knew John wouldn't tell him even if he did.

"So, how's the lady down the hall treating you?" Nick asked. "Still keeping you busy?"

"As busy as she can." John's grin disappeared. He looked down into his lap and seemed sadder than Nick had ever seen him. "You can't keep someone in a wheelchair too busy, know what I mean?"

Nick got water from the refrigerator. John drank his and put his empty glass on the window sill and receded deep into his thoughts for a minute. Then he said, "I remember the fight that should've been my last, Nick."

"Which one was that?"

"Against a guy named Burt Carlyle. You wouldn't remember. You was just a little pup."

"How did you know it should have been your last?"

"Because I was scared before it and I was scared during it. I knew I didn't have it anymore and that's what made me afraid. You can't fight that way. You gotta have fear, but you can't be scared."

"What's the difference?"

John's black eyes set on Nick the way they used to set on an opponent's midsection before he tenderized it with his fists.

"You shouldn't have to ask me that, Nicholas. You know the fear is the fear of losing. Every fighter's gotta have that. But scared is scared of getting hurt. You can't be scared of getting hurt. That's when you ain't a fighter no more. That's when you quit."

"So, why did you keep fighting?"

"Because I won the Carlyle fight somehow and I needed the money. If I didn't need the money I would've quit."

Nick wasn't sure what his uncle was trying to tell him, or if he was trying to tell him anything at all. Maybe it was that he was scared again, but in a different way. Maybe he was scared of growing older in his apartment with no one except Nick and the woman down the hall to help him?

"But I don't have no regrets, Nick," John said, looking down at his lap again. "Yeah, I have a few, but you can't carry regrets with you. They just weigh you down." He put his big hand on the back of Nick's head and, as if he was reading all of Nick's thoughts and knowing everything on his mind, he said, "You gotta do what you gotta do, Nicholas. You always gotta do what you think is right."

Nick nodded with the weight of his uncle's hand on his head. He stayed for another half hour but they didn't talk much anymore. They didn't have to.

X

Before returning to Alice's apartment, Nick walked over to the river and noticed for the first time in weeks how beautiful the slate-colored water looked with the tepid, new daylight playing off its surface. Knowing that the daylight, like the Postal trucks, would always come no matter what, unleashed a distinct sense of relief that hit Nick like a shot of Seagram's after a hard run. Tears welled in his eyes, but his vision stayed clear and sharp.

He blinked the tears away and walked east on 27th Street and was glad to hear the trumpet, each sad note distinct and perfectly formed. He searched the edges of the warehouse rooftops and what he thought for a moment was the trumpeter turned out to be a chimney upon closer inspection. He would have stayed there and listened longer, until the sun gained strength and the trumpeter stopped playing, but Alice would be up soon. He didn't want her to wake and find him gone.

He continued walking west toward 10th Avenue and then south to 25th Street. He let himself into Alice's apartment and crawled into bed and wrapped his arms around her. And it felt safe and comfortable to have her in his arms, as if nothing bad would happen as long as he stayed there with his arms around her. Alice burrowed her face into him and murmured heated breaths against his throat. Before falling asleep, Nick wondered if uncle John somehow knew about his deal with Jimmy and the trip to Atlantic City even though it was impossible that he did. He held Alice tighter and decided what John had said about doing what you have to do was the truth. As the fight approached, Nick was becoming more sure of that.

CHAPTER EIGHTEEN

THE SMELL of leather and sweat and the rhythmic pounding of the speed bags provoked a rush of anxiety that extended from the base of Nick's throat to the pit of his belly. It seemed like longer than four days since he'd been in the gym. He felt like someone returning to his hometown after many years and finding it the same but also unfamiliar.

With his duffel held in the crook of his index finger, he made his way toward the locker room and was nearly there when Leon came out of his cluttered little office and said, "Where the fuck you been?"

"Resting," Nick said.

"You're s'posed to rest before a fight, but not like you been restin'."

"Yeah, well, I'll be all right."

"It don't matter to me if you're alright or not. I still get my cut of the purse."

After asking Nick if he'd paid his dues yet, Leon went over to where the heavy bags hung from the ceiling like huge sausages and demonstrated a left hook to a fighter Nick had never seen before.

In the locker room, Nick dressed and wound the cotton wraps tightly around his hands. He tied them at his wrists and punched each fist into the opposite palm to make sure his knuckles were protected. Two fighters sat on the long, wooden bench, both lathered from their workouts. The tall, skinny one with a white scar running from below his right eye to the corner of his mouth said, "I'm gittin' some pussy tonight if it kills me."

"You know that shit'll weaken you, man," the one with the shaved head warned. He squeegeed away sweat beads clinging to his lopsided skull with the edge of his hand.

The skinny one sucked his teeth and said, "Dat's jess a miff them trainers tell you 'cause they can't git none themself. Nothin' better fo' you than pussy. I feel weak when I don't git it."

Wishing that pussy was his only worry, Nick left the locker room and started his workout slowly, shadow-boxing in front of the mirrored wall, turning his fists so his knuckles leveled at the last moment, popping his shoulders with each uppercut. For a few minutes, Leon stood behind Nick and watched with his arms folded across his chest. He didn't bark any advice like he usually did.

After jumping rope for ten minutes, Nick hit the speed bag for three rounds. He moved to the heavy bag next and worked it first with his jab before throwing combinations, smooth and easy. He circled the bag, changing direction, targeting the yellow Everlast patch where an opponent's head and face would be. The yellow patch became Leroy Johnson's face, each feature sharply defined. Nick visualized the overhand right coming down at him, slipped beneath it and resumed pounding Johnson's body until his fists began to soften the hard-packed heavy bag.

Leon touched Nick's shoulder.

"I want you to move with Rashid."

Rashid was waiting in the ring, his long arms intertwined with the top rope like last time. He already had his headgear on and his shadowed eyes peered out at Leon smearing gobs of Vaseline on Nick's face.

"Box smart. Don't get hit," was Leon's only instruction to Nick before the bell rang and the two fighters moved to the center of the ring.

"I thought you quit, man," Rashid said, touching Nick's gloves with his own.

"What makes you think that?"

"Throw something!" Leon yelled, impatiently.

They circled each other without exchanging any punches until Rashid took Leon's advice and pumped his jab twice. Nick deflected them away from his face with his glove. Rashid doubled another jab. The second one landed high on Nick's forehead. Rashid followed with a right but Nick moved inside of it and countered with a hook hard to his ribs, pivoting his left foot inward for extra power. Nick restrained himself from hooking him again, higher, to Rasid's head. The round ended and Nick returned to his corner.

"You lookin' pretty good," Leon said. "Good for someone who been layin' off."

"I feel good," Nick said.

The second round started and Nick knew it wouldn't last the full three minutes. For the first time in as long as he could remember, he wanted to fight. The juices of anger flowing in his body were hot, making him want to go to war, to put everything he had into each punch, bust some ribs. He focused on Rashid's midsection and followed him around the perimeter of the ring, cutting off his angles, knowing the moves Rashid was going to make before he made them. Everything else, including Leon yelling, became blocked out of his consciousness. Rashid threw a right. Nick saw the opening on the side of his jaw as if he'd left it there on purpose. He fired his own right. It landed squarely. Rashid's body folded—ass, back, head—to the canvas.

✕

It was hot in Blue Paradise. There could be no denying it and nobody did when Jimmy said, "It's so fucking hot! This fuckin' heat! I'm gonna kill somebody if it goes on much longer!"

"Yelling about it isn't going to make it any cooler," Walter said. "In fact, the hot air from your mouth is making it worse." Before Jimmy could retort, Walter added, "You know the old saying about pissing into the wind?"

"How about I piss on you?" Jimmy said.

No pissing in this bar," Paddy snapped from the pool table. "Piss on him outside if you want, not in here."

The hottest June on record. That's what the weathermen were now saying. But nobody in Blue Paradise cared very much about records.

"Maybe I'll get an air conditioner next year," Paddy said, his voice tinged with an uncharacteristic sigh.

"How about this year?" Frank said.

"I'm talking about my apartment, not the bar. Nick, get Frank some Jack Daniel's."

"Oh, no. None for me, Nick. I'm not falling for that shit anymore. Gimme a glass of water." Frank shot at the ten ball and missed. "Pour me a Jack, Nick. A short one. Don't let me have any more."

Paddy and Frank were playing for ten dollars, but not very hard. The TV was vacuuming the attention of the rest of them sitting at the bar. The evening news ended. The jury was out in the Fifth Avenue Rape Case. Still no verdict. Just a blonde-haired reporter outside the courthouse on Centre Street, trying to look professional and pretty and collected under the glare of an expectant city.

"Isn't there more news on, Nick?" Frank asked. "I wanna know if something happens."

"No more news until eleven. Don't worry. They'll cut in if something happens."

"I hope not," Stanley said. He was watching the sitcom that came on after the news, about a little girl with no mother and two fathers. "This is a good show."

Walter swirled his port. The purple liquid pushed up the sides of the glass. "Stanley might be right for a change," he said. "I'm beginning to think it's better to anesthetize one's self with sitcoms instead of watching the news. Either way we're screwed, I suppose."

"It never hurts to know the truth," Jimmy said.

Walter stared down into his whirlpooling wine, bracing for another unpleasant encounter but unable to restrain himself.

"And what is the truth?" he said.

"Like I been saying all along, the truth is those skels are guilty. They raped that woman and everyone knows it."

"Here we go again." Walter rolled his eyes up to the ceiling. "I know you've heard of the concept of innocent until proven guilty, regardless of race. We've already discussed this."

"Yeah, I heard of it. And finding one of the little fucker's semen inside the lady is proof enough for me. Evidence don't lie."

"But people do."

"What the hell is that supposed to mean?"

"Has it ever occurred to you that maybe all of them weren't there? Maybe just that one did it and the woman imagined the other four were there too."

"How the fuck could she do that?"

"I don't know. It's possible. Maybe she's lying. Maybe she was disoriented while it was happening or suffered from Post-Traumatic Stress Syndrome afterward."

"She's a rich old lady, not a goddamned Vietnam vet!"

Walter stopped swirling his port long enough to take a sip.

"It's too hot to argue," he said. "I'm tired of arguing. I just hope the verdict comes tonight instead of next week."

"By then they'd declare a hung jury," Frank offered.

"The only thing they better hang are those little niggers," Jimmy said.

Nick refilled Walter's glass fuller than usual and rapped his knuckles on the bar to indicate a buy back.

"Thank you, Nick," Walter said, grateful for the free port and an excuse to drop the argument. "So, Nick, are you ready? Do you feel you've prepared as much as possible?"

"For the fight? Yeah, I'm ready."

"Are you ready for all the pussy?" Frank asked, resting against the bar, drinking his one Jack Daniel's. "I hear boxers have it lining up outside the dressing room."

"An ugly guy like Nick's gonna have to win big to get any pussy," Paddy said.

"I'm not too worried about sex right now," Nick said.

"Even if Nick loses, he'll get plenty of trim" Jimmy said. "It all goes back to caveman days when the cavewomen went with the caveman who could beat the shit out of all the others. Nowadays women say they're attracted to kind, sensitive men. That's a steaming load of crap. They're attracted to brute force."

"I don't think that applies as much today," Walter said.

"I know it doesn't. That's my point." Jimmy said.

"Women like money these days. Today, money's what brute force was back then. Isn't that right, Nick?"

"My girl don't care too much about money," Nick said.

"Everyone cares about money." Jimmy polished the crystal of his Rolex watch with a cocktail napkin. "Everyone does."

✕

Stanley was watching "The Honeymooners" when the special report interrupted Trixie chasing Norton around the kitchen table with a rolling pin. The anchorman had his serious face on, the one he reserved for stories he knew were supposed to be important. After announcing that a verdict had been reached in the Fifth Avenue Rape Case, he cut directly to the reporter being jostled by the mobs outside the courthouse. She held a mike to her mouth and pressed a hearing device into her ear.

Behind her, relatives of the defendants were leaving the courthouse with wide smiles on their faces, some with their fists pumping victoriously in the air. The reporter didn't waste any time. No need for any more analysis or speculation. Nick turned up the volume so they could hear her announce the "not guilty" verdict. The jurors had some reasonable doubts and believed the police may have falsified evidence to wrap up the case clean and quick.

"The Honeymooners" resumed in progress after a few comments by the anchorman and a McDonalds' commercial. Nick turned down the volume. Only Stanley kept watching. For a while no one spoke or looked up from their drink. Jimmy went into the bathroom, came out a few minutes later and paced around the pool table twice before he could sit again.

"Well, we can't second-guess the jury," Walter said.

"They're a bunch of pussies," Jimmy muttered. "I gotta get the fuck out of this city. I swear to fuckin' God."

Paddy and Frank played another game of pool without the usual arguments. Halfway through it, they decided to call off the bet and even shook hands after finishing, feeling a special, unspoken bond in the face of the disappointing verdict. Frank and Stanley left together, both going separate ways once outside on the sidewalk. Paddy went upstairs. He creaked across the ceiling. The creaking stopped and it became quiet.

"You want another port, Walter?" Nick asked, hoping Walter would stay for one more even though he had a growing feeling that Walter's failure as a writer would somehow rub off on him.

"No. I have to go, Nick."

"Gonna do some writing?"

"I'll try. The novel's coming along. It's really taking shape. I think I have to flesh out some of the characters, but the story line is finally falling into place."

"You still haven't told me what it's about."

"Oh, it's too complicated to explain. I'm afraid you'd die of boredom anyway." Walter put on his jacket and made sure his collar was folded down properly. "At the risk of sounding trite, Nick, good luck. I have to work the dinner shift Friday night. Otherwise I'd watch the fight."

"Don't worry about it. Get some writing done."

Walter shook Nick's hand and held onto it.

"I don't believe in God," he said. "But I'll say a prayer for you anyway."

Walter's eyes lingered on Nick's face for a moment. He let go of Nick's hand and left.

A few minutes later Dog shuffled out of the bar, leaving Jimmy and Nick alone once again. Nick put

Dog's two dollars in his tip cup. Jimmy watched Dog cross 11th Avenue.

"Did you bring your money, Nick?" he said as soon as Dog was far enough away to be out of possible earshot.

"You want another beer, Jimmy?" Nick asked, trying to ignore Jimmy's question.

"I've drunk my fill for tonight. Do you have the money?"

The odds were still ten to one. The money Nick was hoping for, ten thousand in chips, would become a hundred grand as soon as the final bell rang and Leroy Johnson's hand was raised in victory. No way this will fail, Jerry had said about the chips. No way you can lose, Jimmy had said about the fight plan. But for the first time, Nick considered that it was really Jerry and Jimmy who had nothing to lose. You, Nick, you're the one who's putting your body and your pride and your peace of mind on the line. His eyes met with Jimmy's and Jimmy said, "How far do you think you're going to go as a boxer, Nick?"

Nick didn't answer.

"Do you have the skill to be a champion?" Jimmy continued. "Do you wanna fight that bad? Look, it don't really matter to me whether you bet anything or not, I'll make my money just the same. Ain't that right, Nick?"

With Jimmy's words hanging in the air, Nick thought of his morning sparring session with Rashid and the right hand that had put him down.

"I don't know. Who the fuck am I?" Jimmy continued. "What the fuck do I know? You always seemed like a nice guy to me, Nick, but you can't be a nice guy in boxing. You have to be a killer to go all the way. Think about it. The money you can make throwing this fight is probably more than you'll ever make boxing, and you won't have the bad kidney's and cauliflower ears and bruises to show for it. It'll be like having your cake and eating it too. Think of that, Nick."

Nick was thinking about it, about his health, the pain of taking the hits. But mostly he thought about the money and Uncle John who needed it, but wouldn't touch it if he knew where it came from.

"You ever consider opening your own bar, Nick? You'd be good at it. People like you. Take a dive and tell Paddy to shove this dive up his ass."

Jimmy turned away from Nick and looked out the window, using the pause like a lawyer creating drama to influence a jury. The neon Budweiser sign gave his ruddy skin a demonic glow.

"What's the deadline again?" Nick said.

"Like I told you, anytime before the fight but I wouldn't wait too long. You can do it now and get it over with, Nick. Put your mind at ease."

"Well, I didn't bring the money tonight, Jimmy. I'll have to get it to you later."

"Later, huh."

"Yeah."

"Later like when?"

"Soon. I gotta do a few things."

Jimmy's forced smile couldn't completely hide his anxiety. "You're not backing out on me, are you, Nick? You already said you were gonna do it."

"I'm not backing out. I just didn't bring the money. I'll get it to you before the fight."

Nick could tell Jimmy was trying to think of another way to convince him.

"You know where to find me," was all Jimmy finally said before leaving Blue Paradise.

✕

Nick closed the bar and stretched his legs on the side-walk for a few minutes before starting to run. It felt good to leave the bar and run the deserted streets, knowing that for the time being, for tonight at least, he was still an innocent man. The streets were empty except for a few taxis. The traffic lights that usually swung over the intersections, if only in pendulums of a few inches, were completely still.

This morning the thick pollution didn't labor Nick's lungs. He boxed the air in front of him and his punches didn't pull him forward or off balance like they sometimes did. He worked his way south, enjoying the familiar route, letting each block measure his effort. The exertion was bringing certain thoughts to the surface, making them clearer.

Margo didn't come to Blue Paradise tonight and as Nick approached 33rd Street, he knew she would be there. No doubt about that. He considered passing 33rd Street because if he did stop and speak to her, he would have to ask her why she didn't show. Of course, he could avoid the question by making small talk and ignoring the fact that she was out there turning tricks, ignoring that things were different between them now that they'd slept together.

Nick turned the corner and stopped running. Margo was there with most of the cross-town block between them. Nick leaned against the wall, peered down the tunnel-like street and watched her walking the line of trucks and buses. He couldn't quite put it into words what the change between them was, but there was now something instinctual telling him to stay away from her before she sucked him in and took him down with her.

He considered calling to her but her name caught in his throat along with his breath. Margo stopped for a moment and Nick was sure she sensed he was there. He moved away from the wall, out of the shadow to the middle of the sidewalk where she could see him if she turned around. She reached down and pulled a wrinkle out of her stocking, then continued walking away from him.

Nick cupped his hands around his mouth and was about to call to her when she paused again and spoke to an unseen driver sitting in the dark cab of his truck. The door opened and the driver's hand reached down to help Margo in. The door shut with a loud, dull thud that lingered before being swallowed by the early morning air.

Nick took his hands away from his mouth and started running again. At 26th Street, his usual destination, he kept running, free of the desire to stop and walk. He zig-zagged between the highway and the avenue as far as 14th Street, the edge of the meat-packing district where the smell of carcasses stained the air.

He stopped running, took off his T-shirt and wiped his face and torso with it, then turned around and walked back up the highway toward the van yard. "Listen, Jerry," he said out loud because no one was there to hear him. "Why don't you see if Big Bob will lend us a van? You and I'll get the hell out of this stinking city for the day. No, I mean really out, upstate or something. Atlantic City doesn't count."

Up there, on some breezy mountain top, he decided he would tell Jerry what he was going to use the Atlantic City money for. Because he knew he couldn't back out now and, even if he could, he couldn't argue with Jimmy's logic no matter how hard he tried. But someone else had to know about it before it ripped him open from inside. And he knew Jerry would understand, better than anyone.

CHAPTER NINETEEN

Nᴵᴄᴋ ᴅʀᴇᴡ his tongue across his dry lips and exhaled sharply to relax the tension tightening his shoulders and his gut. Suddenly he had an urgent need to go to the bathroom. In the Atlantic City Bus Terminal mens room, he held a lungful of rancid air while lining the toilet with tissues and letting some of his anxiety escape into it.

Afterward, he felt better and a little calmer. He drank some water from the sink, washed his face and patted it dry with a paper towel. Satisfied that nothing else having to do with his body would interfere with the business at hand, he headed to locker twenty-four.

The few people in the terminal—the ticket seller, the two blue-uniformed drivers and the bum lying like a dead body on the bench—were watching him. Nick was sure of it as he walked quietly, almost on tippy-toes, across the main floor. The key in his hand, already covered with sweat, reminded him of sixth grade square dances and the girls with nervous, clammy palms.

Upon finding number twenty-four among the morgue-like stack of lockers, Nick crouched down, slid the quivering key into the hole and pressured it to the right, then the left. The lock clicked and the door popped open an inch. After making sure no one was actually watching, he opened the door fully, took a deep breath and reached inside. He touched the back, the ceiling, the floor, and the walls, then pulled his arm out and stared into the darkness of the empty locker, blinking a few times to be sure he was awake and not dreaming a bad dream. He reached in a second time and once again grabbed at nothing.

Jerry ordered a shot of Seagram's and scanned the crowded casino floor, methodically searching the black jack tables, up one row and down the next. The table Robert had worked the last two times was now manned by another dealer. Jerry thought his absence strange, but it didn't concern him much. Probably got switched to a different shift or took the night off. Jerry didn't bother looking for Susan, sure that she'd soon emerge from the swarm of gamblers and come to the bar to fill her drink orders.

He decided to drink while waiting for her, pace himself, one round every twenty minutes. Three rounds an hour should do the trick without getting him drunk. Don't want to be drunk when Susan finally showed up. After an hour, Susan still hadn't appeared and Jerry considered with disappointment that she too might have been switched to another night. But maybe it was better this way, because in a week his face would be looking more normal. And in a week he'd have more money too, once they cashed the chips Nick was in the process of retrieving right about now.

"Say, buddy," Jerry said to the bartender. "You don't happen to know a girl named Susan, do you? She's a cocktail waitress here."

The bartender, a soft, doughy type with a wide, characterless face, shook his head and said, "I'm sorry. I don't believe I know anyone here named Susan."

"You don't know her? Pretty girl. Nice legs."

"I don't know. They might have fired her along with the rest of them."

"Fired who?"

"I shouldn't complain. That's how I got this job. The bartender before me and a lot of the cocktail waitresses were drinking on the job, a real no-no around here. From what I understand, management planted some spotters and caught them with their hands in the proverbial cookie jar. Susan very well may be one of the ones that got fired. Pretty much all of us now are new, including the dealers."

This last comment nearly stopped Jerry's heart. "The dealers?"

The bartender nodded solemnly as if he truly cared. Jerry knew he didn't and felt like punching this fat, smug, self-satisfied sonofabitch in his puffed up face. Sure, you got your job. Why should you worry about anyone else?

"They did fire a bunch of dealers too," The bartender continued. "I heard through the grapevine they were scamming, but I don't know much about that. All I know is I intend to keep my nose clean. It's hard getting a job these days. I looked for over three months. Luckily I live with my mother and she didn't mind. Sometimes I think she'd prefer if I didn't work. As a matter of fact, the other day I said to my mom, 'Mom, you really ought to . . .'"

Jerry wasn't hearing the bartender anymore. Boring motherfucker. Just being near the guy made him wish he'd drowned along with Susan's phone number that night in the Hudson. If he had, he wouldn't be sitting here now feeling like a second-class loser listening to a first-class one. At least if he still had Susan's number he could call her, but what good would he be to her now? His face was bruised and lopsided. He had no money, didn't own a restaurant, and had never even been in the same room as John Kennedy Jr. or Mickey Rourke.

The bartender was right, though. Most of the workers on the floor were new and, like him, they all looked so damned happy to have jobs. Suddenly Jerry hated happy people more than anything in the world. He stayed at the bar and tried to drink away his hate until a sourness came up from his stomach, followed by an acidy bile taste. But Jerry didn't make any move toward the bathroom. If he was going to vomit, he decided he may as well do it here.

CHAPTER TWENTY

The SIDEWALK at the corner of 6th Avenue and 43rd Street rocked beneath Jerry's feet. Nick had gone home after the bus arrived at the Port Authority, and now Jerry stood alone and unsteady, staring up at the National Debt sign keeping track of how far and fast America was falling into the financial hole. The whizzing digital numbers on the giant billboard were making him dizzy as the amount every American family would have to pay rose from $45,564 to $45,565 to $45,566.

Someone else'll have to foot my bill, Jerry thought before stumbling and regaining his balance against a mailbox. The rising from the pit of his stomach was accompanied by saliva dripping from the roof of his mouth unto his tongue. He bent over and unceremoniously vomited the remainder of the eight beers and six shots he didn't vomit at Caesar's.

After spitting the residual puke from his mouth and wiping the back of his hand across his lips, Jerry's head began to clear and the sidewalk no longer heaved and rolled like a ships deck. Still, he clung to the mailbox and decided not to move until he knew where he wanted to go.

Then he knew. The idea came to him like an old friend bringing relief and renewed hope. Jerry pushed off from the mailbox and walked the two long blocks back to Eighth Avenue where Angel's picture beside the Show World doorway greeted him like a shining beacon of comfort in the middle of a dark, dark night.

Inside Show World, Jerry didn't waste any time before following the directions of the familiar voice on the PA: *"It's showtime, gentlemen. C'mon upstairs, up the stairway to heaven. Meet your fantasy in the flesh. Tonight the queen of adult films, a real live angel is waiting to dance for you. C'mon upstairs and see the one and only, nasty and nice, A-N-N-G-E-E-L-L!"*

Jerry pulled himself up the stairs, gripping the banister tightly to keep from falling backwards. A sullen woman with a hair-sprouting mole on her upper lip sat in the box office. Jerry handed her a ten, pushed through the turnstile and sat in the front row of the theater where a preliminary dancer, skinny with a boyish face, was doing her best to squeeze dollars from the pockets of the meager audience. She came over to Jerry, turned around and waved at him between her legs. Reluctantly, Jerry stood and handed her a crumpled dollar, then sat and looked away from her lifeless eyes that were telling him in no uncertain terms that he was worth nothing, less than his grudging tip.

The stripper moved to the other end of the stage and Jerry slumped further into his seat, careful not to touch the armrests. He focused on his fragmented image in the mosaic mirrors clustered into crude hearts on the side of the stage and decided his injured features looked better cut up this way. Another stripper took the stage and jiggled her hips like a belly dancer, yet Jerry hardly saw her. His mind was on Angel.

Feeling dizzy and somewhat nauseas again, Jerry was thankful not to have to sit through more preliminaries after the second stripper left the stage. The taste of vomit still filled his mouth and a headache was spreading from the top of his skull down to his temples. He cursed his fast metabolism that always caused him to suffer the consequences of sobering almost immediately after he stopped drinking. He stood to go to the bathroom and immediately felt lightheaded. His vision clouded and then cleared just when he thought he might black out. The man next to him moved his legs only enough to let him pass.

In the bathroom, ammonia stung into Jerry's nostrils, reviving him a little. The bald man from last week occupied the urinal next to him. He smiled at Jerry and said with a lisp, "Better pee fast. It's almost Angel time. I don't bother watching the others. It's like comparing Little Leaguers to the Yankees."

The man hurried out of the bathroom and when Jerry returned to the theater, he was already seated, leaning forward like last time with only the top of his perspiration-covered head visible. The music started again and a wave of nervous anticipation passed through Jerry's body, as if he was the one about to perform. Then Angel appeared in her short, satin robe, skipping down the aisle to the stage. Half-way through the song, she took off the robe and lingerie beneath it. Jerry watched her intently, at the same time trying to figure out what he was going to tell her when the music ended.

✕

Angel's show lasted for three songs. Afterwards, the same slit-eyed photographer posed her in the hallway outside the theater.

"One shot for ten dollars, guys. Three for twenty,"

he said. "Remember, gents, Polaroids last forever. Show these to your grandkids and say, 'Kid, when I was your age I used to get pussy like this every night.'"

A line of men waited patiently for their turn to cop a feel while Angel posed for pictures on their lap. The ones who couldn't afford a picture leaned against the wall, watching her hungrily.

"This is valuable stuff," the photographer assured them. "Angel signs it and it's a collectors item. Sell it in fifty years and you'll be a rich man."

Jerry stood at the end of the line, gently rubbing his eyelids to keep them from closing. The boozed-up photographer said, "These pictures stay wet forever, fellas. Angel's the only one who can do that to a picture."

The bald man's turn came and the photographer said, "You again, Eagle?"

Eagle grinned proudly and answered, "I'm starting an Angel photo album." He sat in the chair and said, "Tonight, Angel, I want you to pretend to be sucking me off. Is that a possibility?"

"That should be easy," Angel said. Giggling like a little girl, she sank to her knees and put her mouth a few inches from Eagle's crotch. Eagle spread his legs and rolled his shifty eyes back with his head. The flash blinded the room for a moment.

When Jerry's turn came, he pulled a twenty from his pocket and handed it to the photographer who now had an unlit cigarette dangling loosely from his mouth.

"Three pictures?" The photographer asked, the cigarette bouncing up and down between his lips.

"The fantasy booth," Jerry said.

"You got fifteen minutes with her, fella." The photographer took Jerry's money and pointed to a door. "That's your side. Have fun." He smiled humorlessly, as if to add, "But no funny stuff."

Jerry went into the small booth, pulled the door

shut behind him and pushed the lock button in the middle of the knob. In front of him, a full-length window looked into an identical but unlit room. The cushion of the bar stool he sat on farted stale air out of its cracked vinyl covering.

While waiting for Angel, Jerry tried to rehearse what he wanted to say to her. After a few long minutes, the light in the room on the other side of the window went on and the door opened. Angel slipped in, wearing the same robe she'd worn briefly at the beginning of her show. She shut the door without locking it, sat on her stool and crossed her legs so her robe parted high on her thigh. She picked up the phone receiver attached to the wall and motioned for Jerry to do the same.

"Hi," she cooed into the receiver pinched between her shoulder and cheek. Her voice sounded far away and flat, like a long-distance call. "What's your name, honey?"

What Jerry had planned to say was now sentence fragments floating incohesively in his head.

"Don't be shy," Angel said. "You tell me what you want me to do. It's your money. You paid for it."

Jerry coughed and swallowed a ball of phlegm.

"My name's Jim," he said.

"Hi, Jim." Angel stood, pulled the bow out of her robe tie and shimmied her shoulders. The robe fell to the floor. "That's more comfortable," she said, leaning forward and flattening her breasts against the filmy glass. "I hate wearing clothes." She leaned back and cooed, "Oh, Jim, I'm so hot for you. Dancing for you and having you look at my nude body makes me want to cum. When I saw you at the show I was hoping so bad I could dance for you privately."

Angel inserted her index finger into her mouth, shut her eyes and pushed it in and pulled it out like a kid savoring a popsicle. Next, she brought her wet finger down to her crotch, rubbed her clitoris and nearly brought herself to a fake climax. Her eyes sprung open and she whispered, "You like that, Jim?"

"Yeah," Jerry answered, although he felt more detached than lustful right now.

"Why don't you show me what you got, Jim?" Angel said, fixing her gaze on Jerry's crotch. "You skinny guys always make up for it someplace else."

Jerry stood and fumbled with his zipper until he managed enough grip to pull it down. Angel crouched on her side of the glass so her face leveled with his open fly.

"Take it out, lover."

Jerry obeyed and felt foolish standing there while Angel simulated a blow job from the other side of the window. After a minute, she stopped and pulled away, leaving smears of red lipstick on the glass.

"Maybe there's something else you want me to do," she said to Jerry's frightened penis.

"That's why I'm here," Jerry said, putting it back in his pants and zipping the fly. "I don't really want anything right now. But I was thinking maybe you and me could get together tomorrow night after you finish here. I was thinking we could get a room at the Marriot with some champagne, on a high floor with a good view. You wouldn't have to worry about nothing. I'll pay for it all." Jerry remembered the pound of Chico's cocaine he could sell. Better to get rid of it anyway, before Chico's boys found it. Maybe he'd keep a few lines to go with the champagne.

Angel sat on her stool again.

"You want to spend the night with me?" she said, the seduction in her voice replaced by mundane practicality. She laughed shortly and picked her robe off the floor. "Everyone wants to spend the night with me." Angel took out a pack of cigarettes from the robe and lit one. Smoke filled her side of the booth.

"Where are you performing next?" Jerry asked, unable to think of anything else to say.

"Someplace in Florida or Arizona or someplace. I don't remember." Angel waved smoke away from her face, causing it to swirl in mini-storms around her side of the booth. "My agent knows. He takes care of that stuff."

Their eyes were angled just enough to avoid meeting. Angel looked at the watch she was now wearing.

"If you want me to do anything else you better tell me now," she said.

Jerry switched the phone to his other ear and cleared his throat. Before he could speak, Angel said, "Did you get beat up or something?" She sounded even more distant in this ear.

"No, I had an accident." Jerry touched his sore cheekbone. "It's okay now."

Angel put her robe back on and said, "Are you coming to see me next time I'm here, Jim? I love to see my regulars."

"You sure you don't want to come to the Marriot with me?" Jerry said. "We could go somewhere else, the Hilton if you want. It's just that . . .to tell ya the truth, I need your help, Angel."

"Help?"

Jerry swallowed again and said, "I need someone to teach me."

"Teach you what?"

"Well, you know what I mean—how to be with a woman."

Angel's laugh chilled Jerry despite the close heat of the booth.

"Honey, if you need to be taught then maybe it ain't what you want in the first place."

"Yes it is. Believe me, it is," Jerry said, on the edge of panic now.

"I get paid to dance and make movies." Angel's voice hardened. "I don't do that sex therapy shit."

"It wouldn't be therapy. It'd just be a night. One night."

"Listen, it's been a long day," Angel yawned. "I have to do one more show. If you got a problem you should go somewhere else. No one here's gonna help you. That's not what this place is about. And by the way, I work for tips. You can put mine in the slot there."

"A tip? For what?"

"C'mon, honey, don't tell me being cheap is another one of your problems."

Jerry pushed his last ten-dollars through the slot. Angel returned the receiver to its cradle and took the money. She unfolded the bill, read it as if to make sure it was real, and said, "Thank you, Jim."

She left her booth. The door shut and the light went out. Jerry stayed on his stool for a few minutes, studying his shadowed reflection in the darkened glass and Angel's lipstick marks that would remain on it until the guy they paid to clean the booths came with his rag and spray bottle of disinfectant. Before leaving the booth, Jerry checked his watch and noted that he'd been with Angel for only ten minutes.

"How was it?" Eagle was waiting outside the booth when Jerry emerged from it. "I thought we might compare experiences. I had a private session with her last night that was fabulous."

Jerry pushed past Eagle.

"She's performing again in thirty minutes!" Eagle called after him. "The last show of the night is always the best! Sometimes she does an extra song! Are you going to watch it? We could watch it together!"

Jerry stopped and turned around.

"Which way outta here?" he asked, anxious to get the hell out of Show World.

Sadly, Eagle pointed to the exit. On his way toward it, Jerry passed a door with "Keep Out" written on it. The door was partially open, allowing him to look in and see Angel sitting in a canvas director's chair, smoking a cigarette with her head pushed back by the force of her laughter. The photographer was seated across from her on a green, metal desk. He held a bottle of cheap whiskey and was laughing too. Jerry knew they were both laughing about him and fantasized smashing the bottle of rotgut over the photographer's head before slashing Angel's face with it. He imagined saying: "You should drink good stuff, like Seagram's," while they both bled for their sins. Still, he wouldn't have minded a mouthful of that whiskey right now, no matter how awful it was. He wanted a mouthful badly.

Under the streetlamp, Nick bobbed and weaved and threw some easy punches into the air. He didn't know why he had decided to go running tonight when he no longer needed to. A lone car passed on the highway. Nick stopped shadowboxing and let his arms hang limp at his side. Drops of sweat clinging to his fingertips, clear as rain water, captured the light from the streetlamp.

He started walking north along the highway, his breathing slowing to a normal rate. Soon he heard the trumpet, faint at first, stronger as he came closer. Tonight someone was singing along with it, a familiar voice, the incoherent words coming from the other side of the highway, rambling without tone or pause or punctuation.

Nick crossed over toward the singing and found Jerry sitting with his feet dangling over the edge of the rotting pier, a nearly empty bottle of Seagram's squeezed upright between his legs. His head was tilted back as he serenaded the moon, nearly full except for a slight flatness on the upper right side. Nick forced a cough and Jerry stopped singing. He turned around and said, "Nick, I'm glad you're here," as if he had been expecting him. "I wanted to talk to you."

Nick climbed the cyclone fence and sat next to Jerry. He looked down into the water that was not moving in any particular direction.

"You're not gonna jump in the river again, I hope," he said.

"Been runnin'?" Jerry asked, invisible alcohol fumes wafting from his mouth.

"My last one. I think they're right. It's better not to run in this pollution."

"You're finally lissnin' to reason, Nick. Sweet, fuckin' reason!" Jerry put his arm around Nick's shoulder. "Say, buddy, it's good to see ya! Damned good to see ya!"

"How long you been here, Jerry?"

"I don't know. My whole life. You hear that trumpet playin'? Pretty good, huh?"

"Better than your singing."

"He's damned good. I wish I was damned good at somethin'."

"He's good because he plays every night. Every fuckin' night. That's what you have to do if you want to be good at something."

They listened without talking for a few minutes. Then Jerry said, "Nick, I been watchin' the ships go by and I was thinkin'. I came up with a plan."

"Oh, no. Not another one."

"No, this is a good one, dammit! This one can't fail. Jes' lissen. Me and you'll stow away on one of them cruise ships that go down to the Caribbean."

"Stow away?"

"All we have to do is pretend we're visitin' some relatives on the boat before it shoves off. Then we hide in a linen closet or somethin' 'til we're out to sea. Then we jess hang in the bar 'til we get to one of them palm tree islands."

"What do we do then?"

"We get off and stay there. Tha's what we do. You can get a bartendin' job. They're always lookin' for New York City bartenders down there. They think you're hot shit for some reason. And I'll think of somethin' to do. I always do. Imagine, Nick, us livin' the rest of our lives on an island."

"We already live on an island."

"There's no palm trees here. It's not an island without palm trees."

Jerry drank some Seagram's and held the bottle out to Nick who pushed it away.

"Not drinkin' tonight, huh?"

"No, no drinking."

"Not even a sip?"

"No."

Indignation spread across Jerry's face.

"Wha', are ya too good to drink with your buddy now? So it didn't work out. Big fuckin' deal. I'll think of somethin' else. Am I such a low-life loser that even you won't drink with me now?"

Holding onto his temper tightly, Nick said, "I'm supposed to have a fight coming up, Jerry. You know that, so why do you offer me that poison all the time? It's like you're always trying to drag me down to you're level."

"Down to my level? Nick, you're no better'n me and you know it. 'less we stow away on one of them boats, you and I probably won't ever be goin' nowhere. We'll still be sittin' here on this pier when we're old men."

"Speak for yourself," Nick said. He got up and walked to the fence and hooked his fingers through the wire links.

"Hey, where ya goin', Nick?" Jerry called out to him.

"I'm going to bed. You're drunk. I forgive you. You're drunk."

"Wait, Nick. There's somethin' I wanted to talk to ya about. I need your advice. I'm sorry, Nick. I don't know what's wrong with me lately. I didn't mean to say you're no better than me. You are, man. You are!"

"Talk to me about it tomorrow, Jerry. I'm tired. And you're right. I am no better than you. I'm no better than anyone."

"No, you are better, Nick. You're better'n everyone. Hey, Nick, I hate to ask you. Can you lend me twenty 'til next week? I'm broker'n shit. I'll get it back to you next week."

Jerry pulled his pockets inside-out, like some kind of vaudeville bum.

"Is that what you wanted to talk to me about?" Nick asked, unamused.

"No. I wish it was." Jerry sounded more sober now. "I wish it was."

Nick pulled a damp twenty from his pocket and threw it to Jerry.

"Here. Don't buy any booze with it," he said. "I'll come by in the morning. I got the night off. See if you can get us a van for the day. We'll go upstate, breath some fresh air for a change."

Nick climbed the fence and crossed the highway. On the other side he heard the trumpet which became louder as he headed east into the warehouse canyon of 27th Street. He heard Jerry start singing again and wished he'd stop. It sounded so goddamned lonely and depressing, especially if he was going to be listening to it for the rest of his life.

CHAPTER TWENTY-ONE

JERRY WRAPPED his arms around a pine tree and rested against it while trying to catch his breath.

"Too much Seagram's!" Nick called down to him from further up the trail.

"Too much mountain!" Jerry gasped. "We almost there?"

Nick checked the map he'd bought in the bookstore on Main Street.

"We got some more climbing to do. I think we're about halfway there." He folded the map. "C'mon, we'll rest when we get to the top."

"You're supposed to be taking it easy, Nick."

"This is nothing. Just a walk in the woods."

Nick found the next trail marker and, within a few minutes, Jerry had again fallen behind and out of sight. He stumbled over a log and shouted, "Motherfuckin' cocksucker!"

"You all right, Jerry?"

"What the fuck did they put a log right across the trail for?"

Jerry got to his feet and Nick leaned into the steep incline, his leg muscles propelling him up the mountain without any strain. He took off his T-shirt and tucked it into the waist of his jeans.

A few hundred yards higher, the trail came out of the thick woods onto a ledge that provided a wide view of the Hudson River below. Before Jerry's curses caught up to him again, Nick was alone with only the Hudson and the rounded mountains it wound through. He watched a wide barge floating a hill of gravel push through the silver-blue water toward Albany, as unhurried as the river itself.

"Hey, Nick!" Jerry yelled through the densely packed trees. "They don't have bears up here, do they?"

"No! Only deer!"

"Deer aren't dangerous, are they?"

"If you piss them off, they are!"

This reminded Nick of the deer he'd once seen. He couldn't remember exactly when, but it was at the upstate cabin his parents used to rent for a week each summer. That evening his mother and father were playing poker and drinking beer with the couple from next door. Standing on the porch while a purple dusk eased over the lake, Nick heard his father through the window saying, "He's cheatin'! He's lookin' at my fuckin' cards!"

Nick walked away from the window and his father's rising temper, down to the narrow beach and out onto the dock where the boat that left splinters in his ass every time he rowed it was moored. He sat on the dock and took off his sneakers and skimmed the soles of his feet over the smooth surface of the lake that was punctuated only by the small ripples of landing insects.

He stared into the water, trying to see the bottom, until something, not a sound nor a sight, made him look out to a point of land that extended tongue-like into the lake. At the very tip of the point, a deer was drinking, as silent as a dream, its graceful neck sloping down to the water. The deer stopped drinking and looked directly at Nick for what seemed like a long time before turning and disappearing into the green, summer woods.

Nick's parents stopped renting the cabin when his father lost his job. But back in the city, Nick often thought about that deer which came to represent the peace and tranquility and beauty his life in Hell's Kitchen lacked. Sometimes he wondered if it was still alive and drinking at the lake. He wanted to see a deer today, but knew Jerry's racket was making the chances slim.

The stream bubbled over and around smooth, worn rocks, the larger ones partially exposed and baked dry on top by the sun. Nick crouched to the fast-running water and splashed some on his face and the back of his neck. He lowered himself onto his hands and drank directly from the sweet, icy stream until his forehead ached as if a solid punch had landed there.

A few minutes later, Jerry appeared, the color of his face resembling that of a boiled lobster.

"You think it's clean?" he asked, sinking to his knees. Without waiting for Nick's answer, he drank and between gulps, added, "I don't care if it's not. I eat enough shit. What's the difference if I drink it?"

Nick soon reached the top of the mountain and sat on a boulder spray-painted "Lou loves Debbie." A steady, unobstructed wind blew into his face and, far below, the river looked flatter and narrower, dwarfed by the mountains on each side. Train tracks hugged the winding bank and the sun glinted off the rails guiding a train that looked like a child's model and made a clacking sound that seemed to float free and independent of its origin.

Jerry flopped down on the rock next to Nick who continued to study the panorama of overlapping mountains, the furthest one fading in a smoky haze of humidity. Beyond the mountains, the land evened and he noticed two grey strips standing only a half inch high on the distant horizon.

"Jerry."

Jerry propped himself on his elbows and squinted in the direction Nick was pointing.

"Yeah. Nice view. I'm going to sleep."

"Try looking a little harder."

Jerry did and said, "Oh, shit! The World Trade Centers! Look at them ugly fuckers!"

They slept with the descending sun's rays warming their faces. When Nick woke, the sun had dropped to only a few feet above the mountains on the west side of the river. The sky had turned pink and orange and would soon become black.

"That climb was a ball-buster." Jerry's voice sounded slightly hoarse. "You didn't tell me it was gonna be that hard, Nick." He sat up and plucked a blade of wild grass growing from a crevice in the rock, then peered at the tiny twin towers and said, "The city can burn for all I care."

Another train came up the tracks and Jerry watched it, happy that no one in it knew he was looking down at them.

"I tell ya, Nick," he said. "It's like I can't see straight when I'm in the city. Not like up here." He held his pinky a few inches from his face and closed one eye. "From up here my fuckin' pinky's bigger than both World Trade Centers."

"What was it you wanted to talk to me about last night?" Nick asked.

"Last night?"

"At the river."

"At the river? Aw, it was nothing. I've been having some problems, that's all."

"What kind of problems?"

After debating whether to tell the truth, Jerry lied and said, "Cash flow problems. You know. The usual. I must have been upset because I had to borrow from you again."

"That was it?"

"I was drunk," Jerry said with an edge in his voice. His tone softened. "Yeah, that was it. I owe you twenty. I'll get it to you."

Jerry lay back on the rock and enjoyed the cooling air, the first cool he'd felt in almost a month. He couldn't do it. Any other problem he could talk about but not this one. And not stone sober. There was no way Nick could help, anyway. The only one who can get you laid is yourself. The best thing to do is to keep going, escape the city and the bad memories, start over in a new place where failures aren't hanging over you like a dark cloud.

"Why don't we keep the van, Nick?" Jerry said. "Go somewhere with it?"

"Keep the van?"

"The tank's almost full. We got a few bucks between us. I'll find a way to make some more."

Nick shook his head.

"That's stealing. Besides, I have to fight tomorrow night. Where do you want to go?"

"I don't know. Someplace, for crissakes! Forget about the fight. It doesn't seem like you really want to fight anyway."

"What makes you say that?"

"I can see it in your eyes. I know people, Nick, and I know you best. Maybe you're going soft. I'm not saying that's a bad thing, but something's making you soft. Maybe it's Alice."

"It's not Alice," Nick snapped. "You're the one who's soft, Jerry, not me. Soft in the head, that's what you are."

He had planned to tell Jerry all about it. Now he didn't feel like talking about throwing the fight, not like he thought he would. Going to the top of some nameless mountain doesn't necessarily change anything or make it easier to tell secrets, even ones about to burst out of you. Nick looked straight up into the darkening sky, at the faint, white pinpoint struggling to be seen.

"Check it out, Jerry."

Jerry looked up.

"First star I've seen in a long time," he said.

Trees blocked the remaining light on the way down. Nick led the way, carefully picking his footing among the rocks obstructing most of the trail, walking slowly so Jerry wouldn't fall too far behind. A few times he was sure he'd gone the wrong way and they would spend the night wandering deeper and deeper into the forest. He disappeared around a bend in the trail.

"Nick?" Jerry called out.

"I'm here. Don't worry, I'm here."

Twenty minutes of decent seemed like an hour until Nick spotted a break in the woods and heard a car passing. They emerged from the trees onto the road and the bluish dim remaining from the day was enough to guide them back to the van parked on the shoulder. Walking toward it, Jerry stepped on an abandoned Budweiser can that curved around his foot, reminding him that he wanted another can, a full one, though.

They climbed into the van and Jerry drove to the town of Cold Spring. He turned down Main Street, his eyes shifting from one side to the other until he spotted the Downtown Bar and Grill. He pulled against the curb, said, "Just a quick one," and was out of the van and into the bar before Nick could protest.

College pennants and deer heads covered the wall, their dead eyes looking down on two locals playing pool. One wore a Cat Diesel Power cap and a white T-shirt stretched tightly over his ample belly. The other had a steel wool beard that hung from his chin down to his adams apple. He wore a pair of faded, denim overalls with the knee patches coming off.

"A shot of Seagrams with a beer back," Jerry told the bartender. "And a seltzer for my friend."

The round arrived and they drank quickly. Jerry ordered another and leaned close to Nick.

"You been playing much pool lately?" he whispered behind his hand.

"Just a little."

"That don't matter. We can beat these slobs."

Jerry took two quarters from Nick's change.

"How about we play you guys next?" he said, stacking the quarters on the edge of the pool table. "Just a friendly game. We're not very good."

The one wearing the Cat Diesel cap looked at his partner, shrugged and said, "Awright."

Jerry inserted the quarters into the money tray, pushed it in and racked the balls. The game went quickly and Jerry and Nick lost miserably. Jerry missed three straight-on shots in a row during the next game, helping them lose again, even more easily this time.

"The Seagrams must be getting to me," Jerry said after his last shot rolled wide. "We've been hiking all day. You fellas ever go hiking on that mountain?"

"No." The bearded one said before sinking the four, the three, then the six ball.

Nick sank two balls but Jerry scratched his next turn. He slammed the end of his cue against the floor in mock anger.

"What the hell are you doing?" Nick whispered when Jerry came back to the bar. "You ever hear of withdraw?"

"Gotta invest money to make money, Nick," Jerry explained with a wink. "In this case it's only a few quarters."

The locals won the third game almost as effortlessly as the first two.

"You guys up for another?" the bearded one asked.

"No, we gotta go," Nick said, but Jerry had already slipped two more quarters into the tray.

He racked the balls and the bearded one broke and ran the table until only four solids and the eight ball remained. Noticing that the stripes were in fairly good, unobstructed position now, Jerry shook his head with fake concern. When his turn came, he shot the nine ball against the back of the pocket, hard enough for it to pop back out onto the table.

"Damn! I'm sorry, Nick. Maybe I'd play better if there was money on the game."

"The way you play I wouldn't put anything on this game," Diesel said with a grin.

"Twenty bucks says I should," Jerry countered.

"Where's yours?" the bearded one said, taking a twenty from his wallet and placing it on the edge of the table.

"Right here," Jerry answered. He put his own twenty, the one Nick had lent him the previous night, on the table, then stood back and watched Diesel sink the four remaining solids with brutal efficiency. Without pause or smile, Diesel lined the eight ball with the corner pocket and as he pumped his cue in preparation, Jerry said, "Let's double it."

Diesel straightened up, rested the end of his stick on his foot and stared at Jerry and his twitching right eye.

"It's your money, pal," he said.

"I know it's my money. And it's your shot."

"Put your money on the table first," the bearded one said.

"How about putting your money on the table?" Jerry challenged.

"You upped the bet, not us."

"What do you care if the cash's on the table or not?" Jerry said. He turned to Diesel. "Just take the shot, big guy. I'm sure forty bucks goes far in this town."

Diesel glared at Jerry, then shot forcefully but with enough withdraw to keep the cue ball from scratching. The eight blurred across the green felt and disappeared with no argument from the corner pocket. The bearded one scooped up the two twenties and held his hand out to Jerry. "You owe us twenty more, pal."

"Well, that may be a problem," Jerry said, backing away and watching Nick slide off his stool, then the bearded one's tight fist rushing toward him. Then darkness.

Nick loaded Jerry's semi-conscious body into the passenger seat, found the keys in Jerry's pocket, then turned over the ignition and jerked the van away from the curb. He accelerated up Main Street and at the intersection, a partially revived Jerry gasped, "Step on it."

Heading toward the city on the Taconic Parkway, Nick gripped the steering wheel tightly with shaking hands. He kept his eyes glued to the road that wouldn't stay straight for more than a few yards at a time. He listened to the evenly spaced telephone poles swishing by the open window like someone with his finger to his lips, going "Shh! Shh! Shh!"

"I didn't know you could drive," Jerry said through newly busted lips.

"I can when I have to."

"I'm sorry, Nick. I thought I could bluff him, make him nervous. If he'd missed the eight ball we had three easy shots. You saw it. I was just trying to get the twenty I owe you."

"I don't need it that bad."

"I almost had him psyched out. His cue was shaking."

"You shouldn't gamble with money that doesn't belong to you, Jerry."

Although Jerry disagreed with this, he didn't tell Nick. Instead, he said, "You hit the one with the beard pretty good."

"He hit you pretty good first."

"You could have killed them, Nick. Those yokels were nothing compared to Chico's boys."

"I probably could have, but you shouldn't always rely on it."

"Man, if I could fight like you I'd have fucked them up good myself."

"But you can't fight like me and now you're the one who's fucked up."

From the corner of his eye, Nick monitored Jerry's sorry condition, his bleeding nose and swelling lips.

"I would've liked to see you kill those guys, though," Jerry said. "Take them down a few pegs. They probably think they own that crummy little town."

"You're the one I should have hit! They didn't do anything wrong!" Then Nick said, more calmly, "I didn't want to hurt my hands."

Jerry leaned his throbbing head against the side window and watched the guard rail rush past, the supporting posts whooshing identical intervals. A wave of sadness hit him suddenly, causing his breath to catch in his throat and his bruised cheeks to flush with heat. Nick's right, he admitted silently. He might have hurt his hands. Can't box with injured hands.

Nick noticed Jerry slumped against the window.

"How you feeling, Jerry?"

"I'm a loser and you know it. That's how I'm feeling. Nothing I do ever works, so why dontcha just tell me I'm a loser? It's the fuckin' truth."

"You're not a loser. But it's probably better that none of your scams work."

"Plans, not scams."

"Whatever. Either way, it's better that they don't." Nick glanced at Jerry and saw tears welling in his eyes. He tried to think of something to make him feel better, to help him somehow. "I didn't mean that about hitting you, Jerry," he said. "I just meant you have to be more careful about things. You only live once and hustling pool isn't the way to do it."

It only made Jerry feel sadder that Nick felt the need to tell him this, so sad that he started crying and didn't stop until he felt empty of tears and a little cleaner inside. As the van crossed into Yonkers on the Henry Hudson Parkway, he sniffled the last of his snot and turned on the radio. But after a few songs, he shut it off and sat still, staring straight ahead at the approaching and growing Manhattan skyline, neither flinching nor blinking when the big, summer flies dove into the headlights, committing suicide against the windshield in front of him.

Nick pulled off the highway at 59th Street and drove south along 11th Avenue. A red light stopped him on the corner of 44th Street outside Blue Paradise where Gracie was working the night shift, where he would mostly likely be back working the same night shift after the fight. Blue Paradise always looked different to him on the rare nights he wasn't working, lonely and a little sad. The light turned green and Nick continued on 11th until another one stopped him beside the postal plant that the mail trucks were feeding as if nothing different had happened and nothing ever would. It was almost midnight when Nick pulled into the van lot and parked against the rusted cyclone fence.

"You okay, Jerry?" he asked gently.

Jerry nodded and put his hand on Nick's shoulder and said, "You have to win for us tomorrow, Nick. I can't see you losing."

"You gonna be there?"

"Hell yeah, I'll be there. I got my ticket. You'll hear me yelling even if it hurts like a motherfucker."

"I'll be listening.

Nick helped Jerry out of the van and into the office shack.

"You sure you're okay?"

"I'm always okay."

"I'll see ya, then."

Nick walked nearly to the gate, but something made him turn around and come back. He poked his head in the door. Jerry wasn't startled by his reappearance.

"If you ever want to talk about anything, Jerry, just let me know."

"I will," Jerry said. "The same goes for you."

"Okay. I don't have anything I want to talk about now, but I'll keep it in mind."

Nick turned to go again, but Jerry called after him.

"Hey, Nick?"

"Yeah?"

Jerry struggled for the nerve to say it, then said, "I love you, man."

"Yeah, well, you're a good guy too."

"That's what I meant."

"I know. Put some ice on your face."

Nick stepped out of the office shack and Jerry said mainly to himself, "Hey, Nick, I think I'm gonna fill out that Post Office application tonight. I got nothing else to do."

Nick was already gone, so Jerry took the application from the filing cabinet and found a pen. This shouldn't be too hard, he thought. But after printing his name on the first line, he lay on the cot, closed his eyes and was asleep almost instantly.

Nick headed west toward the river, but stopped when he reached the corner of 27th Street and 11th Avenue. The music was there as always, floating in the air like a seagull. And for the first time, he saw the trumpeter, at the edge of the warehouse roof, silhouetted against the city sky with his trumpet tilted toward the mostly full moon.

Nick watched him and felt as if he knew him like a close friend. He listened carefully to each perfect note and when the trumpeter finally stopped playing, Nick's legs took him to Alice's apartment. He climbed into her bed and with his arms around her, he said, "Alice, maybe getting that bigger place isn't such a bad idea."

"I saw a nice one today," Alice murmured, barely awake. "Do you want to look at it?"

"Sure, I'll look at it." Nick kissed the side of her head. "Did you fix any stiffs today?"

"No. I guess no one died."

"That's good. I hope no one does for a while."

Too tired to talk anymore, Nick shut his eyes and before falling asleep, he saw the fight in his head, clearly for the first time. He knew it wasn't going to be easy and there would be consequences, maybe serious ones, but there didn't seem to be much choice anymore. He slept deeply and well that night and had only one dream, but in that dream he beat Leroy Johnson, knocked him out, in the first round.

ABOUT THE AUTHOR

MATT BLOOM is a native New Yorker. He has worked as a bartender, amateur boxer, migrant laborer, and truck driver. *Blue Paradise* is his first novel.